It's Raining Men

A ROMANTIC
COMEDY

BEATE BOEKER
& GWEN ELLERY

Night Bloom Books

Anatole

Paris

April

She was dying, and we both knew it. But while my heart felt ready to crumble, she still seemed full of pluck and plans. Maybe I shouldn't have been surprised. After all, this was Charlotte. She had never given up in all the eighty-six years of her life, and though her skin now was wrinkled and pale, and her white hair a mere shadow of how it used to be, she still exuded that special energy that had always drawn me to her. She was almost fifteen years older than I was, but there had been times when I had been half in love with her—maybe more than half, if I was totally honest. However, she had never had eyes for anybody but her husband, Hubert, who had died half a year ago. I swallowed, remembering her agony.

"Hubert might not have wanted it, but I'm going to do it nevertheless," Charlotte suddenly said and nodded her head in that determined way she had. The pillow shimmered white beneath her hair.

I blinked. Maybe my mind had drifted off somewhat. "Hubert would not have wanted what?"

"My will, Anatole." She frowned, and her hands moved impatiently on the white bedspread. They made a faint, rustling sound in the quiet hospital room. "Weren't you listening?"

"I was listening. You said Hubert would not have wanted something, but you didn't say what it was that he would not have wanted."

"I'm making a new will. That's why I called you."

I rallied quickly. You had to if you wanted to keep Charlotte's respect. "You should have told me. I didn't bring any paper."

"But you've got a fountain pen with you, don't you?"

"Of course." What an idea, to leave the house without my trusted fountain pen.

"Well, this hospital will have some paper somewhere. Go and get it. But hurry. I won't be around much longer."

I double-checked to see if the well-known twinkle had appeared in her faded blue eyes, but she was dead serious. *Oh, Charlotte.*

Five minutes later, I returned with the paper. She was lying on her back, her head turned to the window. It was an expensive hospital close to the Parc de Belleville, and the best rooms offered a fantastic view of Paris. In summer, a haze of smog sometimes blurred the outlines of the city's famous skyline, but on this crisp April day, you could see the Eiffel Tower in the distance, outlined against the sky as if stenciled in by a remarkable hand.

"Are you all set?" She asked as if we were preparing for a fun day at the sea, ready to head out to Erquy, as we had done so often in the past.

"All set." I pasted on a smile that cost me more strength than avoiding red meat for a month.

"Don't look like that." She smiled at me. "Life will go on. For you." Suddenly, the famous twinkle was back in her eyes. "And it will be fun."

Fun didn't seem likely for me, but I wasn't about to argue the point. I uncapped my fountain pen. "Go ahead. I'll note your ideas, then I'll adapt them where necessary so everything will be legally correct, and in the end, it's best if you write down the final version by hand yourself, unless you'll find it too tiring."

"I can do it." Her chin went up. "Now let's start. This is the last will of Charlotte Lemont, *née* Dupont, born August seventh, nineteen—" She broke off. "But you know the year. I needn't repeat it."

I suppressed a smile. She was eighty-six and still vain. But why not?

The room was warm and quiet, and the soft scratching of the fountain pen on cheap paper was the only sound we could hear. A sudden shiver came over me, a feeling of something big to come, something that would shift my universe. I ignored it and finished writing the first sentence.

Charlotte continued with quiet determination. "I leave everything I have in equal parts to my four grandchildren."

"Everything you have?" I lifted my head. "But you—"

She smiled. "I know, Anatole. Don't ask."

I couldn't help myself. "What about your children?"

"They all got enough when Hubert died, and we both told them that my personal property would go directly to our grandchildren. They know, and they approve. I asked them to confirm that in writing, so we'll have no unpleasant scenes after my death. You will find the four letters in the left drawer of my desk at home."

"That was clever of you."

She smiled. "Thank you, but I'm not done yet." She took a soft breath. "The nature and extent of the inheritance will only be disclosed to the heirs one year after my death."

I continued writing, though it felt as if my fountain pen wanted to go on strike.

"During that year, as an absolute condition to qualify for their inheritance, every single one of my grandchildren will have to carry my umbrella with them, everywhere, for three months, before passing it on to their cousin."

My fountain pen stopped writing all by itself. "Your umbrella? What kind of nonsense is that?"

"No nonsense at all." She lifted her chin. "Write. You're here to write down my last will, not to question it." Her mouth had disappeared into one obstinate line.

I now remembered why I had never been fully in love with her. She was as difficult to shape as baguette that has been around too long. "I've never heard of that umbrella," I said. "What umbrella?"

"It's a very special umbrella." Charlotte's face softened. "It was a prototype. You remember the umbrella factory Hubert and I had, way back when?"

"I remember it well."

"It wasn't very large, of course, but we loved it. A pity we went bankrupt." Her smile vanished.

"That was a very tough time for you."

"Indeed. Hubert took it to heart and felt it was his fault, which wasn't true at all. In fact—" She broke off and made a small move with her wrinkled hand. "But that's old history. Luckily, he found his feet again, and I kept the umbrella. It was especially made for me, a gift from Hubert for my thirtieth birthday. It's red with white dots, and collapsible, but with a heavy wooden handle because that's how I liked them."

I shuddered. "And you want your grandchildren to run around for three months with this ugly umbrella because . . . ?"

"Just because." Her mouth closed with a snap. "Stop questioning me, Anatole. I have my reasons. Just write it down."

I didn't budge. "What happens if they refuse?"

"Then they will be excluded from the inheritance."

"*Mon Dieu!* Isn't that a bit eccentric?"

There was the twinkle again. "Who said I wasn't eccentric?"

She had me there. "Well, nobody."

"There you go." She pointed at the paper. "Go ahead. Write it down. And make sure it can't be challenged. I'm absolutely sane."

I smiled, and this time, it came from my heart. "Nobody dares to say differently, Charlotte."

"Good." She returned my smile. "I knew I could trust you. I first want the umbrella to go to Travis. It's a bit risky as he's the most likely to lose it somewhere, but I have a feeling that he needs it most."

"But isn't Travis the one in California?"

"Yes, that's him." She smiled at something that seemed to amuse her.

"Have you never heard of that song 'It never rains in California'?" I asked. "There's a reason why that song was written, you know."

She tilted her head to one side. "You should have listened to the rest of the song, Anatole. It says 'But it pours, man, it pours.' And I sure hope that it will pour when Travis has the umbrella with him in California."

I shook my head but decided to drop the subject as she was obviously unwilling to disclose more. "Do you have the addresses of all your grandchildren?"

She shook her head. "No. Travis is always on the road because he's a musician, and that's another reason why he should have the umbrella first. You can give it to him at my funeral."

"Will he come?" I couldn't recall seeing Travis in Paris. The others, yes; I had met all of them on and off in recent years and had known them well as children. But Travis had not been to Paris for a long time.

"Oh, yes, he will come. I sent them e-mails and invited all four."

I choked. "You sent your grandchildren e-mails and invited them to your funeral?"

"Yes." She gave me a sunny smile. "I couldn't tell them the precise date yet, of course, but I informed them that I expected them to be present at any cost, and I gave them your address for all details as well as the address of my travel agent so she could book their tickets. I will pay for them. Travis wouldn't have enough money to come over otherwise, and it would be unfair not to invite Carlo and Ainsley. Josie, of course, doesn't need to fly in. She'll take the *métro*, as she always does."

"Josie will miss you."

For the first time, Charlotte's lips trembled. "Little Josie. I'll miss our Sunday lunches, too. But she'll be fine. She just has to learn to trust her talents. She's quite a brilliant designer, you know, but it's hard to earn recognition nowadays. She'll be the third to get the umbrella. After Travis, I first want Ainsley."

"Ainsley in Edinburgh?"

"Yes."

"Well, at least she'll need an umbrella in Scotland."

Charlotte nodded. "Ainsley is a good girl; in fact, she's the most organized of them all, but she urgently needs to loosen up and enjoy life. That's why she should have the umbrella after Travis."

"And the umbrella will do just that?"

"Don't get cheeky with me, Anatole. Did you write it down? First Travis in California, second Ainsley in Scotland, third Josie in Paris. You've got that?"

"I do."

"The last is Carlo in Florence. I'm not sure if he really needs the umbrella."

"Florence is known for its nice weather."

"Oh, the weather . . ." Charlotte waved it away. "I wasn't talking of the weather."

For one crazy instant, I wondered if Charlotte was having a strange flight of fancy after all, but then I saw her sharp gaze resting on me, and I duly suppressed the idea.

"Carlo needs to be liberated."

I lifted my eyebrows. "Liberated from what?"

"Liberated from his own expectations of himself. Do you remember his older brother ?"

I swallowed. "Yes, I do."

Her face turned sad. "My little Amélie was shattered when the accident happened. It was a horrible time for all of us. There's nothing worse than losing a child, but you know, it's also bad for the children who survive. Carlo was only five when his brother was killed, but from then on, he did everything to make his parents happy. And that's unnatural."

"Is it?"

"Oh, yes. A little rebellion is healthy and necessary."

"I see. And that little rebellion is supposed to break out when he's carrying around an unfashionable umbrella?"

Charlotte chuckled, but she didn't reply to my question. "He'll suffer, poor boy. Carlo is a true Italian, always dressed to the nines. However, he'll survive."

I shook my head, but I finished my list with Carlo's name. "Is that all?" My voice sounded faintly ironic.

She leaned back into her cushions, a satisfied smile on her face. "That's all, Anatole. You'll find the umbrella in the bottom drawer in my desk, at the very back. I guess it's a bit dusty because it wasn't taken out for years and years, but it should still work just fine."

Five days later, the dreaded news came. Charlotte had passed away. After I heard this, I walked around all day like a man on drugs, not feeling where I was going, clumsy, disoriented. Without her, my life seemed to have lost its purpose. I had always adored her. She had always been the spice in my life. What now? What was left for me?

With a heavy heart, I started to organize the funeral. No, that's wrong. I didn't organize it; I just set the thing in motion. Charlotte had everything organized already, and when I had nudged it into action, the whole thing unrolled smoothly, like a huge roll of black velvet.

Probably Ainsley in Edinburgh had gotten her gene for organizing everything straight from her grandmother. She was the first to confirm her attendance at the funeral. Little Josie had run to my house when she'd heard the news and had cried on my shoulder. It had torn my heart. Carlo sent an e-mail from Florence to confirm times and places, brief, to the point, like the businessman he was. I had not heard from Travis, but I hoped he'd gotten my message. Maybe his phone service wasn't working.

I felt as if I was breaking in when I went into Charlotte's house and extracted the umbrella from her desk drawer. It was smaller than I had expected—a collapsible model. With caution, I shook it and opened it above my head, then sneezed. I was standing in a billowing cloud of dust that twirled around me in the rays of sunlight coming through the tall windows.

The umbrella was a truly ugly thing. Bright red with plenty of small, white spots, and the large wooden handle clumsy in my hand. It felt good to the touch, though. Polished wood always does. It had a dark nut-wood shade that gave it a bit of dignity that it otherwise lacked. I twirled the umbrella a bit and watched more dust gliding to the floor. In my mind's eye, I saw Charlotte walking around with this odd accessory, and I wondered why on earth she had made such a strange will. "Oh, Charlotte. This is not going to be easy. But I'll do my best to explain everything to your grandchildren. I promised. And I've always kept my promises to you."

When I left the house on the corner of the Rue de Versailles, it started to rain with fat, heavy drops. Typical April weather—a minute ago, we'd had sunshine. For an instant, I hesitated, but then I shrugged and opened the umbrella. Might as well use the thing until I got home. I went down the stone steps and had just crossed the street to get to the Métro station when I heard a screeching sound behind me, like metal scraping over stone at high speed. It made my blood turn cold. I whipped around as fast as I could and stared with wide-opened eyes at a heavy Harley Davidson machine that was rushing around the narrow street corner in an almost horizontal position. I knew I should have made a run for it, but for some reason, my legs didn't react. I just stood frozen in the middle of the street and watched death hurtling toward me, bright and fast and pink.

The machine bucked but was brought to a standstill by a gloved hand, then stopped so close to me that I could have touched it by stretching out my fingers. My mouth was half open, and my hand clutched the umbrella, all muscles contracted in fear.

The leather-clad figure on the hellish machine pushed up the visor of the helmet and looked at me. "I hope I didn't scare you."

My jaw sagged still further. The leather-clad figure was a woman. And she wasn't a young woman. She was well into middle age, to go by the laugh lines around her blue eyes.

I couldn't move.

She bent forward and touched my shoulder. "Are you all right? You should go to the sidewalk. Any minute now, a car might come and run you over."

I managed to lift my eyebrows in mute astonishment. Being run over by a car seemed pretty unlikely, after I'd almost been run over by a motorbike for the first time in my life. I mean, how bad could it get?

She shook her head and dismounted, then pushed the heavy machine onto the sidewalk. I followed her, still in shock.

She turned around and put her hands onto her hips. "Good. So you can still move. My bike didn't touch you, did it?"

"No."

She bent forward and peered at my face underneath the umbrella. "Are you sure you're all right?"

"I'm a bit rattled," I said with dignity.

She shook her head again, obviously not approving of me. "You shouldn't stand around in the middle of a street."

Well, if that didn't beat all. "You shouldn't fly around corners as if Nemesis was on your heels," I said with asperity.

Her eyes widened. "Nemesis. Why should Nemesis pursue me?"

"Because you're driving like the devil?"

She laughed. "You got me there." She pulled her helmet off and pushed a hand through her short curls.

They were white, and with a shock, I realized that this bundle of energy in front of me was probably not much younger than I was.

The rain intensified. It made a hard, spattering sound on the old umbrella above me, and without thinking, I stretched out my arm to protect her from the elements.

She took a small step closer and smiled up at me.

Something inside me moved. I'd never seen a smile like that.

"There's a café around the corner," she said. "Can I invite you for a cup, to make up for the scare?"

I'd never been invited by a woman I barely knew before. It seemed this was a day for several firsts. I smiled. "I'd like that. My name is Anatole Plessis."

She returned the smile. "How funny. We have the same initials. I'm Anne Pluchot."

Two days later found me still unable to believe what had happened. I felt wrung out by all the ups and downs in my emotions—amazing heights and happiness when I'd been with Anne, utter devastation and grief during Charlotte's funeral early this morning. I took a steadying breath and looked around Charlotte's living room. Her heirs were assembled here, just as she had wanted. With an effort, I focused my attention on the four young people in front of me. Travis had arrived the day before. His message to me had gotten lost, probably a problem with whatever messaging app young people used these days. At any rate, I was glad he was here—Charlotte had been concerned about him, and now that I got a good look at him, I suddenly knew why. If I mentally erased all that hair he'd grown (it was really much too long for my taste), then he was the spitting image of Hubert, right down to the way he moved across a room. It was uncanny to see a man who was the exact replica of his grandfather. Genes are a curious thing.

A sudden pang of regret shook me. If we had been younger, Anne and I might have become parents, too. But fate—or whatever it was—had decided differently. Never mind; the important thing was that we had met at some point. And these children in front of me—or young adults, I should say—were close to my heart, almost like my own children. This was thanks to the enchanting summers we had all spent together in Charlotte's and my home town. Every year in August, the family had met in Charlotte's ancient fisherman's cottage in Brittany. Outside all day long, the kids had played and fought and made up, and we, the adults, had cooked and talked and rested. I had marveled at how much the kids had changed from year to year, and how different they all were from one another. Those summers had helped us to grow close, and sometimes, the kids had come to me with their little

worries and questions. I wondered if they still recalled the nickname little Josie had given to me when
she'd been small—her call for "Toli" had often been
on all of their lips.

Now, when I remembered those summers, I had a
deep ache in my heart. Over the past few years, the
visits had stopped. I couldn't really tell why. Maybe
they were all too busy with their own lives; maybe the
distance had proved to be too much after all that
time—I didn't know. I sighed and recalled myself to
the present. Time to read the unusual last will of
Charlotte Lemont.

Her four grandchildren were sitting in a semicircle
around me. We were in Charlotte's living room, and
for some reason, it felt as if she was here, too, invisible, but hovering and making sure that I did everything right. I wiped my brow and took a deep breath.

Carlo leaned forward, his elbows on his knees, his
handsome dark head turned toward me. "We're here
for the reading of Grandma's will, is that right?"

"Yes, that's right."

"But why weren't our parents invited?"

"Because they already got their part of the inheritance when your grandfather died. For example, this
house—it was split up among your parents, and
Charlotte only had the right to live here as long as she
wanted. That's why she specified that you four be the
sole beneficiaries of her personal inheritance. Your
parents are aware of that. In fact, they have agreed to
it in writing."

I looked at their faces, which appeared expectant, a
bit excited, curious. Very natural sentiments in the

circumstances. Unfortunately, their grandmother's last testament would be a stark disappointment. I steeled myself and started to read Charlotte's words. When I'd finished, I looked up.

A blank look from Ainsley. A confused one from Josie. Smothered laughter from Travis. Disgust from Carlo.

"You're saying we won't get our inheritance until we've all carried around an umbrella for three months?" Travis shook with laughter. "How awesome. Grandma really was something else."

Josie looked around. "Where is this umbrella?"

"It's right here." I opened my briefcase and brought out the gadget in question, handing it to Josie.

A stifled gasp from Carlo. "It's red! With white dots. And that huge handle, totally out of proportion! It looks terrible."

"I'm afraid so."

"Why, I think it's pretty." Josie shook it out and opened it, then twirled it around.

Her cousins stared at her in utter silence.

I wasn't sure if I should draw a relieved breath or if it was too early for that. I had expected a storm of protest.

"What exactly is our inheritance once the year is over?" That was Ainsley. Cool and collected and going straight to the marrow of the matter, as always. Her large eyes focused on me with intelligence.

"I'm not at liberty to tell you," I said. "In fact, I don't know myself. I only know her wishes. She specified that we all meet again in one year—a bit more than that, actually: She said it should be on the 15th of May."

Josie's face softened. "She organized it all."

"That's all you know?" Ainsley asked. "But if you don't know more, how are you going to tell us what we'll inherit?"

I smiled. "Your grandmother organized that part as well. She told me that a sealed letter will reach me just in time."

Carlo jumped up. "I don't like it! What kind of joke is this?" He frowned at the umbrella. "Why are we supposed to make a laughing stock of ourselves? Does she want to humiliate us?"

"I don't think so," I said. "It was her conviction that it would do you good. At least I got that distinct impression."

His chest swelled. "Do me good? Why should it do me good to run around with a ratty, old umbrella? You must be kidding me!" He stopped in his tracks and focused on me. "Are you one hundred percent sure that she was in her right mind when she made that will?"

"One hundred percent." I allowed myself a smile. "So much so that she even said you would take it the hardest."

"Pah." He dropped onto his chair again, then lifted his head. "But why now? Why didn't she give it to us sooner? I mean, looking at it, this thing is at least twenty years old, isn't it?"

"Even older. It's a unique prototype from your grandparents' first factory and as such, quite valuable. Your grandfather gave it to your grandmother as a birthday gift for her thirtieth birthday." I didn't tell them about my sneaking suspicion that Charlotte had submitted to her husband's wishes in keeping the umbrella hidden all those years. I could still recall her words "Hubert would not have wanted it. . . ."

But Hubert was dead, and it had been important to Charlotte that her four grandchildren take the umbrella into their lives. She had her reasons. I suppressed a smile as I recalled her insistence about the matter. A clever woman, Charlotte. She knew that a message from her after her death, linked to an inheritance, was far more binding than any other request she might have made—since the youngsters had no chance to protest.

"There's just one more condition," I said. "You're not allowed to talk about your experience with your cousins during the next year—until we all meet again in May, that is."

"Our experience?" Carlo lifted an eyebrow. "What on earth did Grandma mean?"

I hesitated. This condition in Charlotte's will had made me extremely uneasy, as it would be virtually impossible to prove one way or the other whether the young people went along with her edicts. But she had been adamant, and so I tried to pass on her wishes now without showing what I felt. "She said to me that you're not to discuss the umbrella or anything that happens to you during those three months. Those were her exact words, and that's all I know."

They blinked in surprise, but didn't comment anymore.

"I'm afraid I can't tell you anything else," I said. "She didn't take me into her confidence. I was only chosen to pass on the information."

"Thank you, Toli." Josie smiled at me. "I know how much you loved her."

To my surprise, I felt my eyes fill up. "That's quite all right."

Carlo sighed. "All right, then." He held out his hand to Josie. "Give it to me. Since we seem to be stuck with it, I'd like to get it over with as soon as possible."

I took the umbrella from Josie and gave it to Travis instead. "I'm afraid that's not possible. Your grandmother specified who should have it first. Travis, you're the first. And she said you should take care not to lose it."

Travis grinned. "I'll do my best." He turned the umbrella, now folded up again, in his hands. "Leave it to Grandma to come up with a crazy scheme like this. What was she thinking?"

"When your three months are up, you have to send it directly to Ainsley in Edinburgh," I said. "Make sure it's an insured dispatch with a tracking number, so we won't lose it when it crosses the Atlantic. After Ainsley, it's Josie's turn. Then Carlo's."

"Wouldn't it make more sense to send it to Carlo before it goes to Josie? Then she could bring it directly to our meeting, and we'd have one less chance of the package being lost in the mail." This practical suggestion came from Ainsley, of course.

I shook my head. "I'm afraid not. Your grand-mother was very specific about the schedule, and I want you to stick to it."

Ainsley got up. "Well, let's do it, then. If it's the only way to get the inheritance, then we haven't much choice, have we?"

Shrugging, they all murmured their agreement, some more reluctantly than others, and kissed me good-bye before filing out of the room.

When the door had closed behind them, I looked around, strangely relieved. Charlotte had gone, too. Don't tell me how I knew. I was free now to go back to Anne. Maybe we could still grab a late lunch somewhere.

But when I turned, I saw something red out of the corner of my eye. The umbrella. It was on the floor, next to Travis's chair. I grabbed it and ran after the departing cousins. Thank God I caught up with them before they had gone more than a few steps down the Rue de Versailles. "Travis! You forgot the umbrella!"

Travis

On the Road

June

It started with a bang. Literally. The beginning of the end of my single life started with a resounding pop. I was driving down Highway 101 at about five a.m. with my band members in tow. Stinky and Jud were crashed out in the back with our equipment, and because I was the designated driver, I'd been up all night chugging super-sized cups of coffee and squeezing eye drops into my eyes, or what my friend Bo likes to call "ocular orbs" (as opposed to testicular or mammarian orbs, as Bo would also say). Bo himself sat sprawled in the passenger seat beside me. He and I had been having one of our typical conversations.

"Dude, will you stop singing that song?" he said. "You're driving me nuts."

"Sorry, was I doing it again?"

"Only every other McDonald's sign. Which is to say, approximately every ten minutes. They're spaced pretty evenly in this area."

I didn't have to ask if he'd been timing the distance between the billboards. Of course he had been. That was Bo.

It never rains in California. Duh-da-duh-da-duh-da-da.

Bo threw an empty paper cup at me. "You're doing it again! Stop singing that song."

"Hey, I'm trying to drive here. Don't throw shit."

We would have probably gone on like that for the next hour if it hadn't been for a sudden, loud thwack-bang behind us. All at once the van lurched and swerved, skidding out of control.

"Turn against it! Turn against it. Don't turn with it!" Bo shouted.

We hit a rain puddle and started hydroplaning. It was like the magic teacup ride at Disneyland, only this time I wasn't a kid anymore and I was spinning on an empty stomach.

Then the weirdest thing happened. As we were sliding toward the center divider, I had a kind of dream or hallucination. A part of me got up out of the bucket seat and drifted to the back of the van, where I saw Jud and Stinky sitting up with freaked-out expressions on their sleepy faces. They didn't notice me drift by. I floated over the drum set and the guitar cases, and hovered above something red in the corner. It was sticking out from under a drop cloth.

For an odd second, I thought it might be somebody's blood, but then I zoomed in on it, the way you do in a dream, more of a jump cut than a slow approach. Now I was right on top of it.

I was looking at a dirty, folded up, wrinkled umbrella, the compressible kind that some women carry in their handbag. It was red with white polka dots. Where had I seen it before? Oh, yeah. It was the one Grandma bequeathed to me and my cousins. I'd stuck it in the back of my van about a month and a half ago after bringing it home from Grandma's funeral. She'd insisted in her will that I carry it around with me to get my inheritance, and my cousins seemed to think ignoring it would be bad luck, but that was a bunch of bull. I'd thrown the thing in the back of my van and forgotten about it.

Until now. It was as if *it* had remembered me.

Man, I must really be dying if I'm in a car wreck, looking at the last thing Grandma was obsessed about before she died. Maybe the next thing I'll be looking at is her and the pearly gates. Or whatever other clichéd imagery my brainwashed lobes can come up with.

I was still musing along these lines when I noticed that the van had come to a halt. Jud and Stinky jumped up.

"Oh-my-god, oh-my-god," Jud said.

Bo jumped up from his seat and hit his head on the van roof. He rubbed his crown. "Travis," he yelled at me. "We're sitting in the middle of the road. Get us to the side before a big-rig slams into us. Travis? Travis?"

All of a sudden, I was looking at him again from the driver's seat. It was as if I'd blinked, and everything was back to normal.

The engine had died. I started it again, and the van wobbled to the highway shoulder, coming to a stop in front of a sign that somebody had shot holes in. It read *Now Entering Gilford, The Garlic Capital of the World.*

"Vampire population, zero," I said in a daze.

"Human population, whatever it was, plus four," Bo said.

Jud's face looked as white as my knuckles did on the wheel. "What if the population hadn't grown?" he said. "What if it had stayed the same. . . ."

"Then we wouldn't get laid tonight by some smokin' hot, garlic-scented babes," Stinky said, coming forward in the van.

With a nickname like Stinky, you wouldn't expect him to get laid much at all—and it was true he almost never did, but that was because of his personality, not his smell. He actually smelled fine. We called him Stinky because when he was at a loss for words in an argument, he spoke with his stinky finger.

"We're not staying here," I told them. "I have to be at work this afternoon."

"Let's assess the damage first. Then we'll talk." As usual Bo was thinking clearly. At least one of us could keep his head during an emergency.

Not me. I'd been running on pure instinct and intuition, like some newbie Jedi mainlining the Force.

And there *had* been a force. That's what was so weird. There had been a freaking force in the van that had kept us alive. I didn't know how to bring this up with my friends without them scoffing at me, so for now, I kept it to myself.

We piled out of the van and into the pouring rain.

It never rains in California. Duh-da-duh-da. Duh-da-da.

Bo halted beside the van and looked over at me with a strange expression on his face.

"Did I do it again?" I said. "Sorry."

His eyes got kind of shiny. Was he going to cry? Bo the brain, cry? He rubbed the back of his neck, and his hand came away slick with rain. "I never thought I'd say this, but I now officially love that song, and I want you to sing it every day. Every freakin' day. That stupid song is now our song, got it? And if anybody gives you a hard time for singing it, I will personally argue that person into the ground until he hasn't got a thesis to rub against his antithesis."

I couldn't believe it. Bo the ultimate music snob loved a schmaltzy radio hit from the seventies. Our car accident must have gotten to him too.

"Thanks," was all I could manage. My throat had swollen up inside. I hurried toward the back of the van, head bowed. Most people don't know this about me, but I'm a crier. I can usually control it until I have a chance to sneak off and get it out of my system alone. But today was different. Anything could set it off now. And I wouldn't let it. If I lost control of my emotions, I wouldn't be able to help change the tire. And if we couldn't change the tire, I wouldn't be back in Santa Barbara by noon. With the economy in the state it was, I was not about to go through another four-month job hunt against the three hundred other people applying for the same positions.

Behind the van now, I checked the tires. Yup, the situation was as I'd suspected; we had a flat.

"Uh-oh," Jud said.

I glanced over. He was looking behind me, not at the tire but down the highway. "What?"

"It's the cops. Some trucker must have called in our accident."

I followed his gaze. Sure enough, through the sleeting rain, two headlights and the top-lit blue bar of a patrol car were approaching.

"Why did you say uh-oh?" I asked sharply.

Jud's gaze slid from mine. "I'll just hang out in the van while you guys talk to the cops. If anybody needs me, I'm hiding the weed."

"Weed?" I sighed. "You said you'd quit."

His sheepish look told another story. "I did. But then I didn't anymore. Then I did. Then I didn't. It's complicated."

"I can see that," I said. "Get the hell in there, slowly, and pretend you're looking for the tire iron, and come out again slowly. Don't panic, okay? Don't do or say anything suspicious."

He turned to go, walking in extreme slow motion.

"Not that slowly," I said, rolling my eyes. Jud had smoked way too much of the green stuff in his short puff here on earth. It was a wonder he could still shred the guitar at lightning speed.

But, as I'd learned in the back of the van just now, the human brain moves in mysterious ways.

"Oh, and there's a red umbrella in the back of the van. Bring it back with you," I added. "We're getting soaked."

Jud nodded and rolled off, a bit less snail-like than before.

"O-o-o-oh, a lady cop. I like," said Stinky, our resident Casanova-wannabe. He craned his neck to peer around me. "And she's stacked under that vest. Look at the way she pops out a little on top. It's like a corset."

I resisted the urge to thwack his arm. "You. Say nothing," I told him. "Bo and I will handle this."

I turned around to see—oh wow, even I had to admit we were out of our league. Hell, we weren't even in the same species as the woman who sauntered toward us. She had long legs, red hair, and huge hazel eyes that assessed us with a swift, intelligent glance. Just looking at her, I felt like something that had been scraped off the highway by an orange-suited prison worker and presented to a goddess for inspection.

"Morning, officer," I said. "We had a blowout, then a spinout. But we're okay."

She shined her flashlight through the raindrops at our faces, and then at the back corner of my van, which sagged pathetically onto one hubcap, looking like an elephant that's having a hard time getting comfortable for a nap.

"You're lucky to be alive," she said. "Vans tip easily."

We nodded our agreement, Stinky the most emphatically, probably because he was feeling the luckiest at the moment to be able to gaze at her without interruption.

"You fellas have Triple A?" she asked.

For a second, I thought she was talking about a bra size, and I could only blink at her. Then I remembered the good old days when I could afford membership in AAA, the statewide auto club and emergency road service.

I shook my head. "Nah. But we know how to change a tire."

Or, at least I hoped so. I'd never changed one before.

Her flashlight played over the back of the van. In the window Jud's face appeared briefly, looking confused, but that was nothing new.

"That other back tire looks bald too," she said. "You'd better get a new set right away. There's a place in town that'll do that for you while you wait."

How could I tell her I couldn't afford it? I'd only just started working at an online catalog company for minimum wage, and I couldn't ask my friends to pay for the tires. They had less money than I did.

"We're kind of in a hurry," I said. "We have to be in Santa Barbara by noon."

Stinky pulled himself up to his full six feet and said gallantly, "I'll cover the tires with my credit card. And lunch too." He ogled the lady cop. "You should join us when you get off work. We're in a band. You'd probably like our music. It's a fusion of classic rock and modern angst, with the occasional romantic ballad thrown in for the ladies."

I gave Stinky my *I thought I told you to keep your trap shut* look, but he completely missed it.

The lady cop darted a similar look at him, but of course he missed that one too. This was Stinky's tragic plight in life. He could not read body language until the body language was in his face, yelling, snarling or slapping.

"Is this a tire iron?" I heard Jud say behind me. I turned to see him holding out the red umbrella.

"No, Jud," I said. "It's an umbrella. How about you go back and look some more?"

Jud rummaged in his loose pants pockets, swaying slightly.

Oh, God. Was he high? When did this happen? I flashed back to our last gas station visit and remembered how furtive he'd been when he'd returned from the restroom.

"I could have sworn I had it," he said. "Is this it?" He pulled out a plastic baggy through which was clearly visible a handful of dried, green buds.

He was showing the lady cop his pot! I stiffened, unable to speak. I could only hope the drugs would be hard to recognize in the dark.

Too late. Her flashlight beam zipped to Jud's hand.

"What have you got there, partner?" she said.

Jud looked down at his hand and then burst out laughing, but when he saw the rest of our panicked faces, he stopped. "Spirulina?" he said, all innocence. "I found it on the ground."

The cop was already on her radio, calling for backup, and within minutes two other cars had pulled up, tires splashing in puddles. My band members and I watched, helpless, as two of the cops rifled through everything in the back of my van and the other two kept an eye on us. Luckily, the only illegal thing on hand was Jud's baggy.

They dragged out our travel bags and unzipped them in the rain. As I stood there watching, a black cloud moved in fast from the west. Moments later, rain poured from the sky, even heavier than before.

Jud was handcuffed. His long hair was getting drenched, falling into his eyes. He stood there, grumbling about not being able to see anything. The lady cop must have felt sorry for him because she got a kind of "this is so pitiful" look and picked up my umbrella, opening it above him as she finished telling him his rights.

That's when it happened. She stopped mid-sentence and just stood there beside Jud, her head poking in under the umbrella beside his, looking at him as if she were trying to place his face. Maybe she'd recognized him from one of our album covers from when we'd been mildly famous for a week, many moons ago.

"Do I know you?" she asked. And then, get this, she reached over and moved the wet clumps of hair out of Jud's eyes.

Jud said nothing.

I said nothing.

Stinky and Bo said nothing.

The lady cop jumped back from Jud and shook her head, like a wet dog. The whites in her eyes showed as she glanced around.

The three back-up cops were too busy patting down Stinky, Bo, and me to see what had just happened.

Of course none of my band members said anything about it, gentlemen that we are. The lady cop kept her eyes down during the rest of the formalities and then asked one of her colleagues to drive Jud into town. I could imagine what she was thinking: *Are these guys going to make a case out of this and get me fired for inappropriate conduct?* And when she wasn't thinking that, she was probably asking herself why the hell she'd touched Jud's face. I know I was.

"Man, what was that all about?" Bo asked me after he and I were installed in the back of one of the other cars. The cops had offered to take the rest of us into town and had kindly arranged to have my van towed for free to the repair shop. At the moment, our particular patrol car was rolling along the dark and empty main street of Gilford beneath a flashing yellow traffic light. I'd barely heard Bo's question. I'd been too busy staring at the sky, spaced-out with memories from the accident. The spinning van. The drifting feeling. The hallucination about the umbrella. Nothing like that had ever happened to me.

"Travis? Are you okay?" Bo asked when I still hadn't replied.

My body jerked. "Huh? Fine, fine."

"Can you believe that cop? What could a woman like that possibly see in a guy like Jud?"

"Hell if I know," I said, and new images bombarded my mind, these ones accompanied by worries; I could already picture my ex-girlfriend's expression when I'd have to tell her I'd lost another job due to tardiness. She'd get that tight-mouthed look that always reminded me of a pinched butthole and she'd tell me to move out of her apartment. I could totally understand why. She'd been more than generous, letting me stay with her rent-free after our breakup until I'd found my current job. She believed in my music, so she'd continued to waive rent every month even after I got my first paycheck. Thanks to her, I'd been able to pay for my band's marketing and travel expenses. But even she had her limits. And her issues.

And my "passive-aggressive lateness," as she called it, was definitely an issue for her.

Bo, meanwhile, was still talking away beside me in the patrol car, caught up in his own train of thought. "I mean, it'd make more sense if he were rich or good-looking, but he's obviously neither."

"Mm-hmm," I said, still lost on thought.

"I don't get it. A puny guy like Jud. She has to be at least five inches taller than he is. And she definitely washes her hair more often."

"Maybe she has a thing for criminals."

Bo sat up. "I've read about that. I think it's called the Bonnie and Clyde Syndrome. People who can only get turned on by thugs."

"Mystery solved."

As I said this, our car passed a beat-up, warehouse-style building made of prefab material. The sign on the front of it read *Greyhound*. Seeing it, I thought of a solution to my job problem. I leaned forward to rap my knuckles on the Plexiglas between us and the cop in front. "Excuse me, do you know when the Greyhound bus stops in town, heading south?" I asked the guy.

He told me they leave every day at eight-thirty and ten-thirty a.m.

I thanked the cop and leaned back, grinning. "This is so cool. I can catch the first bus. My shift starts at three, and I can walk to work from the bus station."

Bo chewed on his lower lip. "Three things. One, the money we pool for your bus ticket should probably go toward Jud's bail. And two, who's going to pay for the new tires if we use it on the ticket or Jud? I'm pretty sure Stinky's credit card is about to max out."

My shoulders tensed. I'd forgotten about the bail money and Stinky's questionable credit line. "We could call Jud's parents."

"Because that worked so well last time."

I sighed. Bo was right to be skeptical. Jud's parents were worse potheads than their son, forgetful about pesky little things like grocery shopping and where they'd left their only baby boy. "What was the third thing?" I asked.

"Thirdly, if you leave town without us, our band will probably break up."

The cramp in my shoulders intensified. "The band is not gonna break up."

"Don't be so sure. Jud's a super-sensitive guy. He can't handle brutality. If he spends too much time in jail, his nerves will be shot, and he'll lose the will to play."

I had to hand it to Bo; he understood Jud, and he'd thought this thing through. "Oh, man. This sucks."

I was racking my brain for a better plan when our car passed under a banner spanning the street. The sign read: *Let's Get Spicy! 15th Annual Gilford Garlic Festival, June 10-17.*

"A garlic festival?" Bo snickered. "These people are desperate for tourist money."

From the look of the closed storefronts, I could see why. Every other shop had been boarded up, and the ones that were in business had seen better days. We passed a 24/7 laundromat with rust-covered machines, the window fronted by a crooked *Open* sign.

This was followed by a hairdresser's shop featuring faded posters with hairstyles from the previous century.

"What a sad sack town," I said. "I wouldn't last a day here."

"You'll have to. We're staying the night."

"What?"

"I saw a sign for a campsite by the highway. We should set up the van there until Jud's out on bail."

I turned in my seat. "But if I lose my job, Chrystal will kick me out."

"I know, I know. But you can't leave. You're the heart of the band."

I flopped back on the car seat. He was right. Without me, the other guys had no purpose or vision. Or any original songs.

Not that I'd come up with any since my breakup, but that was another story. I sighed. "Okay, I'll stay."

"That's what I'm talking about!" Bo held up his palm for me to high five, but as usual we flubbed the cool move. It didn't matter, though. We were alive, and together as a band.

And we were all I had.

Two hours later, the sun crested the hills in the east, and the clouds had cleared enough to let sunrays angle into town. Bo, Stinky and I had angled into town as well and could be found in the 24/7 laundromat wearing only our boxer shorts. We sat lined up across from the dryers, shivering on the orange plastic seats, watching our clothes tumble. Back at the police station, Jud had been fingerprinted and was sitting now in a holding cell, waiting for his arraignment. The rest of us had decided to dry our laundry right away, since the police had laid out all our bags on the roadside during the search and our clothes were all damp.

"At least they paid for the dryers," I said, jingling the quarters the police had given to us.

Bo nodded. "Local tax dollars at work for itinerant minstrels."

"I'm sick of living in the cracks," Stinky said, addressing the universe in general and us in particular. "Remember when we used to stay in four-star hotels on tour?"

We were still sitting there when the glass door to the place swung open, and a brunette woman wedged herself inside, a plastic laundry basket in her arms. Her long, brown hair was mussed from the wind, hanging mostly over her face, and her shapely body was covered in a form-fitting lavender track suit with white flower decals across her bust.

It was just after seven in the morning. What was she doing in here? I, for one, felt my face grow warm. The guys and I hadn't expected anyone to come in and see us stripped down to our shorts. Mine had holes on one side.

The brunette shook her hair back from her face, and her eyes took us in with a sweep. They widened when she saw our naked torsos above the row of washers. Stepping back, she reached for the door.

"It's not what it looks like," I called in a joking voice. "We're wearing shorts. We're just drying our wet clothes."

She paused, and her gaze locked with mine. Her eyes were large compared with the rest of her face, not comically large, but enough to give her the look of someone much younger. Those eyes held mine with a trance-like quality, as if she were looking beyond me at something she was remembering about me.

"I hope you guys know there's a police station around the corner." Her voice had a surprisingly husky quality and unusual authority for someone so petite.

I quickly explained that we'd been at the police station because our car broke down, and the police had helped us in the rain. I left out the part about Jud and his baggy of green gold. I was just winding down with my account when outside a thickset man and woman showed up. The girl stepped aside for them, letting them enter.

"Morning, Leila," the stout woman said to her.

"Morning," she said, and her shoulders relaxed.

The older couple went to a door at the back of the shop, and the man pulled a set of keys from his pocket. He and his lady friend barely glanced at us as they rolled up a metal curtain from the counter and switched on the back room lights. I guess they'd seen people here in their underwear before.

For some reason, the idea of ending my conversation with Leila made me panicky. "Do you work here?" I asked her.

She shook her head and moved around me to the nearest dryer, where she stashed some wet clothes.

That would have been the end of it if she hadn't suddenly started sniffling and wiping her eyes.

"Everything okay?" I came around the row of washers toward her, with the unfortunate consequence of revealing my boxers. They were decorated with red hearts, a present from my ex in happier days.

Leila's eyes flicked to my shorts, and she paused mid-sniffle, a faint smile on her lips. "I'm fine. It's just stress."

"Did something bad happen?"

"Yeah." She turned to watch her clothes as they circled inside the dryer. "I can't believe I'm telling this to a half-naked guy in a laundromat."

"Think of me as partially clothed."

Tiny curves played at the corners of her mouth, and for the first time I got a good look at her lips. They were full and naturally rosy against her pale skin.

But what was I doing? Staring at her mouth like some lovelorn Romeo. I gave myself an inner kick. It was so rare that I was really attracted to someone, I'd forgotten how it felt. I had to snap out of it. For one thing, I was leaving town soon. For another, there was no way that a girl with an expensive haircut and manicure like hers would go for someone broke like me. Girls like her were looking to move up in the world, not to live in a van.

"There are so many things stressing me out," she said. "It's hard to pinpoint a single one as the main cause."

As she said this, the heavyset lady who worked here stepped outside and stood on the sidewalk, lighting a cigarette.

In the next moment, Stinky, wearing only his boxer shorts, joined her outside and from his gestures, I could tell he was bumming a cigarette. The rain started coming down harder, and Stinky retrieved my umbrella from where it was drying near the entrance. He opened it over the lady smoker, and she took off her raincoat to drape around Stinky's shoulders. I turned back to Leila.

"This weather isn't helping," I said. "It's enough to get anyone down."

"I know what you mean," Leila said. "My basement is flooded, and the clothes I left to dry got soaked. All before I've had my coffee."

Coffee. I sure could use some right now. I blinked, and tried to focus on what Leila was saying.

"Not to mention the festival opens tomorrow night," she said. "I'm scared no one will show up in this weather."

"You mean the garlic festival?"

She grinned, and her look said *Is there any other kind?* "That's the one."

God, was she beautiful. She had a dimple on one side of her face and a smile that lit up her eyes.

"Are you a vendor at the festival?" I asked.

She shook her head. "It's my first year as director, and it's been one disaster after another."

"Director. Wow. That must be a great job."

She laughed, an edge to her voice. "Yeah, right."

"That bad, huh?"

She nodded, brushing a damp curl from her fore-head, and then, leaning against a dryer, she proceeded to tell me a tale of woe about a land permit that had expired, electrical power sources that had gone out, and a rock band that had tried to sue the city.

I'd been nodding sympathetically through it all. At the mention of a rock band, I perked up. "Why would they want to sue your city?"

Her sigh was so heavy I felt bad about prying. "It's complicated," she said. "I'm not sure where to begin." Her voice was shaking, and her eyes were fixed on something outside. "God, I need a cigarette," she said. "I wish I still smoked."

I followed her gaze to see Stinky and the lady still huddled together. Stinky took a drag from his ciga-rette. He handed it to the lady, and she puffed on it too.

My eyes went wide. Had I just seen what I thought I'd seen?

Leila glanced to the back of the shop. "I hope her boyfriend didn't see that."

"The guy in back is her boyfriend?"

"Yup."

I looked again at Stinky. He'd put his arm around the woman's shoulders! And she'd let him. She gazed up at him as if he were made of chocolate and she had the munchies. They made an odd pair. She looked to be in her mid-forties, with a sagging waist and fine wrinkles around her eyes. And Stinky, well, he was Stinky. Twenty-three, muscle-bound, and pudgy.

"I'll be right back." I nipped outside and cupped my hand near Stinky's ear. "Hey," I whispered, "sorry to rain on your parade, but you need to know that the guy behind the counter inside is the lady's boyfriend."

"He is?" Stinky looked down at the woman beside him. "You have a boyfriend?"

Her eyes got wide. "Oh, my God. I forgot!"

"You forgot that you had a boyfriend?" I asked.

She hurried inside, shaking her head to herself, her cheeks flaming red. Stinky and I were left outside.

Stinky still had her coat on his shoulders. He pulled it more tightly around his neck. "I don't know what happened. One second we were smoking, the next second, I had this urge to put my tongue down her throat."

"The way she was looking at you, I think she might have let you."

He shook his head in wonder. "Do you believe in love at first sight?"

"I believe you're referring to lust. And yes, it does happen right away."

"No, this was different." He collapsed the umbrella and stubbed out his cigarette in the ashtray by the door. "We can't leave town until I get her to come with us."

I gaped at him, unsure whether to laugh or groan. "Hello? She. Has. A. Boyfriend."

"We all make mistakes."

"Didn't you see the muscles on that guy? I would not mess with him."

Stinky shrugged. "*Que será será.*" He thwacked his chest with his open palm. "If I can't have her, I'll die trying."

"What are you gonna do? Challenge him to a duel? This is crazy talk. You just met her."

"A man's got to do what a man's go to do." He handed me the umbrella, his gut jiggling over his blue-and-black satin boxers. "It's kismet, baby." He sauntered inside.

I looked down at the umbrella, remembering how I'd floated above its red-and-white self during the spin-out. I thought of the lady cop, the way she'd brushed the hair from Jud's eyes when she and he shared the umbrella, and the smoker lady when she was under the umbrella with Stinky. She'd set her coat over his shoulders as if he were precious to her.

And then all at once, I understood; either I was in limbo having an elaborate hallucination to end all hallucinations or this freaky little piece of cloth and steel had special powers.

I fought the impulse to cast it from me, as if it were infected. Get thee behind me, red thing! Hadn't this umbrella almost killed me out there on the highway this morning?

But the more I turned it this way and that, shaking it out and folding it into a bundle, the stronger my desire grew to protect it, if only to make sure it didn't fall into the wrong hands. I glanced around at the glistening street and storefronts. Early morning workers walked past, heads bent and purposeful. An older man hobbled along the sidewalk across the street, looking a bit lost. A tough-looking guy with a neck tattoo lumbered in the other direction. For all I knew, these guys were probably kindhearted people, but what if they weren't? What if they were bad eggs who would just love to get hold of a way to persuade some thirteen-year-old to do something dangerous or emotionally damaging? I wouldn't let that happen. I'd guard the umbrella's secret to make sure no one got into any bad situations.

But then again, has it hurt anyone yet? A little voice in me asked. *Experiment with it. See if you can find a woman for Bo. The guy has been moaning about not having a girlfriend for at least two years. He deserves some happiness and fun. Plus, then he'd be less of a hard-nose. It'd be good for the morale of the band.*

I blinked. Was I seriously considering using the umbrella on Bo? What had gotten into me?

As I was obsessing like this, two clouds parted above me, and a patch of sunlight lit my spot on the sidewalk. The umbrella took on an almost surreal quality in the clean air, bright and intensely crimson, the curved wood handle gleaming with many shades of brown. I'd never seen an object in such detail before. I shook my bangs from my eyes and blinked, and the umbrella seemed to pop out at me even more from the background of the dark sidewalk. I shivered, half scared, half amazed.

I didn't want to be paranoid or anything, but this baby was alive.

My hands shook as I went back inside the laundromat to fetch my cell phone. I had to call Anatole, my family's lawyer in Paris. Maybe he knew something I didn't about Grandma's weird weather accessory. Cell phone in hand, I returned outside and clicked on Anatole Plessis's number. All I got was his voice mail, so I left a message asking him to call me back about the umbrella, reminding him of our time zone difference of nine hours.

I stashed my phone and cast a wary glance at the umbrella, which was still gripped in my left hand. Maybe I should find a locker at the bus station for it, like some criminal with a money stash. Or maybe—

"A penny for your thoughts," someone said behind me. I turned to see Leila coming out of the laundromat. God, she looked great in this light. Her skin practically glowed, and her eyes glinted with the same blue as the patch of sky above her in the east. She held a black garment in one of her hands. "Your dryer finished its cycle. I thought you might want this."

I recognized the shape of my cotton hoodie. As I reached for it, our fingers brushed. Her skin felt cool against mine, but not too cool. My ex had had cool hands too. She'd used to call me her bed warmer.

I put on my hoodie, transferring the umbrella from one hand to the other. No way would I set it on the windowsill for even a second.

Leila watched me through eyes that were hard to read. Was she looking at my bare torso between the zippers of my hoodie? "Your friend told me you guys are in a band," she said. "I feel so rude. I don't have my list of performers with me. You're here for the festival, right?"

I hesitated. How do you tell a beautiful woman that your friend got arrested for possession of contraband drugs? I opted for the edited version of the truth. "We're not part of the festival. We're on the road from San Francisco, heading south." Then I told her about the car accident. Well, most of it. The fact that Jud was in jail didn't make it into the director's cut. "But as soon as we get the van fixed," I concluded, "we'll be heading to Santa Barbara."

Her eyes bugged out a bit. "Do you believe in fate?"

"No, why?"

"You know that band I was talking about, the one that's suing the city for the puddle in their rehearsal room? Well, the judge dismissed their claim as frivolous, so they left town yesterday. And now I have no one for opening night. And here you guys are."

"Sorry, but we have a gig the day after tomorrow in L.A. and we need to regroup in Santa Barbara tomorrow night."

By regroup, I meant trying to salvage my job and my rent-free situation, but that's not something I felt like advertising.

"Won't you consider staying on? The pay is good."

I shook my head, and we exchanged a couple of good-natured excuses and arguments.

She'd just launched into a third round when behind me on the sidewalk I heard a man shout, "You leave my woman alone!"

It was the owner of the laundromat, pointing at Stinky. The tall guy pushed Stinky against the storefront window. Big mistake; you do not push Stinky.

Before I could do more than say, "Can we discuss this calmly, guys?" a full-fledged fight was underway.

"Stinky!" I yelled. "Run to the police station and stay there till I come to get you."

He ignored me, taking a swing at the big guy and missing by a foot.

The tall guy charged at him, and Stinky dodged, backing into the empty street. His attacker followed.

I jumped onto the attacker's back to slow him down, but he easily threw me off. Now they were both in the street, circling each other in the rain.

"Bo!" I looked around for the only other person nearby strong enough to help me stop the fight. But Bo was nowhere in sight. Why didn't he come out of the laundromat to help? Hadn't he heard us?

A sudden screech of car brakes drew my attention back to the street. A silver Mercedes was heading toward the tall guy. The car swerved, missing him by a hair's breadth, only to careen onto the sidewalk and smash into a metal newspaper dispenser. A blond woman in a skirt suit burst from the driver's seat and strode toward us, eyes flashing in anger. "You'd better have insurance, Clayton."

"Hey, Jenny!" This was Leila talking. She went up to the angry blond and set a hand on her arm. "I'm sure we can work something out. You're not hurt, are you?"

The blond ignored this and started arguing with Clayton. "Forget the insurance," she said."Let's settle this right now. Write me a check."

At that moment the clouds darkened and huge raindrops started splatting all around. I'm talking steady, cold sheets of water that splashed like little explosions on the sidewalk. My hands, I realized, were empty. *The umbrella!* It must have fallen during the fight. Panic seized me as I scanned the wet concrete. "Anyone seen my umbrella?"

"Right here."

Bo was holding the umbrella, unfurling it, angling it to cover the blond business woman.

"No-o-o-o!" I moved my legs, leaping at Bo, but it was as if I were in slow motion. A century later, I tackled him to the sidewalk.

Too late. The umbrella had spent a timeless moment hovering above Bo and the angry woman.

Bo struggled out from under me and got to his feet. "What is your problem?"

"Are you okay?" I said.

"I'm fine. What the hell did you do that for?"

Scooping up the umbrella, I made a lame excuse about mistaking Bo for the Clayton guy. No way was I going to tell him I thought the umbrella had magical powers. He'd think I'd gone off the deep end.

Maybe I had.

"You've been working too hard lately," Bo said. "You need some serious rest and relaxation."

"You're right, man. You're right."

We were still brushing mud flecks from our arms when I noticed the middle aged lady that Stinky had fought for hugging him. He hugged her back, looking every inch the bruised victor claiming his spoils.

The laundromat owner grunted in defeat and went into his store, leaving the blond business woman to pocket a business card she must have gotten off him. The blond then trotted up to me and Bo, her formerly hair-sprayed curls now plastered around her head. Her eyes shone at Bo in adoration.

"I wanted to thank you for your help," she said. "Your diplomacy calmed Clayton down, and your offer of an umbrella was the most chivalrous thing someone has done for me in, well, ever."

I gave an inner groan. This uptight woman was clearly smitten with my bedraggled, bohemian friend. The umbrella had done its magic.

Bo put his arm around her. "You're soaked. Let's get you inside. I'd offer the umbrella, but my buddy might flip out again."

Everyone went inside the laundromat, and I stood on the sidewalk for a minute, like a zombie. My life was starting to go pear-shaped, spinning out of control, and it was all the fault of the stupid umbrella. I had to figure out how to take back control of my fate, but I didn't have the first clue where to start. All I knew was I had to get somewhere warm and dry, pronto. Shuffling my feet, I went inside to join the others.

"Why so glum?" Stinky thumped me on the back. "Here's something that'll cheer you up. We got a gig for tomorrow night. Opening act. It pays five times more than we usually get, including free accommodations."

"What? No, no." I glanced at Leila. Had she gone behind my back when I was out on the sidewalk just now? "We have to be down south by tomorrow night. I thought I made that clear."

She smiled. "You did. But your friends saw that poster." She pointed at a bright orange sheet hanging in the laundromat window, emblazoned with the words *Garlic Festival Guide*. "They asked whether I had any open performance slots. I told them I did. They insisted I give you guys a shot."

A chorus of assent came from the business lady and the laundromat woman, who both clung to their new men's arms, gazing up at them as if seeing gods. Stinky and Bo returned their gaga looks, eyes wide in wonder.

Oh, brother. They were goners. I leaned close to Bo's face.

"Bo, listen to me. This is not going to work. We can't do a gig without Jud."

He broke off his trance-like gaze with the blond, turning to me. "That's the beauty of it. Leila agreed to pay us in advance. It should cover Jud's bail."

I hesitated. What a heel I'd been! In my eagerness to get away from this Podunk, I'd closed down my mind to options.

"Right, of course," I said.

And so our fate was decided. We would stay two nights in Gilford.

Only two nights, I told myself as I packed the umbrella into my bag and headed with the guys to Leila's house (our free accommodation). Somehow I would get my band members out of this town and back on the road to real life and better opportunities. This was just a temporary setback. Like all the other hundreds of temporary setbacks we'd had to endure in our failure to make a comeback. But we *would* make our comeback. We would get down to L.A. even if I had to drive us there from dawn to dusk on the day of the gig.

L.A. was my El Dorado. That's where real opportunity knocked.

✦

That evening found me stretched out alone on Leila's living room sofa, waking from a long and dream-filled nap. Leila had gone out to her festival office, leaving me to catch up on some much-needed Z's. When I'd asked her why she trusted me enough to let me stay alone in her house, she'd smiled and said she could read shifty types like an open book, and I wasn't one.

"Not an open book or not a shifty type?" I'd asked, and just as soon, I wished I could kick myself. I was flirting with her, and I hadn't meant to.

"A rock-solid, half-open book" was her reply. Then she'd fluttered her lashes at me and whisked out to her car.

I groaned at the memory. The last thing I needed right now was a complication with a woman who'd either a) freak out when I left town or b) dump me when she figured out I was an emotional mess. There was no such thing as a strings-free situation between me and a woman. There were always tears and accusations in the end. And sometimes the tears were mine.

I rolled over on the sofa, checking my cell phone on the coffee table. The display read 6:08 p.m.

Glancing around the living room, I saw Stinky's duffel bag on the floor beside me. It looked out of place next to Leila's rose and lilac décor. I continued scanning the room. Jud's sticker-covered guitar case sat propped against an armchair. The stickers struck me as gaudy compared with Leila's framed posters on the walls.

I checked my phone messages. I had one from Bo and one from Stinky. Both said they'd be spending the night at their girlfriends' places and would come for their bags tomorrow.

Great. The guys were moving in with their women. Which meant our band might be breaking up even now. I plonked my phone back on the coffee table a little harder than I should have. True, I'd sometimes fantasized about going solo as a singer-songwriter, but I'd always been scared I'd lose momentum without the guys. Just the idea of discussing our situation with them made my gut twist. I hated change, and more than that, I hated conflict.

I glared at the red shape nestled beside me on the sofa. There it was, my constant companion. The umbrella. I'd decided to keep it within view at all times. That's what Grandma had requested, and I was starting to see why.

I must have dozed off, because a few seconds later, the front door clicked open and Leila came in, but the room was much darker than I'd remembered it.

"Evening, sleepyhead." She laughed as she switched on a light.

I sat up and blinked into the bright entryway. "Welcome home."

"Thanks." She was carrying two grocery bags.

I leaped from the sofa. "Here, I'll get those bags for you." I gently took them from her and carried them to the kitchen. "I'd love to cook dinner for you, too," I said. "To thank you for your hospitality."

"And not because you like me?" A charming smile spread over her lips, dimpling one cheek. She blushed and lowered her eyes, as if surprised by her own boldness.

Dang. She was flirting with me again.

"That too," I said, hoping to sound neutral.

"How about we go to a restaurant instead? There's an Italian place a few blocks away. I could use the walk."

I paused. I couldn't ask her to pay for my dinner, broke as I was. Besides which, I didn't want her to think we were on a date. I glanced into the grocery bag we were unpacking. "Or I could cook you my famous spaghetti *à la* scrumpdiddly-umptious and after that, we could go on the walk."

She grinned. "Deal."

So I put on the flowered apron I found on the hearth, and I whipped up the one dish I could do without a recipe. When we sat down at her kitchen table, I was thankful to see she hadn't dimmed the lights or brought out any candles.

While we ate, I asked her about the garlic festival, figuring she might need to blow off some steam about her stressful job. I was right.

"I'm doing the work of three people," she said, twirling a forkful of noodles. "I really, really needed an assistant, but the city council didn't budget for one. They spent everything on the entertainment and advertising."

"Is there anything you can do to lighten your load?"

She shook her head. "Nothing short of quitting. I've thought about looking for similar work in San Francisco. But I won't quit. I love this town, and I love that the festival has put it on the map."

Naturally I didn't mention that I'd never heard of the festival until today and that for most people, Gilford was only a dot on the map.

After dinner, I stashed the umbrella in my backpack, and we headed outside. Most of the clouds had blown away, but the sidewalks were still wet, reflecting the streetlights—streaky stars in a black asphalt sky. I stepped on one of reflections, and it exploded in ripples.

Leila stepped in the next puddle, creating more waves of light. "Stinky told me your band was semi-famous for a while. Sorry I hadn't heard of you."

"Not a problem. Most people haven't."

"He said you guys can do rock ballads?"

Flattered, I told her about the various styles my band tried to emulate and to transcend in our own original way. "But we're never cynical about it. If a song is too ironic, it's like it's afraid to feel. Music like that will never truly move people. But if a song is too sentimental, it descends into pre-packaged emotion, which makes the people listening to it into, well, emotional robots. It's a very fine line, and I never know if we've crossed it until we've rehearsed and rewritten a song to death." I stopped talking, suddenly aware I'd gotten carried away. "Anyway, that's the ideal case. Lately, we're like a broken record. No new material. That's almost as bad as a robotic song."

She drew in a slow breath, as if weighing her next words. "Hearing you talk like that, I feel guilty about tomorrow night."

"Why would you feel guilty?"

"I wish Bo had told you sooner. He said he'd talk to you, but then he reneged, so now I'm left holding the bag."

I stopped in the middle of the sidewalk. "What do you wish he'd told me?"

She stopped too, facing me but unable to meet my eye. "We have a lot of young teens coming in with their parents tomorrow night. It's a special theme night, and the kids will be wearing the T-shirts and signature styles of their favorite boy bands."

"You want us to be a boy band?"

She nodded. "The kids are expecting covers of songs by their favorite artists, and older songs in the same style. The city has gone all out and sprung for the performance licenses." She glanced at me. I said nothing—too much in shock. She forged on, speaking faster. "Stinky and Bo said it would be okay. They said they're quick at picking up a tune and can pull everything together during rehearsals tomorrow. I'll provide the lyrics for you guys on a *karaoke* screen as well."

My mouth finally was able to move again. "Why didn't you tell me this morning?"

"Bo promised he would, but then he called me at the office and asked me to tell you instead, since he was—busy."

Huh. I bet he was busy, love-struck goofball that he had become. Evidently, all Bo could think about today was his new yuppie princess.

On the other hand, knowing Bo, he probably hadn't wanted to go head-to-head with me over this issue. He would want to break the news to me gently through the mouth of a beautiful woman he hoped I'd end up sleeping with.

I puffed out a sigh. Our band used to have such effortless teamwork and a fair decision-making process, and now Stinky and Bo were riding roughshod over me, blinded by "lurv" and steered by their dicks.

Stupid umbrella. I could feel it poking into my shoulder from inside my backpack.

"I wish he'd told me sooner too," I said.

"Do you still want to look at the contract?"

"Don't worry. I'll sign it."

She sighed. "That's a relief. Your expression looked horrified."

"Let's just say that style of music is not my cup of tea."

"Think how happy you'll make the fans who do love it." She smiled.

God, how beautiful she looked, lit up from the side by the street lamp, the hollow of her cheek in shadow. Her hair stirred in the wind, and I resisted the urge to touch it.

"That's a generous way to put it," I said.

"And who knows? Maybe you can bring out the raw emotion anyway."

As she said this, a raindrop hit her cheek. And then another. A second later, I felt the drops too on my bare head.

"We'd better go back," I said, hands in pockets.

She slid her arm through the crook of my elbow. "I love summer rain, don't you?"

"Sometimes."

The drops were coming down faster now, and harder. A warm rivulet ran down the nape of my neck into my shirt. I pulled up my collar.

Leila snuggled closer to my arm as we walked. "Hey, didn't you pack your umbrella?"

I paused. "No."

"Yeah, you did. I saw you."

"I'm pretty sure I didn't," I said, walking faster.

She laughed. "How much do you wanna bet? I have a clear memory of you wrapping the little strap around it and putting it into your bag. Here, hand me your pack. I'll show you."

"Now I remember. I did pack it, but it won't help. It's broken."

"It's got to offer at least a little protection." She shivered against me. "Please? I'm getting soaked."

"It's broken."

She looked at me sideways. "Why would you lie about something like that?"

I hesitated. "I'm not lying."

"You forget. I can read people like open books."

Crap. She knew I was lying, and she knew that I knew she knew. But if I admitted the lie I'd have to explain why. A quick search of my gray matter for a good excuse yielded nothing. Meanwhile, our hair and our shoulders were drenched. A drop of water had gathered at the end of my nose. I wiped it off.

"I'm sorry," I said. "I'm superstitious about the umbrella. I can't say why, but I can't lend it to anyone."

I could feel her gaze on the side of my face. "I believe you," she said.

After that, a chill set in between us. We race-walked the rest of the way to her house, exchanging strained small talk about the weather and the route home, and by the time we reached her place, the warmth that had once been between us was gone.

"Ta-da!" Bo waltzed into the festival rehearsal tent, where I'd been working all morning. It was the day after my fiasco with Leila, and I'd been up early, the lyrics of a new song pressing themselves into my mind. All I had so far was . . .

> *You want my shirt*
> *I give you my coat*

I literally could not get these words out of my head. They'd woken me up at around five a.m. in a mental play-back loop, including a snippet of melody. Whenever that happens, I have no choice but to listen to the lyrics and write them down. It's the only way to get the words to stop for a while, so I can move on to the next section of a new song.

But today I was getting nowhere with the snippet. Story of my life lately. I'd accrued hundreds of these play-back loops, but none had flushed out into a full song. And our band needed new material to make our comeback.

It was maddening.

I set aside my guitar and focused on Bo and the rest of the people trooping in behind him.

My jaw dropped. *What the--?*

All three of my other band members stopped in front of me, including Jud. How had he gotten out of jail? And more mysteriously, where had he found that pair of god-awful ugly, gold-colored spandex jeans?

The other guys were dressed in the same style of tight and shiny trousers, and they each wore wigs that were short in back and long in front, their bangs hanging into their eyes.

Bo tossed his head, swinging the wig bangs out of his eyes. "Check out the new look. We're gonna rock those teenies' world." He struck a pose, lowering his face to give me a smoldering look through his bangs. "Pretty cool, huh?"

"It's pretty something," I said, unable to elaborate for the moment. I could not take my eyes off of their sequined shirts. And the belt buckles! They were huge and metallic, in the shape of lightning bolts.

I shook my head, trying to focus on the fact that our lead guitarist was now out of jail. I got up and gave Jud a hearty thump on the arm. "So! What happened? I thought your arraignment wasn't until this afternoon. I was gonna be there."

Jud grinned, his wig hair falling over one eye. "They let me out early."

"Why?"

"My new girlfriend couldn't bear the idea of me being locked up. She told the judge she planted the pot as false evidence. She claimed she had 'unresolved anger issues' about criminals or something like that." His eyes took on a dreamy quality that was more glazed than his usual glazed and dreamy look. "She's an angel."

I gulped. "Wait, are you telling me the lady cop lied for you? That could cost her her job."

"No worries. They set her up with some kind of counseling for a while. But between you and me—" He leaned close and said in a stage whisper, "—she told me she hates her job. She's gonna resign and become our band manager."

A sudden cough closed my throat for a second. "Okay, let's not get ahead of ourselves. Since when do we make unilateral decisions about the band? We're supposed to discuss things and put them to a vote."

"Actually," Bo said from the sidelines. "The vote is already three-to-one. Stinky and I are on board with the idea."

"What?"

"Believe me, you'll love Alice," Bo went on. "She'll make a great manager. She's well-organized and works hard. Check it out." He plucked at one of his sequined sleeves. "She bought these outfits with the money we saved because we didn't have to pay Jud's bail."

All three of the guys struck theatrical poses, flexing their pecs and triceps, and then they broke out into a song I'd never heard before, crooning and twisting their faces as if constipated.

Don't call it puppy love
It comes from above
So what if I'm sixteen?
You know what I mean
Are puppies so bad?
They don't make me sad

Their love is true
Like my love for you

When they stopped, they looked at me expectantly.

I stared back in undisguised horror. The song had quite possibly been the worst piece of music I had ever heard, and their rendition of it had been like squeezing honey from a gooey rag.

"Well?" Bo said. "What do you think? I wrote it last night. I thought we should do at least one original piece for our fans tonight."

Our fans? I continued goggling at them, adding an open mouth to my medley of expressions. Speech was not at option at the moment.

"We were thinking of doing some cool visuals up on the screen behind us," Stinky added in his baritone. "I found a bunch of royalty-free pictures of puppies on the net. Super cute. Check it."

He whipped out his phone and held it before my traumatized eyes. Pictures of brown-eyed Labrador puppies, black-eyed pugs, and whimsical Chihuahuas flashed by on the screen. All puppies, all of their eyes larger than life, as if digitally enhanced.

The other guys had gathered around to watch the slideshow.

"Aw-w-w-w-w," Jud said. "Look at that one."

"Hold me back," Stinky said. "I'm having a cute attack."

"I'm gonna get a real puppy tomorrow," Bo said, sighing. "Their love really is innocent and pure."

"Whoa, whoa, whoa." I held up my palms in a stop-sign gesture. "Where is the puppy going to pee? I don't have a litter box in my van."

All three turned to me, astonishment in their eyes.

"Your van?" Bo said.

It was as if I'd been talking about a newly sighted but probably invented flying saucer.

"I got my van out of the shop this morning," I said, "so we can leave right after the show tomorrow night and drive all night straight to L.A. We can sleep the next day on the beach and be fresh for our gig."

"Whoa, whoa, whoa," Jud said, repeating my phrase. "I need to think about this."

"Me too," said Stinky.

"Me too," said Bo.

They screwed up their faces and looked off in various directions.

"There's nothing to think about," I insisted. "We have a gig in L.A. the day after tomorrow. We have to be there."

"Not necessarily," said Bo.

"Yeah," said Stinky.

"Yeah," said Jud.

I drew in a slow breath. "Don't tell me you want to stay here."

"I want to stay here," said Stinky.

"Me too," said Jud.

"Me too," said Bo.

What were they, wind-up toys? They could barely think for themselves. Had the umbrella taken away their free will?

"Guys," I said, coming to a quick decision; I would reveal all about the umbrella. Maybe that would help them snap out of their state. I hated to risk being seen as nuts myself, but these guys were so far gone, I had to follow them there to haul them back. "You know this crazy feeling you have? This new passion for kitschy songs, unknown women, and baby animals? It's not real." I pulled the umbrella out of my backpack, and in rapid-fire speech, told them about my near-death experience in the van and my observations of my friends when they'd been under the umbrella with their new flames. "Don't you see? It's like a love charm," I concluded. "Eventually it should wear off. Or at least I hope so, because, look at yourselves. This is not the bad-ass crew you were meant to be. I mean, Spandex? And, guys, what's with the rhinestones and the lightning bolts? You guys *know*, deep in your soul, this is not your scene. So, what do you say? Shall we hit the road tonight and rock L.A.?"

Winding down, I was feeling pretty good about my speech. I wasn't a natural leader for nothing. Under normal circumstances, I could pep-talk just about anyone into just about anything.

But these weren't normal circumstances.

"Are you finished?" Bo asked.

I nodded, and Bo launched into a counter argument that obliterated each of my points. Using his famous logical abilities, he explained that I must be having some sort of mental breakdown, because what I was claiming was impossible. Inanimate objects do not have animate powers, and my brain cells contained nothing more than electrochemical charges, without any sensors or awareness outside of my body. "I hate to break it to you," he concluded, "but you're hallucinating. I don't want to say the 'S' word, but I'm thinking it."

"I do not have schizophrenia."

"I'm just saying . . ."

"Okay, forget all that about the out-of-body experience. How do you explain your sudden awful taste in music?"

"It's not awful. It's a love song. When you're in love, you feel things and see things you never noticed before." He turned to the other guys. "Am I right?"

"So right," said Stinky.

"So very right," said Jud.

They gathered around me, concern etched in their faces, and patted me as if tending a terminally ill patient.

Jud put his hand to my forehead. "You haven't taken any drugs, have you?"

"I don't take drugs."

He nodded. "Why don't you lie down over there while we set up for rehearsal? I'll bring you some lunch, okay? We got Taco Bell. Veggie burritos, your favorite."

Stinky patted my shoulder with a heavy hand. "I'll help you memorize the songs for tonight. I brought index cards!"

"Everything's going to be fine," Bo added in a soothing voice. "There's medication for this kind of thing. I have a cousin who's a politician back east. Totally off his rocker. But with medication, he's like you and me. I mean, like me and the guys, I mean—oh, never mind. Sorry."

It was not worth the effort of arguing with them. I could only hope the matchmaking magic would wear off soon or lessen, and they'd get their ear for good music back.

We had just sat down with our bags of tacos and burritos when the rehearsal tent flapped open, and Leila came in. She carried a clipboard, a phone, a computer tablet, and from the slope of her shoulders, I'd say the weight of the world.

I stood up at once, something my French grandfather taught me when I used to visit him and my cousins during summers as a kid. When a woman enters a room, and a man is seated, he should stand and offer her a chair or at least remain standing until she sits down.

Leila's cheeks were flushed, and her eyes glassy. Had she been running? Crying? I pulled out one of the folding chairs at our table for her, and she sat down.

"Thanks. I can't stay long. I came by to check on you guys. Do you have everything you need? The *karaoke* machine should be delivered here within the hour." She gave a sudden sneeze, barely covering her nose in time. "Pardon me!" She grabbed a napkin from the table and dabbed at her nose. "I think I'm coming down with something."

A pang of guilt ran through me. I'd have bet anything she was sick because I'd refused to bring out the umbrella last night. My hand went to her forehead. "You've got a fever. You should be at home in bed."

"I'm fine. It's just a little cold." She sneezed again into the tissue.

"A fever like that is a sign of the flu," I said.

"I can't have the flu. The festival opens tonight."

Bo perked up at the card table. "Those two statements are not logically consistent. How can the festival cause you not to have the flu?"

"Actually," Stinky said around his mouthful of burrito. "If a person has something important to do, his immune system sometimes can put off getting sick until the big event is over. I guess our ancestors needed that when they crossed the Alps or whatever."

They started an argument about pure logic vs. implied logic, and I turned my attention back Leila.

"Let me drive you home. My car's out of the shop."

She sighed. "I can't. I have about a hundred things to do. Speaking of which, if everything's fine here, I'd better get going." She stood up, and then weaved a bit to the side. She put her hand on the table to steady herself, sinking slowly to the chair. "O-o-o-h."

Guilt zinged through me, tensing my gut. She wouldn't be ill if I hadn't been such a clod about the umbrella. In a flash, I thought of a way to make it up to her.

"You said once you needed an assistant? Let me be that person today. I'll do the groundwork while you're resting at home. Look, I even have one of those ear phones. I'll keep it on at all times."

"What about your rehearsal?" she said.

"A couple of hours of prep and the *karaoke* machine should be enough for me. I don't play any instruments during performances."

She looked at her clipboard for a moment and then at me, eyes bright. "This could work. I could talk you through everything. Mostly it's meet-and-greets with the vendors and trouble shooting anything that comes up."

"I love to trouble shoot." I held out my hand for her. "Let me walk you to the car."

I drove her home, and for the rest of the afternoon, when I wasn't reviewing new songs, I was Leila's eyes and ears at the fairgrounds. I had to admit, if only to myself, we made a great team. Usually, I'm so independent I don't like taking direction from anyone, but with her, it was different. She had a genuinely polite way of making her requests. She used a lot of expressions like "would you mind" and "could you," and she included thank-yous and please. If she'd asked me to wash her car and pick up her dry cleaning, I was so charmed by her voice purring "thanks so much," I just might have done it.

"That was wild!" Late that night, I stumbled into the backstage area beside the main show tent, sweat dripping from my brow and laughter pouring from my throat. Stinky, Bo and Jud tripped in right behind me, whooping and pumping their fists in the air.

I couldn't help but join in with the celebration, mostly because our boy-band ordeal was over. The songs had been trite—I'll be the first to admit it—but we'd brought something primal to the performance that hadn't totally sucked.

I mean, if you're going to do something, even something stupid, do it with conviction. So I'd worn the smudged eyeliner and the long-banged wig. And I'd crooned out the song texts as if they were poetry for the ages. At one point, I even ripped off my shirt and threw it into the audience.

They loved it.

I'm talking teenie boppers swooning and tearing at their hair. It was pretty amazing. You could have sailed a ship on that sea of adoration.

"Did we rock or did we rock?" Stinky shouted too loudly. His hearing always goes out after a performance.

"It's not an either-or question," Bo yelled joyfully. "It's an *and-and!*"

"Oh, ye-e-e-e-ah," said Jud, drawing it out in his blissful, fried-brain way.

"Why can't we get that kind of response to our own material?" I asked.

"Our old audience is more reserved," Bo said. "Left-brained, city hipsters who don't like physical contact." He thumped his chest. "I am whereof I speak. But, man alive, I have smelled me some teen spirit, and that stuff is potent. There were enough hormones out there to sprout the next generation."

"Ye-e-e-e-ah," said Jud. "Totally."

"Did you see what they did to your shirt?" Stinky asked me. "I wouldn't have been surprised if they ate it."

Bo grinned. "Good move with the shirt. I'm gonna get buffed so I can do that next time too."

"Me too." Jud flexed a scrawny arm, groping it for firmness.

I stared at them, reality setting in. "What do you mean, next time? We're not performing for this audience again."

"Not this one exactly," Bo said. "But one like it."

"Oh, no, no, no, no." As I said this, my boy-band wig swished across my eyeballs. I took off the wig. "I am not gonna write songs like this. I couldn't even if I wanted to."

"You don't have to," Bo said. "We'll write them. Right, guys?"

The two others nodded, bangs swaying.

I sighed. "This is not going to work."

A panicked look passed over Bo's face. "Come on, Travis. You're the soul of the group. Without your voice, we're just a bunch of guys banging on instruments."

I couldn't believe it. He was talking as if our band was breaking up. Maybe it was. "Let's sleep on it, okay? Let's go to L.A. tomorrow, do our usual thing, and then we'll talk."

Bo hesitated. "Speaking of L.A., I have a confession to make."

I stared at him. Had they all decided to stay in Gilford? "You're killing me! What now?"

"See, I—"

He didn't get to finish his sentence, because just then the tent door flapped open and our former agent walked in, hair gleaming with pomade, eyes unreadable as always. Tall, lean, and clever, but too little kind, Garret Proudie had been our agent for three years during our heyday, but as our sales had waned, he'd lost interest in us, ignoring our messages and basically consigning us to the dustheap of musical history. Luckily, the indie scene had started taking off around that time, so we could try our luck with streaming and digital downloads, not that we'd had much luck, but at least other routes had become potentially lucrative, and we could move on. To places like Gilford.

"Garret," I said. "This is amazing. What are you doing here?" But I didn't have to ask. I could tell from Bo's lowered gaze that he must have called our ex-agent and begged him to drive down from San Francisco to check out our new sound.

Garrett pulled at his shirt sleeves so that they poked out of his jacket at exactly the same distance. I remembered that tic of his well. His gold cufflinks glinted in the uncertain light of the bare bulb above us. "That makes two of us asking that question. What the hell am I doing here?" He turned to Bo. "I was promised something original. What I was just subjected to was run-of-the-mill, crank-it-out pop. It was all covers! You of all people should know better, Bo."

Bo's eyebrows had risen and disappeared under his bangs. "One of those songs was an original piece. Didn't you see how the girls swooned over 'Puppy Love'?"

"That was the worst of the bunch!" Garret said.

"To be fair," I interjected, "it doesn't matter what we think. What matters is what the fans feel, and those fans were feeling it."

Garrett made a dismissive gesture and looked at his watch. "I'm out of here."

Stinky, Bo and Jud all turned to me, begging me with their eyes to say something more. I suppose they thought I'd miraculously converted to their new style of music. I hadn't of course, but I wasn't going to stand there and let Garrett insult my friends. Besides,

I'd be a fool not to pitch my new song ideas to him. I didn't have to like Garrett to know that working with him might bring us more revenue streams via his performance venue contacts abroad.

"Wait," I called after Garrett, and when he turned, I said, "That's not our new sound. We filled in for another band tonight, and we wanted you to see how we connect with a younger audience. But that's not the main reason we asked you down. We wanted to tell you about some new tracks I've been writing."

Garrett pursed his lips in a skeptical expression, but maybe he was more desperate than he let on. He had after all driven more than an hour to hear us. He might have fallen on hard times. The music industry was in turmoil after all. "Go on."

"We want to fuse our old darkness with more heartfelt love songs and upbeat dance tracks."

"Play me something."

The guys all looked at me, wide-eyed, and for a panicked moment, I was tempted to run out of the tent. But I'd never forgive myself if I didn't at least try to talk up a new sound.

"Now's not a good time," I said. "I need to be somewhere. Can we email you a sample track?"

He tapped his chin. "I want to hear it live. Come by my hotel tomorrow morning around nine. Just you and your guitar. I'm leaving town at ten."

Did I dare agree to it? I had a wild idea that I could finish a song tonight. I'd done that once before when pressure was on. Could I do it again?

"Will do," I heard myself say.

Garrett shook each of our hands, and sauntered out.

All four of us guys stood there a moment. Then Bo broke the silence.

"You have new songs finished?"

I gulped. I hated to lie twice in a row, but if I told the guys the truth, they'd write me off. I needed a twelve-hour grace period. "Only one is finished," I fibbed, "but it's good."

"When were you planning to tell us?"

"I kept thinking it's not ready. But just now, I decided it is."

"Let's hear it then."

"I can't. I need to go the grocery store before it closes."

"What? Why?"

"Leila needs more juice and cold medicine."

Bo, Stinky and Jud exchanged glances. "You know what I think?" Stinky said. "I think you pitched your stuff to Garrett so you could go solo."

"That's not true."

"Oh, yeah?" Jud chimed in, "then why don't you share the song with us? We could sing back up tomorrow morning."

"Garrett doesn't want too much noise in his hotel room."

Bo's eyes narrowed. "He asked to see you alone. Have you been in contact with him?"

It was like being questioned by a cop. I felt guilty even though I hadn't done anything wrong. Yet.

But maybe they were right. Maybe I did want to break up with the band. If they couldn't snap out of their smitten state, how much of a future would there be for us anyhow? "Is that what you guys want? For us to go separate ways?" I asked.

They shook their heads, eyes bugging out in worry.

I let out the breath I'd been holding. "Me neither." I ran my hands through my hair, suddenly exhausted. "We've got a lot to think about. Let's sleep on it and see what Garrett says tomorrow, okay?"

And maybe by then, the love-magic would have let up and we'd be able to talk reasonably.

All three of them nodded eagerly, and we grinned at one another. It felt great to be a team again, but if I couldn't come up with something to wow Garrett and the guys, it'd be the end of us. They would move in with their girlfriends and take root on their living room sofas and in the garlic fields.

I would not let their talent go to waste like that. I was going to compose like mad, convince the guys to opt for long-distance romance, and haul their love-crazy asses out of this backwater town.

About forty minutes later, I parked my van in the driveway in front of Leila's house. I killed the engine, and sat there a moment in the dark, scrolling through my phones messages. There was one from Anatole in Paris. I clicked on the message.

"Sorry, Travis." His accent made my name sound like *Travees*, emphasis on the *ee*. "I don't know much about that funny little umbrella. Your grandmother seemed to consider it a good luck charm. She even

told me once that the umbrella saved her marriage."
Here he chuckled. "She may have been eccentric, but
it was in a good way, *non?* At any rate, the stipulation
in her will is clear. You must carry the umbrella with
you whenever possible and then pass it to your next
cousin to get your inheritance next spring, though of
course, how can your grandmother or I be sure you
will do this?" Another chuckle. "She used to speak of
you and your cousins with much love. I hope you realize this. I suspect she wanted to remain near to you
through a treasured object—it could have been any
object—to remind you of her love and your own mor-
tality. So please be sure to pass the umbrella on to
your cousin, to—to—Ah, yes, to Ainsley, at the ap-
pointed time. It's only fair that she have a chance to
receive her part of the inheritance as well."

Having heard all this, I stashed my phone in my
pocket, none the wiser, although the anecdote about
Grandma believing the umbrella had saved her marriage was news to me. She must have known of the
thing's matchmaking power. I shuddered at the
thought and went to the back of the van to check on
the umbrella.

There it was, as innocuous-looking as could be,
wedged behind Stinky's drum set where I'd hidden it.
I'd have liked nothing more than to destroy it or bury
it somewhere outside of town, but my cousins would
give me hell if I did that. So I grabbed my grocery bag,
climbed out of the van, and locked all the doors.

I let myself into the house with the key Leila had
given me, and went to check on her. Her bedroom
door was ajar, but darkness filled the room. I could
just make out the shape of her body under the covers,

her chest rising and falling slowly. I found myself stepping closer, enchanted by the sight of her face. Her eyelashes looked like two dark moons in a luminous sky, and her hair was spread out on her pillow like a black sea.

Watching her, I lost track of time.

I shook my head to clear it. What was I doing here staring at her? I had work to do. But I didn't want to wake her up with my music. I would work in my van.

I went to the kitchen and started a pot of coffee. I was going to be up all night.

I jerked awake to a sudden honking sound. What the—? Bolting upright, I looked around, blinking into the darkness. My van's dashboard lay before me where I sat in the driver's seat, the front window streaming with raindrops, the steering wheel a round shape below. I groaned. I must have fallen asleep on my van's horn.

Rubbing my eyes, I clicked on my phone screen. The time was shortly after three a.m.

Crap. I was getting nowhere with this song. The last thing I'd remembered before dozing off was obsessively repeating the chorus aloud, nodding to the rhythm like one of those ridiculous, bobbing-head toy dogs.

> *I ain't afraid to love you*
> *I ain't afraid to die*

A light went on in Leila's window. The curtains were pulled aside, and there she was in silhouette, peering into the night. I didn't move. I just sat there in the dark van like something in a coffin. Her light went out again. Still I didn't move.

Finally, I grabbed the damn umbrella from the back and went out onto the sidewalk. I needed to clear my head. Maybe there would be an all-night coffee shop in this town where I could get an omelet and free coffee refills.

I walked and walked. The restaurants were all closed. I kept walking, now in the rain. There was no one around, so I risked opening the umbrella over me. Nothing happened. I felt no tingle or anything. Just a regular old umbrella with a funky, curved handle.

I walked for another ten minutes around the downtown area, past the city hall, the police station, and the laundromat, until I came to a park that took up an entire city block. At its center I found a pagoda. The summer rain was beating down pretty hard, so I took shelter under the pagoda roof and sat down on the bench there.

Alone. In the middle of the night. In the middle of nowhere.

I sat there in a caffeine-induced haze, jittering a bit as I gazed out at the lush greenery. Each tree nearby looked different from the tree beside it, each fronted by a signpost and a plaque. The trees must have been brought as saplings from other regions. I got up and went out to peer at the nearest tree. Its species had originated in Japan.

Huh. All roads lead to Gilford.

I went back to the bench, sat down, and after a while, realized I was still holding the umbrella over my head, even though I was under the pagoda roof.

I laughed, and for some reason, I kept the umbrella where it was, like a small tent.

Looking up at the red canopy and the spokes, I sighed. I couldn't blame this ugly piece of rain gear for the sorry state of my band. Even before the love spells, the guys and I had been on the outs. It's not easy keeping four very different people bound to the same vision and moving in the same direction. Hell, I couldn't even do that with one other person in a relationship.

I thought of Leila, of her insistence she was fine and could still work from bed even though she'd obviously been in no shape to work. She would probably be like that on her deathbed too. "Just one more text message. One more call. I need to do this one thing before I go."

I laughed at the imagined scene, and in that moment, as I sat there under the umbrella, the rest of the song I'd been working on came to me whole, playing out in my inner ear as if by someone else. I could only listen and witness. The song was about lovers torn between losing themselves in each other and finding a separate self in the world. About that feeling of oblivion you get when you're making love.

I jumped up, and rushed back toward Leila's house. I had to write this down. I had to try it out. Maybe it was just a flash in the pan. Maybe it wasn't as good as I thought.

"I'm so sorry to wake you, but I'm in something of a pickle."

It was the next morning around nine forty-five, and I was sitting alone in my van's driver's seat with my phone to my ear, talking to a very groggy Leila, who was back home in bed.

"That's okay," she said. "Where are you?"

I had left a long note for her on her kitchen table, but evidently she hadn't seen it yet. So I brought her up to speed about Garrett's being in town and my having been up all night working on a new song for my appointment with him. "But my van just stalled out in the middle of a puddle in an intersection. I'd call a cab, but the guys in my band spent our advance payment on those boy-band outfits. I feel like a clod for asking, but do you have Triple-A road service? Maybe the tow-truck driver can drop me off at Garrett's hotel in time."

As I said all this, I noticed that my forehead was pressed to the top of my steering wheel and that I had been slowly and softly pounding my head on the wheel, rocking like an autistic person. I sat up and shook my head. Man, I needed to get some sleep soon. I'd sacrificed sleep to finish the song, and last I could remember, the song was pretty good, but then again, I'd had a few space-out sessions this morning while driving. Maybe I was completely out of touch with reality.

Leila's breath sounded heavy in my earpiece, as if her nose was plugged. "Yeah, I've got that service. I'll be right there with my card."

"No, no, you're sick. Stay in bed. I'll jog back and get the card."

"Where are you now?"

I peered at the street signs above me and told her the street names.

"That's too far to jog without missing your appointment. Besides, I think they need me to be there in person to get the free tow service. I'll see you in about ten minutes."

"Wait, let me try my other band members again."

"You told me they're late sleepers, right? They won't pick up."

Wow, she remembered everything. No wonder she was in overwhelm with the festival. Her brain never shut down. "True," I said, "but maybe their girl-friends will be awake."

"In the meantime, I could already have called for the tow truck. Please, humor me, okay? You helped me yesterday. Now it's my turn to help you."

What could I say? "Okay, but dress warmly and take your time. And when you get here, stay in your car. There's a lot of water in this area. I don't want your feet to get wet."

"Deal."

About ten minutes later, Leila's rusty Ford hatch-back pulled up at the edge of the intersection's "lake" in which my van was sitting like an island. I ran to greet her, my feet squeaking in my wet shoes.

She grinned at me. Her hair was damp and sticking to her forehead, and her cheeks were flushed pink. But she was still beautiful. "I'd have driven faster, but the germs formed a little cloud in front of my eyes and slowed me down. They want their host to stay alive."

"I feel terrible about this. I'll make it up to you."

"No worries. How about I drive you the rest of the way right now? We can call the tow truck later."

"If anyone's driving anyone anywhere, it's me, you. Hand me those keys. You can lie down in the back. I'll get you a sleeping bag from the van."

She smiled, a pearly-white crescent. "I won't argue with that."

Within minutes, we arrived at Garrett's hotel. I got out of the car and came around the side to Leila's window.

"I'll be back in about fifteen minutes to drive you home," I told her. "Are you sure you'll be warm enough in the car?"

"I'm so hot if I had air conditioning, I'd turn it on."

I looked down at her from where I stood. She *was* hot, lying there in the back seat with her hair fanned and her lips parted.

You can turn on more than an air conditioner, girl.

Dang. Did I just think that? Lack of sleep had destroyed my mental filters. I gave myself a shake; Garrett was waiting, and I had a song that needed singing.

So I went to the hotel's front desk and waited there for Garrett to be summoned by the clerk. A second later, Leila walked into the lobby instead, cheeks pink, eyes vivid.

"Everything okay?" I rushed to her side and put an arm around her to support her weight.

"I changed my mind. It's too cold in the car. Would you mind terribly if I sat in on your meeting?"

"Of course you can. Of course. Are you sure you're okay? I'll reschedule the meeting."

"No, this is your future. It's important."

"Your health is more important."

"It's just few chills, silly. Nothing to meet my maker about."

"After this, I am going to stay home all day and make you soup."

It occurred to me I'd said "home" as if it really were my home, but I quickly dismissed the thought. Home was just an expression.

"Thanks. You're the best."

Garrett came in, and after exchanging greetings and pleasantries, we went up to his room. "I've got about five minutes," he said, glancing at his watch. "Show me what you've got."

I gulped. I'd performed hundreds of times in front of an audience, but now that Leila was here, my throat was suddenly dry and my stomach jumpy.

I had to admit it; I wanted her to like the song.

I wanted her to like *me.*

But that was nothing new, right? I wanted everyone to like me. So why were my hands trembling so much? I could barely feel the strings on my guitar. Oh, right. The shakes were probably from all the coffee in my system. And *of course* I was nervous. I was trying to make a comeback and save my band from oblivion. Who wouldn't be scared?

Oblivion. Fear. Saving grace. These were the themes of my song. I had to feel them. I had to know them. I had to—

Then it hit me. The song wasn't about some abstract lovers in some big city, as I'd thought it was. It was about me and Leila, right here, right now. How could I not have seen that until this moment?

I took a deep breath, and I sang the song. I sang it for her.

You want my shirt, I give you my coat
You want my time, I give you my life
You slap my hand, I turn my cheek
You cut my cheek, I show you my throat
You want my heart, I give you my soul
You take a part, I'm giving it whole
'cuz I ain't afraid to love you
'cuz I ain't afraid to die
I drop down, hands above me
Couldn't run if I tried
And everywhere you walk is
everywhere we'd run
And every time you balk is
everything undone
And everything that fears is
anything that bleeds
And every time we kiss is
everything to me
'cuz I ain't afraid to love you
'cuz I ain't afraid to die
I drop down, hands above me
Couldn't run if I tried
'cuz I ain't afraid to love you
I ain't afraid to die
When you take me, take completely

Take me, take me alive

When I played the last chord, it seemed to hang in the air for longer than my hearing perceived it.

Another couple of seconds passed. I stared at a leaf design in the carpet, waiting. It didn't matter what Garrett thought. What mattered was what Leila thought. Or said. Or did. Or felt.

Anything could happen now between us. And if she didn't want me, I knew I'd need a long, long time to get over it.

Garret gave a low whistle. "Nice. Very nice. I see what you mean about fusing your old sound with something more upbeat. If you repeat that line about the shirt to the end, you could rip off your shirt during performances and throw it into the mosh pit. Then get down on your knees and raise your arms. 'Stick 'em up! This is the love police.' Yeah, those first lines about the shirt and the 'drop down, hands above me' should be repeated at the end."

Actually, it wasn't a bad idea. It would make the song longer, and that was a good thing during live performances.

"Duly noted," I said in a noncommittal voice.

Leila still hadn't spoken. I sneaked a glance at her. She had her gaze directed at the carpet. We'd locked eyes off and on during the song, but now she looked as embarrassed as I felt.

Garret said something about wanting to hear more in this vein and sending us a contract to consider.

Yes! Garret must be desperate. So much the better for my band. The guys were going to be thrilled. I felt sure I could persuade them to sign on with me. They could even live in Gilford as their home base if they wanted. I wasn't sure where I'd be based. San Francisco maybe? Everything was up in the air.

Garrett gave me his new card, and after we'd all said our good-byes, I helped Leila walk to the parking lot, supporting her on my arm.

She stopped for a moment beside her car and leaned against it, blinking rapidly.

"How are you feeling?" I asked her.

"Sad."

I felt my eyebrows go up. "Why?"

Her gaze met mine. "I can see the future. Well, not actually. But I can make some pretty accurate guesses based on existing circumstances. And sometimes, I just get a strong impression about what will happen, but I don't know why or how to interpret it."

For some reason, I felt the need to whisper. "What do you see?"

"I think you guys are going to go far. And I'm not going anywhere. That makes me sad. Not that I'm envious. It's just . . ."

A lump formed in my throat. Now that the high of the song had worn off, would I be brave enough to stay in Gilford with her? It's one thing to sing about it; it's another to take the actual step and limit your freedom. Limit your possibilities.

But love is infinite. There is no limit.

Were those my own thoughts or the umbrella's? I didn't know anymore, and I didn't care. It was just talk. I wanted deeds.

A gray-bellied cloud had filled the sky above us. A few light drops pattered on the roof of Leila's car. I remembered the umbrella in my backpack. As I brought out the umbrella, my fingers shook worse than when I'd played my guitar in the hotel room. I stepped close to Leila, closer than I'd ever been to anyone before—not in actual fact, but in some new internal sense. Without looking at it, I unfurled the umbrella beside us with a click. It extended and opened in my peripheral vision, and with a slow arc, I brought it above her and me.

A rush of well-being passed from my crown to my toes. I breathed in her scent, and she leaned into me, clinging to my shoulders. She put her lips near my ear. Her breath sent a shudder to my core. "Aren't you worried about getting my flu germs?" she asked.

"I want everything about you, including your flu."

"You'd be housebound for a while."

I trailed light kisses along her cheek toward her mouth. "I'm not going anywhere but here."

She pulled back, eyes searching mine. "You're staying in Gilford?"

"If you'll have me."

"Oh, I'm having you." She laughed and tipped her lips up to mine, and in the same instant I dipped for a sweet and fevered kiss.

Ainsley

Edinburgh

August

Edinburgh, Saturday, August 25

- *Butter*
- *Sugar*
- *Eggs*
- *Chocolate Chips*
- *Shampoo*
- *Washing powder*
- *Breathe*

I stared at the last item on my list and blinked. Had I really written that? Where had it come from? True, I was feeling a little stressed out this rainy Saturday morning, having the shopping to do, my work clothes to take to the dry cleaner, a batch of chocolate chip cookies to bake, and Marie's birthday party to get to by two p.m., and all that after having slept until eleven, but did I really have to note down breathing as if I would forget it otherwise?

I shook my head in disgust. Making lists had become my passion from the moment I learned to write. Lists helped me to clear my head, to organize myself, to make sure I would stay on time in any project. But maybe I was getting a bit over-organized here. Marie already laughed at me because I placed the city and date on top of each list. She didn't see that these were important—because sometimes, I would happen upon an old list, and it had happened that I spent horribly inefficient days just because I was working on an old list, never realizing my mistake.

I stuffed the list into the pocket of my summer raincoat and eyed the rivulets of water streaming down the window pane. It was a cloudy August morning. The gray stone houses across the street, so typical for any residential area in Edinburgh, seemed like insubstantial shadows through the rain that fell straight like a curtain. Even the bright red doors with their brass door knockers looked washed out.

Mrs. McDowell sailed past, as she did every morning, her massive chest sticking out, and pressed against it, her little pug dog Tony. Tony had a squint and was one of the least endearing animals on this planet, probably on a par with a hooded cobra. Officially, Mrs. McDowell walked Tony three times a day. Unofficially, she ruled the neighborhood and carried him because he might get a cold when in contact with cruel rainwater. She lived right next door to me, and if I had known that fact when I signed the contract for my little house, I might have reconsidered. But I had not known it, and now I had to content myself with either being ignored or being talked down to. I watched her turn around the corner of Glenfriar's Street, her long raincoat in tartan print flapping around her ankles. Mr. McDowell had very wisely preferred eternal rest to being married for a prolonged period of time, leaving his wife enough money to stay at home and carry Tony as principal occupation.

Spontaneously, I added another item on my list.

- *forget about Mrs. McDowell*

Then I crossed it out. A list was there to remind me to do something. I couldn't remind myself NOT to do something. How stupid of me. Or was it more than stupid? Was I sick? I probably needed help already. Did we have shrinks in Edinburgh that specialized in listaholics?

I decided to postpone that thought and to start with the first item on my list: butter. Tesco supermarket was just around the corner. Usually, I pulled the hood of my raincoat over my head when I headed out, no matter the weather, but I had forgotten my favorite raincoat at the lab yesterday and now had to take my second best—which didn't have a good hood. With severe reservations, I glowered at Grandma's umbrella. I had tightly closed and leaned it against the wall next to the entrance, where it had been sitting for almost a month like a silent reproach. Umbrellas don't make much sense in Edinburgh; with all the wind we have, they flip inside out and break a spoke and are good for nothing but the trash. I had given up on umbrellas after realizing that I had to put them three times in as many months on my shopping lists. Instead, I had noted a raincoat with a good hood that could be fixed tightly with Velcro, so the wind couldn't blow it off. My new raincoat had served me well, even if it didn't make me beautiful. But now it was sitting at the lab, and I could only retrieve it on Monday. *Drat.*

With a sigh, I grabbed the umbrella, unfurled it over me and stepped outside. At least it had a fun color, red with white dots. I wondered why so many people liked black umbrellas. I for one needed a bit of cheering when walking through the rain. The curved wooden handle felt uncomfortable in my hands. Had my grandmother had huge hands or was I just unused to holding this special umbrella? I transferred my grip to the section above the handle. Better.

When I looked up from my hands, my gaze fell onto my Charles Austin roses. They were in bloom, and in spite of the rain, I stopped for a moment to smell them. Of course, they smelled much less intense today than they did in the sunshine, but even when I had a full work day ahead at the lab, I made a point of smelling my roses every time I walked past. Funny, I had not yet put that on my list. It came naturally. Like breathing.

Feeling better because I now knew that I didn't have to list everything in my life and was still quintessentially sane, I straightened. Out of nowhere, something fell at my feet. With a little yelp, I jumped back.

Where had that come from? I looked around. The street was empty. The rain made a soft pattering sound on the uneven garden flagstones and on the canopy over my head, but otherwise, everything was quiet. I frowned and bent forward to pick up the strange object that had landed at my feet.

Bad idea. The umbrella tipped to the side, and a gush of cold water emptied itself onto the nape of my neck. "Brrr." I shook myself, picked up the hook or whatever it was and looked at it. It was made of polished wood and seemed slightly familiar. How odd. I turned it in my hand, and suddenly, I realized that it belonged to the umbrella. In fact, it was the handle. My family heirloom was falling apart. *Thank you, Grandma.* I sighed and stuck it back on as best as I could. *Dang.* It was facing the wrong way now, pointing directly at me, and as a result, the umbrella was even harder to hold. I tried to take it off, but the handle refused to budge. It would probably fall off by itself again at the most inconvenient possible moment. I gave up trying, sighed and fished a pen out of my pocket, adding one more item to my list.

- *Liquid glue*

Job done, I stuffed the damp list back into my pocket and moved down the street in a hurry to make up for the lost time, only to walk straight into a massive chest with fangs. The chest belonged to Mrs. McDowell. The fangs, predictably, to Tony. Where had they come from?

"Ms. Fraser!" As always, it sounded as if she was about to explode in anger. She would never call me by my first name, Ainsley, not in a million years.

I wobbled back on my heels, trying to get out of reach of Tony's fangs. The umbrella swished to and fro, covering us both, and distributed water over us with gentle fairness.

She opened her mouth.

I cringed in anticipation of her acid words and looked at my feet. When nothing came, I looked up again and found her staring at me as if she had never seen me before.

"That's a pretty umbrella."

My jaw dropped. I blinked water from my eyelashes and managed a half-smile. "Why, thank you."

She actually smiled at me. A real smile, one that not only moved her mouth but also started a light in her eyes.

I had never paid much attention to her eyes, having tried my best to avoid any prolonged contact, but now I noted that they were pale blue, and combined with that unprecedented smile, she almost looked pretty.

"Is it new?" she asked.

"Kind of." I realized I sounded rude. Not wanting to destroy this once-in-a-lifetime neighborly moment, I hastened to add, "Actually, it belonged to my grandmother." In my hurry to be friendly, I forgot to keep my distance and was startled when something wet touched my hand, still curled around the handle of the umbrella. I looked down. Tony was licking my hand.

I almost fainted.

He looked up, and I swear he smiled as much as a pug can smile, a real smile, like the one his owner had just given me, though he still squinted.

Something really odd was happening here. A pre-Christmas moment, love to the world and cheer for everyone? Not likely in the middle of August. What on earth was this?

Mrs. McDowell looked over my shoulder to my precious roses. "I have to say, your roses are magnificent."

"Why, thank you." I realized I had said this before. She would think I was a half-wit. "I love my roses."

Not exactly clever repartee, but at least I didn't sound churlish anymore.

She nodded. "I noticed. My husband adored roses as well. Unfortunately, I don't have a green thumb. I was thinking that you might like to have a look at some of his books on roses, maybe?" She gave me a hopeful look.

With difficulty, I found my voice. "I . . . I'd love that. Right now, I'm stepping out to go shopping, but—"

"Of course, of course." She took a step back. "You'd better hurry. How about tomorrow? We could drink a cup of tea together, around four?"

"That would be lovely." Shell-shocked, I waved at them and stumbled down the street.

I was still in a daze when I arrived at Tesco's. Thank God I had my list, so I could work on autopilot. Mentally repeating the scene that had just happened, and trying to make sense of it, I put all my items into my basket and went to stand in line. Without really paying attention, on some sub-conscious level, I studied the woman in front of me. She had her back to me, and she was unusually tall, but the reason I noticed her most was that amazing ponytail. It was a warm auburn red, very curly, and it almost reached her narrow hips. Plenty of people would kill for that kind of hair, and I guess they could put me down as first in line.

My hair was as boring as the August rain and just as straight and fine. I kept it short because there was nothing else to be done with it, really. For special days, I fluffed it up with a bit of gel.

The woman turned to the side to place a six-pack of beer and a super-sized package of shortbread onto the checkout counter. That's when I realized the redhead was a man.

I swallowed hard. Suddenly, the hair seemed less attractive. *I don't like guys with long hair. They don't do a thing for me. I also don't go for men with super broad chests and rippling muscles.* Which he had, now that I got a closer look at his tight black T-shirt.

The cashier batted her heavily mascaraed eyelashes at him. "Why, how nice to see you again, Taran."

He smiled at her. "Good to see you, lass."

Lass! He behaved as if he was at least sixty when he couldn't be a day over thirty. In fact, he had to be my age, and the girl at the cashier was—what, sixteen? Maybe she did seem like a little lass to him.

He pulled out a black wallet from the back pocket of his nicely fitting jeans and handed her a bill. Then he slapped his forehead. "Gosh, I forgot something." He turned to me. "Would you awfully mind waiting just one minute? I really need to get this."

I hate unorganized people. I hate people who hold up everybody else simply because they can't stick to a schedule. Why didn't he make a list? Why didn't he have a plan? Of course, I couldn't say so. Instead, I looked at my watch, shrugged, and said, "Please hurry."

He flashed me a charming smile, squeezed past me—I got a whiff of a rather heavenly scent, couldn't put down what it was, though—and disappeared behind a toothbrush display.

I sighed and aligned my items by size and type. The heavy stuff first, the fragile stuff later. That would save me time when I had to coax it all into my shopping bag, and it would avoid breakage.

The Highlander was back, squeezing past me again with that stunning smile that shouldn't be allowed on anyone. He probably cultivated that wild look to entice swooning tourists into his arms. Maybe all that hair was a wig. Maybe I could touch it by accident to find out?

He placed three shrink-wrapped toilet rolls in front of the giggling cashier, then gave me a crooked grin. "Needs must."

"Sure." I didn't roll my eyes, but I felt like it. If that was the extent of his weekly shopping, he never ate at home. Well, never mind. It wasn't likely that I would ever see Taran again.

On my way out, I discovered that the exit was submerged in a large puddle that had somehow seeped underneath the sliding doors of the supermarket. Somewhere outside, a gutter had to be blocked. This was a hazard to everybody, and normally, I would have turned around and alerted one of the employees, but I was running late already. They would notice the water soon enough. I took a giant step to get across the mini-ocean and peered into the rain. Nothing doing—I would have to use my umbrella again. I readjusted all of my bags and opened the umbrella. Just as I was about to step out into the rain, someone gave me a mighty shove from behind, propelling me out of the supermarket. I fell forward, straight onto my knees, straight into another puddle. Mud splashed up and covered me. "Ouch!"

"I'm so sorry!" A couple of strong hands picked me up and put me onto my feet again before I could blink.

I stared into the face of Taran. "Didn't you leave several minutes ago?"

He hesitated, then shrugged with half a grin and gestured toward the supermarket. "I forgot something, rushed back inside, saw how many people were waiting, decided I could buy it later, turned around, slipped in that puddle, and inadvertently took you down with me." He winced and gave me a lopsided grin. "I'm babbling. I'm sorry. The fall rattled me."

Like a Saint Bernard dog. Friendly, attractive, clumsy, and totally unorganized. I swallowed and noticed two things. First, he still smelled heavenly. Second, my knee was hurting.

He put his hand underneath my chin and brushed his thumb across my cheek.

I stared at him, my mouth half open.

"You had mud there," he said, as if that explained it all.

I know plenty of men who would have pretended not to see the mud. I know even more men who would have pointed it out to me with an embarrassed cough. But I didn't know a single man with sufficient self-assurance to easily wipe away mud from my face, totally relaxed, sure of his welcome. It spoke volumes about him.

"You're getting all wet in the rain." He picked up the umbrella that had dropped onto the asphalt and opened it above us. Our gaze met.

He took a sharp breath, opened his mouth as if he wanted to say something, then closed it with a snap.

Did I have more mud in my face? I could feel my cheeks heating up, so I turned my face away.

He pressed the handle into my palm and bent down again to stuff my soaked belongings willy-nilly into my shopping bag.

I winced. "Oh, no. The eggs!"

He looked up. "You bought eggs?"

"Yes." I bent forward to pick up the carton that was lying lopsided on the ground and almost lost my balance. "Ouch!"

His hand gripped my arm and steadied me. "Careful. Are you hurt?"

"No, I don't think so." What was he? A nurse?

He looked at my soaked trousers. "Hmm."

First things first. "What about the eggs?"

He picked up the wet carton, opened it and glanced inside. The result was apparently not very reassuring because he looked at me with a comical expression and said, "I could offer to make you scrambled eggs for lunch."

I closed my eyes. "I need those eggs to make chocolate chip cookies."

His face lit up. "My favorite."

"They're not for you." I shook my head. "I've been invited to a birthday party this afternoon, and I have to bring those cookies. I promised."

He cocked his head to the side. "And you always keep your promises?"

"Always."

He narrowed his eyes. "And you're always on time, I would guess?"

"Always."

One eyebrow went up. "One hundred percent reliable?"

"One hundred percent."

The second eyebrow went up. "Your life is organized from morning to night?"

"Up to the last minute." I couldn't tell why he was asking all these questions. Even less did I know why I was answering them, still standing in front of Tesco, clutching that old umbrella like a lifeline, with the rain falling down around us. It felt as if we were on an island, as if the umbrella was shading us from the outer world, from interruptions.

"You are the epitome of everything I abhor." He said it softly, as if he was wondering why he even told me. "So how come I like you so much?"

I blinked. "You like me?"

"I like you." He said it in a decisive tone, as if it was something fate had decreed, something that could not be shaken or changed, no matter what.

"I see." I couldn't tell if I liked him. He made me uneasy, pushed me totally out of my depth.

"So what do we do now?" he asked.

I swallowed. "Buy new eggs?"

He looked into the store. "No way. There are too many people standing in line."

"But I promised . . ."

"I know. You promised chocolate chip cookies." He looked around as if he'd lost something, discovered his own shopping bag next to the puddle, and pulled out the large package of shortbread. "Take this instead."

"I . . ."

He grinned. "That too much of a deviation from your schedule? Shortbread from Tesco's instead of homemade chocolate chip cookies?"

Put like this, it sounded absurd. "Marie loves my chocolate chip cookies. She's expecting them."

He shrugged. "Make her another batch tomorrow."

"I can't take your shortbread. You had a plan for them, and I . . ."

He laughed.

I couldn't help but notice that he had wonderful eyes. Deep brown with a few amber specks.

"A plan!" He shook his head, still laughing. "The only plan I had for this shortbread is to eat it whenever the fancy takes me."

"That's enough of a plan." I felt like defending myself, and for some reason, I could tell him exactly what was I thinking, velvet gloves off. This attitude of his to do exactly as he pleased was liberating, in a way. "Now stop laughing."

"Tell me one more thing." He pushed his face close to mine.

I caught my breath. He was crowding my space, and I liked it. What was happening to me?

"When you buy cookies, do you plan exactly when you will eat them?" His eyes sparkled.

My cheeks heated up. "I do."

He lifted the shortbread and looked at it. "So you're picking a package of shortbread from the shelf and you tell yourself softly, 'I will eat you tonight at 6:35 p.m. after I return home from work?'"

"No, Taran." Impatience gripped me. "I count the pieces, I calculate how often and how many cookies I want to eat per cookie-eating-session, and then I decide how many to buy."

His laughter faded. "Seriously?"

I swallowed. "Something like that." Why was I answering anyway? He was only poking fun at me. "Now thank you for your help. I have to go." I took a step forward and winced. My knee had started to throb.

He took hold of my shopping bag. "I'll accompany you."

I held onto it and rolled my eyes. "Maybe I don't want that."

"You don't want me?" He looked at me with huge eyes.

"Is that so difficult to believe?" The image of the Saint Bernhard dog came back to me. He was really like a large puppy, happy to bounce around my legs, unable to believe that he might be in the way or unwelcome.

Taran blinked. "What's your name?"

"Ainsley." It slipped out before I could stop myself. Why did I continue to talk to this guy? He had already said he abhorred me. We were from different planets.

"Ainsley." It sounded like music when he said it. "May I accompany you home?"

I hardened my heart. "Why?"

"Because I have to make scrambled eggs for you."

"You don't have to do anything. What makes you think that I would invite a total stranger into my house?"

His eyes widened in surprise. "You mean I might be dangerous?"

"Exactly."

"Well, don't you have anybody around to protect you?"

"I can offer a wild dog and a ferocious neighbor on one side, and a policeman on the other side." I decided not to mention that the ferocious neighbor had unexpectedly softened this morning and that the policeman had retired some twenty years ago.

"That should do." Grinning, he pulled the shopping bag from my weakened grasp, took my arm and led me down the street.

I followed his lead, wondering if I had lost my mind. "One moment." I pulled my cell phone from my handbag. Then I took one step back and took a picture of him.

He smiled into the camera as if he was used to media attention. "Taking a memento?"

"Taking proof." I checked that the picture was clear, then forwarded it to Marie with the words "This is Taran. I'm taking him home now."

"Proof? What kind of proof?"

I smiled at him. "I forwarded this picture to my best friend. If anything should happen to me, she can pass it on to the police, so they'll know who the last person was to see me alive."

He shook his head. "I can't believe how your mind works. What kind of work do you do?"

"I've got a PhD in chemistry, and I'm working for an international company that produces wall colors and other paint."

"Jesus."

I lifted my eyebrows. "Excuse me?"

"I hated chemistry in school."

"That's not a very original answer. About ninety percent of the people I meet say that."

He grinned, acknowledging the hit, and gave me a wicked glance. "Well?"

"Well what?"

"Aren't you going to ask?"

"Ask what?"

"What I do for a living."

I continued to hobble down the street, grateful to lean onto his arm every now and then. "I know what you do for a living. You're a freelance painter and you sell one painting for five hundred pounds or so every nine months, if you're lucky. The rest of the time, you manage on beer and shortbread." I couldn't believe I'd just said this. This guy had a strange effect on me and my manners.

"Wrong." His face gave nothing away. "I'm the director of a bank."

I stopped in my tracks. "You're kidding."

"Of course I'm kidding." He laughed again.

I couldn't help myself; I had to laugh too. And that sealed it. For some reason, he felt like a friend.

When we walked through my little green gate a minute later, Mrs. McDowell looked out of her window and waved at me, a big smile on her face. This had never happened before. I smiled back, silently freaking out, and waved at her. This morning would go down in history.

"Is that the ferocious neighbor?" Taran sounded amused.

"You don't know her." I made sure my voice had an ominous ring. "Don't underestimate her."

"Ah." Taran grinned.

I opened my front door and ushered him in.

"Nice door," Taran said. "The red matches your roses."

I smiled, but before I could answer, a shrill ringing sound rent the air.

"Your phone is ringing." Taran looked around my small hall with interest.

"I can hear that." I fished my cell phone from my handbag and saw Marie's name on the display. I should have known that she would call right after seeing Taran's picture. For a second, I wondered if I should let her call go to voice mail, but then I figured I'd better answer personally, or she might alert the police even before I was murdered.

"Ainsley!" She sounded breathless. "WHO is that guy?"

"Hi, Marie! I'm fine, and you?"

"Don't change the topic." Her voice was stern and unfortunately, loud enough to fill the entry hall. Taran could understand every word. "He's delish! Where did you find him?"

I sighed. "I found him at the supermarket. Tesco's, you know."

"Do they have more? If yes, I'll pop right down to the store and get myself one, too."

As he was overhearing every word anyway, I decided to put it all out into the open. "Taran, do they have more guys like you down at Tesco's? Marie wants to know." I held the phone in his direction, so Marie would understand his answer.

He frowned. "I'm not sure. When they created the barcode to scan me, they said I was unique, but you never know. It might just be a clever marketing ploy."

I took the phone back. "See? He might be unique or not. Difficult to say."

Marie gasped. "Did you put me on loudspeaker?"

"Nope. Your voice is loud enough. No loudspeaker needed."

She lowered her voice to a whisper. "Now tell me the truth, Ainsley. What on earth is happening? Do you want me to come over?"

"Tell her to speak up," Taran said. "I can't understand a word."

I felt a grin spreading over my face. This was more fun than I'd had in a very long time. "I'm fine, Marie, really. So far, Taran is staying in line. I made that picture just in case he does anything illegal, so you can send him to prison later."

Marie continued to whisper. "We really have to set up a code word so I know when you're in trouble. In the future, when you call and mention . . . say, chocolate chip cookies, I'll know that I have to come right over. All right?"

"Perfect." I smiled at Taran.

"I'm getting uncomfortable here," Taran said. "I have an uneasy feeling that you're plotting something behind my back; besides, it's getting boring, this one-sided conversation."

"What's he saying?" Marie asked in her normal voice.

"He's afraid that we're plotting something behind his back, and he's feeling bored."

"What a charming guy."

"I know." I chuckled. "Oh, and talking about which, there's a slight change in plans. I'll bring shortbread instead of . . . the other stuff this afternoon."

"That's fine. However, I insist that you bring Taran too."

I lifted my eyebrows. This was getting out of hand. "I'm not sure he'll—"

Taran grinned. "Thanks for the invitation. I'm delighted, and I'll bring a six-pack of beer."

"But I don't like beer," Marie said.

I grinned. "You'd better take it. The only alternative is toilet paper."

Five minutes later, we were hanging out in my kitchen as if we'd been a couple for months already. Taran was whisking the remains of the eggs around in a bowl, and I was watching him from my place at the table, a bag of ice on my knee. It felt surreal, as if I had strayed into a fantastic dream and would wake up at any moment.

"So, tell me about your life, Ainsley." The muscles on his arms looked nice as he added a splash of milk to the eggs.

"What do you want to know?"

"Most of all—" He flashed me a smile. "—I want to know if you're in a relationship."

For an instant, an image of Bruce flashed through my brain, my secret crush at work. However, I had never done anything but adore him from afar, so that didn't count, even though my adoration was pretty hefty. I decided to continue my conversation with Taran as I had started. Brutally honest and straight-forward. "No relationship. How about you?"

He found the pepper and grated some onto the mix. "Ditto."

"Why not?" I asked. This new style of communication was starting to grow on me. Getting to know someone like this was so much better than staying on the surface with inane small talk.

Taran didn't look up. "My wife died three years ago in a car accident. I've pretty much lived for work ever since."

A sudden feeling of being let down hit me in the chest. I had known guys like him before. Guys who tell you a sob story and expect you to fall for it. Guys who manage to look manly while wiping a tear away from their eyes. Guys who build on your soft feelings and are expert at making you fall for them—without ever once making a single scratch on their own hard heart. *How stupid I am!* I had been a fool to invite him in. But he would soon learn that sob stories were no good when it came to mellowing this girl.

I crossed my arms in front of my chest and lifted my chin to hide my feeling of disappointment. Then I launched into full fairytale mode. The more drastic, the better. "Well, since you're so honest, here's my story: My fiancé killed himself a day before the wedding. I shredded my wedding dress and used it later to mop up the floor, but all this happened two years ago, so even those rags are in the trash now." I shrugged and tried to look cynical. "It was pretty useless material anyway."

He slanted me a glance with a half-smile. "You're making this up."

Good answer. He was intelligent enough, this Highlander. "Yup." I cocked my head to the side and watched as he put butter into the pan and switched on the stove. What would he say next?

His smile broadened. "Because you think I told you a sob story."

"Exactly."

"Why would you think that?"

Not difficult to answer that one. "Because you're walking around, looking like a tourist's dream of the Highlander, you're used to charming people right and left without any visible effort, and I bet you believe that the best way to melt a woman's heart is to tell her a moving tale and make her think that you're a grieving widower, and only she can mend your broken heart."

His smile deepened. "That sounds pretty convincing. But wouldn't I go to the supermarket in my clan's outfit if I wanted to charm all those droves of tourists?"

I recoiled. "That would be a bit over the top, wouldn't it? I mean, even the tourists know that we

Scots don't run around in our clan's tartans every day, don't they? What's your clan anyway?"

"I'm a Cameron."

"Sheesh." I rolled my eyes.

"Don't tell me you're a Macintosh," he said.

"Not as bad as that. Your clan was at war with the Macintoshes for—what—three hundred years or so, wasn't it?"

He shrugged. "Something like that." He put his hand on his heart and gave me a soulful look. "But I wouldn't let that stand in the way of true love." Without missing a beat, he turned back to the pan and poured the egg mix into it with an expert flick of his wrist.

"How fortunate." My voice was dry. "But no need to go to such lengths. I'm a Fraser. Our clans only fought each other occasionally."

Taran wiped his brow with an exaggerated gesture. "Phew. I'm relieved. Then the clan won't excommunicate me when we get married."

Married? Ha! This guy was a piece of work. "You shouldn't be too sure. I'm only half a Fraser. My mother was French."

Now was his turn to recoil. "No way. What on earth was your father thinking?"

"I have no idea." I grinned. "So sorry. Will that be a problem when it comes to the wedding vows?"

"I'm not sure. A Fraser's better than a Macintosh, but the French roots on top of that . . . That's a tall order."

I chuckled.

"Lunch is ready." Taran placed the scrambled eggs onto two plates and put them on the table.

I bent forward and started eating. "It's good."

"No need to sound so surprised." He smiled.

I cocked my head to the side. "That's a perfect look. Make sure you use it often."

"What do you mean?"

"This half-smile, showing just a wee bit of hurt because I dared to doubt your culinary abilities. It will melt the tourists' heart in a second."

He grinned. "I know. Cooking for the woman you want to seduce is a great first step." He leaned back and squared his shoulders. "But I have a confession to make."

I tried to get my breathing under control and lifted my eyebrows to mask my real feelings. "Oh, yeah?"

"Yup. Scrambled eggs is the limit. It doesn't get any better than that."

"I see." I pretended to frown in thought. "Now what would be the perfect reply? 'Don't worry, I can teach you, sweetheart?' "

He shuddered. "Ugh. Not sweetheart. That's too gooey. How about—?"

I jumped in my seat and stifled an exclamation.

"What's the matter?" He sounded alarmed.

"Nothing. Don't worry." I waved my hand through the air. "I just remembered that I forgot to take a jacket with a gooey blob to the dry cleaner's." I fished my list out of my jeans pocket. "Of course. I forgot to put it on my list, that's why."

He took the list from my fingers and read it. Slowly, his eyebrows climbed. "Breathe? You're telling yourself to breathe?"

I bit my lips. I had forgotten this morning's aberration. "It was a mistake. I was feeling a bit under pressure this morning."

His eyebrows stayed up as he continued to check my list. "Who's Mrs. McDowell?"

"My neighbor."

"The friendly lady next door? Why do you have to forget her?"

"She wasn't friendly until this morning. Never, not one single minute since I moved in four years ago. Something happened to create a total turnaround, a complete change of heart, and I'm still puzzling over it."

"Do you make a list for every little task you have to do?" Taran looked at me as if I was a new species, something he'd never come across before.

"I need it to stay organized." I shrugged. "See what happens if I don't make a list? The stuff I should do just slips out of my mind." I checked my watch. "Damn. Of course the dry cleaner's are closed now." With a sigh, I held out my hand. "Give me that list. I need to write down that I have to go there on Monday."

"But won't you write a new list for Monday?" His voice was teasing me.

"Of course I will, but at the end of each day, I transfer the points that weren't done to the new list."

He shook his head. "I don't believe this."

My cheeks heated up, and I looked down at my plate. Maybe I was a basket case after all. Spending time with Taran had been amazing fun so far, but now, for the first time, I was feeling self-conscious.

Suddenly, I heard a slight scratching sound and looked up to discover that he was adding something to my list. "What are you doing?"

"I'm noting an important point so you won't forget it." He handed me the slightly crumpled piece of paper.

I read it, and my jaw dropped. Five new words were on my list, written down in decisive handwriting. "Fall in love with Taran."

His warm brown eyes locked with mine. "Think you can do that?"

I cleared my throat. "We'll see."

Several hours later, I was still struggling to regain my inner equilibrium. We were walking toward Marie's home, and I had no idea how this crazy day would end. Marie lived in an ancient house just off Grassmarket, and while it offered a most romantic view of Edinburgh castle, it did not offer any parking spaces; that's why we'd had to park farther away and walk down the wet steps of Heriot Place that led to the old town. It was still raining, but Grandma's umbrella protected us from the worst of the rain. I leaned onto Taran's arm just to be closer to him, pretending that my knee was hurting worse than it did. Maybe my knees really *were* trembling a bit. Truth be told, I was rattled. Since this morning, my life had turned upside down, and I had no idea why.

A man was overtaking us from behind. I could hear his energetic steps, and even before I turned my head, I knew it was Marie's father, Duncan Muir. While it's true he doted on his daughter, he was also very ambitious for her, driving her hard to advance quickly in her career, preferably by marriage. We had a cool relationship because he had put me down as too crazy for Marie, and all because she and I had once decided to dye our hair together, and it had turned out pink instead of blond. My hair had been short, so my pink period was over soon, but Marie's shoulder length hair took more than a year to recover, and her father had taken that as a personal insult. From that day on, he had ignored me, not returning my greetings, looking straight through me, even when I addressed him. When I had crowned my education by getting a doctorate, he had deemed me sufficiently worthy to greet me again, but with never more than two words, and never with anything but an expression of slight distaste on his face, as if I smelled a bit off.

He did not slow down as he prepared to overtake us, but the very second he rushed past, his foothold slipped on the ancient stone steps, and he would have fallen if I had not clutched his arm and pulled him up next to me, jarring my knee again. Taran held the umbrella over both of us and bent forward. "Are you all right, Sir?"

Mr. Muir turned his head with that sour expression I knew so well.

I released his arm and braced myself.

He opened his mouth, no doubt to give his thanks as tersely as possible, when for some reason, his mouth relaxed and he beamed at us in a way that he usually reserved for Marie and Marie alone.

I caught my breath.

He grabbed my hand and shook it until my bones rattled. "Ainsley! How nice to see you. I was lucky you caught me. Thank you so much! How clumsy of me to fall."

It was Taran who replied because I was still speechless. "Not at all. These worn steps can be treacherous when wet."

"Quite so, young man." Mr. Muir beamed at him, then looked at me, obviously waiting for an introduction.

I managed to find my voice. "This is Taran Cameron. Taran, meet Duncan Muir. He's Marie's father."

The men shook hands, beaming at each other.

It wouldn't have surprised me if they'd started to hug and slap each other on the back, but they managed to refrain from expressing their brotherly feelings, and we walked down the last steps together to the house. When Marie opened the door, she looked as shell shocked as I felt, seeing her father acting as if I was his long-lost second daughter and Taran a favorite friend.

Taran handed over his six-pack of beer. "Happy birthday, Marie."

She grinned. "Thanks. Actually, my birthday was on Monday, but during the week, there's never enough time to celebrate." She hugged me and whispered into my ear. "He's even more attractive than his picture! And what happened to my dad? Why is he acting like this?"

I lifted both hands in a gesture of surrender. "I have no idea."

That afternoon passed in a blur. For some reason, it felt good to be at the party with Taran, not awkward at all. I saw a few curious glances, but most of the guests refrained from asking for details about our relationship, thank God, as I wasn't keen on repeating the story about our supermarket pick-up.

The highlight of the party came when Mr. Muir told me that it was time to proceed to a first-name basis after all these years. He smiled at me, lifted his glass and said, "The name is Duncan." When I finally realized that this was not a piece of information but an offer to drop the "Mr.", I almost fainted. From the corner of my eyes, I could see Marie looking like a stag blinded by headlights.

That was it. I had to get out of here before other people started to throw their arms around me in ecstasy, literally or in so many words.

I managed to drink to my new friendship with "Duncan," then jumped up. "I'm not feeling well, and I think I'd better go home now. Please excuse me."

Taran looked at me with concern. "Is it your knee?"

Not my knee. Everything! I swallowed before the words could slip out. "Yup."

Of course Taran left the house with me and accompanied me home. As we walked up the steps of Heriot Place and back to the car, I had the sudden urge to tell him to go. I had to be on my own, had to grapple with these unprecedented events, with nobody around to confuse me, but I had no idea how to tell him so without hurting him. How do you tell a Saint Bernhard puppy that he has to give you some room to breathe?

It didn't take us long to get home. When we came to my little front gate, I put my hand on the latch, then hesitated, my face averted, so he couldn't read me as he seemed to do with such astonishing ease.

I liked him; I really did. And I could feel an attraction, but I was not head over heels in love, and at the moment, all I really wanted was to be alone. I took a deep breath and faced him. "I'm sorry, Taran, but I think I need to be on my own now."

He smiled. "That's fine. We have a lot to think about."

I was surprised. "We? I thought you're used to picking up girls at the supermarket."

Taran frowned. "Why would you think so?"

"Because it was done with such ease, as if you did it every other Saturday."

He gave a small, lopsided smile. "For the record: I have never yet picked up any girl at the supermarket. If it seemed easy, it was because it was meant to be."

I swallowed. His brown eyes held such warmth.

"Can I see you again?" he asked.

I could hear a faint note of insecurity in his voice—the very first hint that he was not quite the happy Saint Bernhard puppy, always sure of being welcome.

My heart melted. "Of course."

"Would you give me your list?" he asked.

I pulled it out of my jeans.

He took a pen from the pocket of his jacket and noted his phone number below the last point. "Don't forget to copy it onto tomorrow's list." He passed it back to me.

"I won't."

He brushed his finger against my cheek, gently. "See you soon, Ainsley."

Then he was gone.

I scuttled into the house and burrowed deep into the cushions of my sofa. Why was everybody suddenly so nice to me? And why did it trouble me? I should be grateful, should enjoy it while it lasted. Instead, I was freaking out. I had no idea what to do next.

When I got up on Sunday morning, I put my new list with Taran's duly copied phone number on the kitchen table. While pottering around the kitchen, I kept glancing at it, circling around it, so tempted to type his number into my phone, but never quite finding enough courage. I still had to come to terms with myself, and that proved to be more difficult than I had expected.

In the afternoon, I had tea with Mrs. McDowell, and it turned out to be surprisingly nice. More than once, I started to ask her why she was so different all of a sudden, and every time, I lost my nerve. She never referred to any unneighborly feelings in our past, so I let sleeping dogs lie.

I went home, busied myself with my laundry, cleaned the house, read a book, watched a movie, and talked at length with Marie, who couldn't answer any of my questions about the sudden change in her dad, either.

I didn't call Taran. I half expected him to show up, but I didn't see a sign of him, and I wasn't sure how I felt about that. I liked that he respected my need for privacy and hadn't turned out to be a stalker. I didn't like that he seemed to have shrugged me off just as quickly as he had slipped into my life. I missed his easy banter much more than should be allowed on such short acquaintance. I was so tempted to call him, but I didn't. I couldn't. If I called him, it would send a message of sorts already, even before I had said one word. A message that I had agreed to something—but to what exactly? I didn't know. I was scared and disoriented and had no clue what to do. In short, I was a mess.

On Monday, it was still raining. I was a bit late for work, so all the good parking spaces were taken. Forced to park at the far end of the street, I hopped out of the car in a hurry, opening the umbrella as I ran.

"Ainsley! Hey, Ainsley!"

I stopped short and turned around. My heartbeat accelerated. It was Bruce. Bruce, with his short brown hair, his black-framed glasses, his slim figure. Bruce, who looked exactly like the up-and-coming bank director Taran had claimed to be. In fact, he worked in the controlling department just down the hall from me, and rumor had it that he would soon be called onto the board of directors. Bruce. The guy I had secretly been in love with for half a year or more. My mouth turned dry.

He ducked underneath the umbrella and flashed me a smile. "Thanks for waiting. Terrible weather."

"You're telling me." I was already turning to continue hurrying toward the entrance, hoping he wouldn't see me blush, when I noticed that he wasn't by my side anymore. I stopped and turned around.

He stood rooted to the earth and stared at me as if bewitched, not realizing that he was getting soaked by the steady drizzle of rain.

I hurried back and held the umbrella over him.

He still stared at me without blinking.

"Em." I cleared my throat. "Is anything the matter?"

He opened his mouth and said in a voice that didn't sound quite like his own. "I've never before noticed your beautiful eyes."

My jaw dropped. And all at once, I understood what was happening. I knew why this weekend had been the craziest in my life. I knew why Mrs. McDowell had suddenly become the neighbor from paradise, why Taran had followed me like a love-sick puppy and Mr. Muir had softened like warm butter. The umbrella had magic power. Everybody who shared it with me was bound to fall in love with me or to be super nice to me from now until doomsday. Or until whenever, who knew? Just thinking about it, I started to shake so much that the umbrella threatened to slip from my grasp.

"Hey. Steady there." Bruce covered my hand with his to right the umbrella.

His hand felt warm and safe. I took a shuddering breath.

He took a step closer to me and smiled, "I'd like to meet you tonight."

Words I had fantasized about for months. I had dreamed that he would say this exact sentence. Now it had happened, and I wasn't sure I liked it.

"Do you like Mexican food?" he asked. "I know a nice little restaurant on The Royal Mile."

"That sounds lovely." My mouth had answered before my heart knew what it wanted. Or maybe it was my heart that had answered, overruling my head? I had no idea. All I knew was that my knees wouldn't stop shaking.

"Great." He squeezed my shoulder briefly. "I'll pick you up at seven, all right? What's your address?"

I gave him my address in a kind of daze. And just like that, I had a date with Bruce. I couldn't believe it!

I went to the lab in a trance. The next hour crept by as if someone had wrapped it in cotton, all sounds muted and muffled. Motionless, I stood next to my desk and stared down at the umbrella inside my open handbag, wondering about it, wondering if Grandma had known about its power. She must have known. But how odd that she had never let on. Why not explain the magic and be done with it? I frowned in thought. Maybe the magic power would vanish if you knew about it? Could that be the answer?

Easy to find out. On an impulse, I grabbed the umbrella and hurried downstairs to the buying department. The head buyer, Mr. Pomp, was the most grumpy man I knew. Just recently, he had almost brought the whole chemistry department to a halt because he had not processed my order for new test tubes. True, I had forgotten to note the internal short code for my department on the ordering form, but he knew who I was, and he could easily have added it. If that had been too much work for him, he could have called and asked me to add it. Instead, he had put it aside and decided to do nothing. I had never even thought to check up on it because for me, the job had been done.

I had disliked him from the word go because it was evident that he tried to do the least possible work in the hours he spent on the job, delaying every single order. When, on top of that, I found out that he had been sitting on my order for ages, I was through with him, and I told him so in no uncertain terms. He then complained to his boss about me, saying that he could not be expected to iron out the mistakes of all his coworkers because he simply had too much to do. To say our relationship was strained was putting it mildly.

With an ingratiating smile, I eased into his office.

Mr. Pomp was bald, and the dome of his head shone like a polished ball as he turned to me with obvious reluctance. "Ms. Fraser." He stated my name as if I was a recurring problem in his life.

Which I was and would keep on being, as long as his attitude about work didn't change. Tough luck. I sidled closer to him and opened the umbrella above us.

His eyes looked as if they were going to fall out of his face.

"I'm having a bit of a problem, Mr. Pomp, and I thought you might be the perfect person to help me. See this umbrella? I really like the wooden handle, but it already fell off once, and I'm afraid that it won't last much longer. Do you have any idea where I could find a replacement?" I stopped and held my breath. If the magic had stopped because I knew about it, he would now bellow a reply that would surely create a new hairdo for me—like the one I'd had when I'd hiked up to Arthur's Seat last Easter, with my head in a gale. And for once, I would have had no complaint about his behavior. I had no business to ask him to source a private spare part for me.

He looked at me with ever-widening eyes and opened his mouth until I could see straight down his throat, all the way back to his moving uvula.

I took a cautionary step back. This was going to be nasty.

His mouth closed with a snap, and his face creased with a smile I had never seen before. "You're not asking much, little lady." He winked at me.

The umbrella dropped from my nerveless grasp. I had to lean against the edge of his desk to steady myself.

"But I'll see what I can do," he went on. "It won't be easy to find this kind of hook. Do you know who manufactured it?"

I swallowed and fought to get my voice back. "Actually, I do. The factory used to belong to my grandparents."

"But how fortunate!"

"Unfortunately, the company ceased to exist decades ago."

His face fell. "I'm so sorry to hear that."

I stared at him, willing him to revert to his normal, unhelpful, phlegmatic self.

Nothing doing.

He picked up the umbrella from the floor and peered at its handle. "It could be mahogany, but I'm not an expert on wood. Maybe, if we take it—"

"Gosh, I just remembered that I know who could do this!" I grabbed the umbrella and held it away from my body as if it could contaminate me. "I'm terribly sorry to have bothered you, Mr. Pomp. Thank you so much for your help. I do appreciate it." With every word, I was retreating to the door.

"But not at all, little lady." He smiled. "Come back anytime."

I made it out of his office before my shaking knees could give in, beat a path to my lab, and closed the door behind me. I rarely lock myself in, but when I do, my colleagues know they'd better leave me alone.

"You are a magic umbrella," I said to the innocent-looking thing on my desk. "And you are highly dangerous." I shuddered. What if it got into the wrong hands? It could create havoc with the world. They say that nothing corrupts you like power. I had an almighty tool in my hands—a magic wand to make anybody like me, even my most determined enemies. This umbrella had the ability to change world politics, to solve conflicts that had shaken humanity for centuries. For a start, I could contrive to get my boss underneath this umbrella. Not that he was against me, but if he suddenly saw me in a golden light, it would no doubt help my career. I touched the fabric with the tip of my hand.

No.

I wouldn't do that. I would put the umbrella away, lock it inside a bank vault. It was way too dangerous. Whatever had Grandma been thinking when she bequeathed it to us? And why hadn't my cousin Travis added a note when he sent me this thing? Then again, sending notes wasn't his style. Nothing unusual there.

Suddenly, I remembered Anatole's words. "You're not supposed to share your experience with your cousins." I wondered why not. Had grandma wanted us to learn something, all on our own? I wished I could call Travis and get him to spill the beans just a wee bit, but it was way too early to call California, even if I overlooked that Travis had probably been working half the night at some gig or other.

I saw a bit of thread hanging from the red canvas material, and an idea flashed through my mind. I pulled at the thread until it had unraveled a bit more, then cut it off and put it underneath the microscope. My scientifically trained mind did not want to accept that this umbrella had magic power. Maybe the magical effect stemmed from the material. Maybe the canopy gave out some sort of odor that made people fall in love. My hands trembled at the thought. *Oh, sweet Jesus.* I ran all the tests I could think of with this little bit of thread, only to learn that it was 100 percent ordinary cotton, covered with some sort of wax.

I dropped my head into my hands. I had to accept the truth now. For some strange reason, the umbrella was responsible for all that had happened. My heart plummeted when I remembered my wildly romantic meeting with Taran. I had felt oh, so desirable. Which was all over now, because his fascination hadn't been inspired by me. It had been created by the umbrella. Taran would have fallen in love with anybody who owned it.

Another thought occurred to me. I now had two guys in love with me, and if I wanted to, I could add half the town. I shuddered. For some reason, that didn't sound like fun. *This is how royalty must feel. When all the world is willing to swoon at your feet, and all you want is real friendship, real feelings.*

Maybe the magic of the umbrella would go away at some point in the future. I had no way of knowing. But did I even want the magic gone? Hadn't the umbrella offered me a way to live my dream? I was having a date with Bruce tonight. What more did I want?

I searched my soul, and for some reason the image of Taran's face floated into my mind. I wanted to talk to him. The more I thought about it, the more urgent the need became. I wasn't sure what I wanted from him, but I had to hear his voice. I dug out my list to find his phone number.

He answered on the first ring.

"Hi, Taran. It's Ainsley." I cleared my throat. I had no idea what to say next.

"Ainsley! I'm so glad you called." He sounded relieved. "Can you imagine how much I paced my apartment yesterday, hoping you would get in touch?"

Something warm flooded me. I was unable to squeeze out a word.

"How are you?" he asked. "Is your knee fine?"

"Yes. Fine," I croaked.

"Where are you? Can I see you?"

"I'm at work. I just wanted to hear your voice for a second."

"What is it? You sound odd, as if you've had a shock. Are you sure everything is all right?"

"Yes." The warm feeling remained. It still felt good to talk to him. In fact, it felt better than ever, and I was thrilled that he could read my mood just by the way I'd said a few words on the phone. But I was scheduled for a date tonight with Bruce, and I couldn't help myself, I just had to go. I had a feeling that the umbrella had destined Bruce and me to be together and that Taran had only been a slip-up in every sense of the word.

"How about tonight?" he asked. "We could go out to dinner."

"Not tonight." My throat was dry. "Listen, I'll be in touch, all right?"

He hesitated. "Did anything happen? Has anybody soiled my reputation? Did they dare to imply that I don't earn five hundred pounds a year with my paintings but only three hundred, and that made you believe I can't support a family? Because I can, you know."

I giggled. "Nothing as bad as that. Besides, I'm not looking for a free meal ticket. I earn enough money to keep a family."

"That's a relief." His voice was full of laughter. "So what do you need a man for?"

"Why, to make me laugh, of course." A niggling doubt appeared out of nowhere. Would Bruce be able to make me laugh? I added in a hurry, "And to make me feel loved."

"Not to help you make lists?"

I could hear the smile in his voice. "Nah," I said. "I'm perfect when it comes to list-making."

"Good. Because I'm rotten with lists."

"I figured." There was a pause. For some reason, I didn't want to hang up. "Taran?"

"Yes?"

I cleared my throat. "Nothing. I have to go."

"Can I call you tomorrow?"

"Yes." I hung up with a warm feeling inside, a feeling that stayed with me for the rest of the day and soothed my nervousness even as I prepared for my date with Bruce.

When he picked me up at 6:59 p.m., Bruce was still wearing the same suit he'd been wearing all day at the office. Maybe he hadn't gone home in between. It figured. But for some reason, I felt let down, as if he hadn't made an effort. While we drove to the restaurant, I found it hard to fill the gaps in our conversation with small talk, but maybe we just had to get used to each other.

However, our chemistry didn't improve much in the next hour. We chose from the menu; we got our food; we ate it; and all the time I felt as if I was cut from cardboard, only pretending to be here and as if the real me was somewhere else.

It didn't help that Bruce was explaining a new tax evasion system to me that was probably thrilling for people who had millions to squirrel away, but it left me cold. My thoughts kept slipping away to the dangerous umbrella. At first, I had wanted to hide it underneath my bed, but then I'd taken it with me, feeling that it was safer to keep it in my vicinity, to have an eye on it. The things one could do with it . . . It was way too scary to think about the umbrella unchaperoned in town.

Suddenly, without apologizing for interrupting Bruce's monologue, I asked, "If you had the power to become extremely popular by some kind of magic, would you use it?"

He blinked. "Say that again?"

I repeated my question.

Bruce looked as if he had discovered something slimy on his plate. "There is no such thing as magic. I'd have thought that you, as a scientist, would not fall for this kind of mumbo-jumbo."

Until yesterday, I would have agreed. To placate Bruce, I waved the magic away. "Then treat this as a theoretical question. If you had the power to make people root for you, what would you do?"

He laughed. "Why, I'd run for prime minister, of course."

"No, seriously."

Bruce lifted his eyebrows. "I am serious. Once you have political power, you can pull the strings in a way that will ease everything else. In fact, you can get away with an awful lot once you're in power."

My throat hurt. "I see." And suddenly, all the magic of our relationship fell away. Bruce had a certain superficial charm, and I could still feel a sort of physical attraction, but now that I knew him better, I realized that he bored and appalled me. He was power hungry, possibly ruthless. If only we had had this date months ago, I could have saved myself so much longing. I tried to catch a glimpse of my watch. How long would I have to stay until I could leave without being too impolite?

Bruce had changed the topic. He was now delivering a lecture about people who had made it. He focused on people who came from poor backgrounds, people who had been smashed to pieces by fate, but who had picked themselves up and had become rich beyond words. It seemed to be a sort of hobby of his, to focus on people who've made it, to analyze how they got there, and, strangely enough, to criticize them as far as possible.

I suppressed a yawn. Had he always been this boring? I loved to hear success stories as much as the next person, but when Bruce talked about them, it seemed he only focused on the monetary value. He didn't mention if the people were happier in the end, or if they made others happy. As he droned on about another great Edinburgh citizen who'd made it to the top, I only listened with half an ear to his ongoing monologue, trying not to feel suffocated by his obvious superficiality.

"So when his wife died, he threw in his job and started his own advertising agency. You wouldn't believe it if you saw him, but he's been heralded as Scotland's most creative man, and the advertising budgets of his customers are large enough to buy half of Scotland and England. He recently won three Lions at the festival in Cannes, and he's making money as if there's no tomorrow, all the time looking like a most romantic Highlander with women swooning over him. I read an article about him in *The Economist* today. Not that I want to look like him, mind you, with his red ponytail and all, but—"

My head snapped up. "What? Did you say he looks like a Highlander?"

"Yes. I think he carefully grooms that image." Bruce made a face. "But they all fall for it, long hair and all. Yuck."

"What's his name?" My voice was sharp.

"But I told you. It's Taran Cameron, and his agency is called TC Creative. You must have heard of him." He bent down, pulled *The Economist* magazine from his immaculate black briefcase and slapped it on the table. Taran looked at me with a half-smile that made my mouth go dry.

Bruce pointed at the cover. "You must have seen that face. It's everywhere at the moment. I read this article about him at lunchtime today. Personally, I don't think the hype around this guy will last, and if he's not careful, all that money will disappear, but—"

I pushed back my chair and jumped up, trying to get my hectic breathing under control. "Bruce, I'm sorry, but I have to go. I . . . there's something I have to do."

"But—"

"I'm so very sorry about this, but I'm— I'm feeling unwell. Thank you for a nice evening." The lie came out before I could stop it. Before he could say more than two words, I grabbed the umbrella and bolted out of the restaurant.

The wind had calmed down, and the rain had stopped. For once, August felt like summer, and the air was positively balmy. I took a deep breath and hurried uphill toward Edinburgh Castle, pushing past the crowds of tourists without seeing anybody, walking on and on and on, never stopping to think.

I'm a horrible person. Tears filled my eyes. How could I have made fun of Taran when he'd told me that his wife had died? How could I have been so hard on him? How could I have assumed so much about him only because he looked different from most people? Talk about being superficial. Talk about being crass. I was so ashamed, I stumbled over my feet.

As I continued to struggle uphill both in the real world and in my mind, I suddenly realized that I had been so harsh because I'd been looking for any reason to reject him in my own thinking—so he couldn't get close. Because getting close would give him the power to leave me, to hurt me, and that scared the bejesus out of me.

But Taran had taken it all in his stride. He had laughed about it, had accepted my queer vision of him without feeling belittled, without feeling the need to shift my image of him. Instead, he had continued to woo me, to charm me, making me fall in love with his true self, with his character, not needing the help of wealth or social standing to make him more important. What a man. What laid-back sincerity and self-reliance, what inner strength.

I swallowed. From out of nowhere, the conviction came and stayed with me that it had happened: I had fallen in love with Taran. With the man himself, with his sense of humor, his way of reading my mind, his gentle teasing. Not with his position in society or his success. I'd fallen in love with him even when I thought he was a dropout. A big smile spread across my face.

But then, a thought darted through my head, and my happiness evaporated. Maybe Taran had only fallen for me because of the umbrella. Maybe the magic had made him blind to my insults. I stopped dead, closed my eyes and tried to make sense of it all, but the more I thought about it, the more confused I got. What was real and what was magic?

I didn't know, but I realized one thing: I had to discuss it with Taran. After I'd had apologized for being so rude.

With trembling hands, I pulled out my phone and called Taran.

"Ainsley! Didn't you say you're busy tonight?"

"I was." My voice sounded husky. "But I'm not anymore, and I wondered . . ." My courage failed me.

"You wondered what?" His voice sounded soft.

Could I ask Taran to drop everything and come to meet me? I had been so incredibly rude to him. I swallowed but couldn't get out another word.

The bells of St. Giles started to ring with three light strokes to indicate the three quarters of the hour. It was a quarter to eight.

"Where are you?" Taran said. "Is that St. Giles I hear in the background?"

"Yes. I'm on High Street."

"I'm not that far away from you. I'm on Princes Street."

I gulped, squared my shoulders, and said, "Would you like to meet me?"

"Of course." He didn't hesitate. "Now?"

"Yes. Please."

"Where?"

"How about the corner of Mound Place and Ramsay Lane? It's halfway between both of us, and it'll give us a spectacular view of the city."

"I'll be there. Give me ten minutes."

I hurried to our meeting place and leaned against the iron fence, looking out toward Princes Street. Dusk had fallen some time ago, and the city was alive with lights. How should I start the conversation? Should I apologize first? Should I tell him I now knew who he was? I was afraid of broaching the subject, as if that would somehow destroy the lightness of our fun relationship. Behind me, people walked past, hurrying home or returning from their shopping, with plastic bags from Tesco's in their hands. Two boys with wave boards used the hill to exercise and rushed by at neck breaking speed, but I hardly noticed them, so intent was I on looking for a tall guy with red hair. My heart beat faster when I finally saw Taran approaching uphill from Princes Street, and I almost ran to meet him.

He stopped in front of me and pushed a strand of hair from my face. "What happened?"

"Taran, I need you to answer one question, and I know it sounds weird, but it's important to me." My heart was hammering inside my chest.

His eyebrows pulled together. "Shoot."

I wanted to ask him why he had followed me home from the supermarket and put up with my rude behavior, but when I opened my mouth, a totally different question came out. "If you had the power to become extremely popular by some kind of magic, would you use it?"

His gaze searched my face. "I think I would. Who wouldn't? Why is that so important?"

I swallowed, and once again, my private Taran-magic kicked in: I could say anything I thought without fear, without wondering if he might misunderstand. "But if you use that power, how do you know which people are your real friends? And what if the magic disappears one day again and you realize that you've been fooled, and it was all a big mistake? Wouldn't you prefer to find the people who are your soul mates instead of using magic and making them all fall in love with you, no matter who they are?"

His expression grew serious. "Wait. Do you think that some sort of magic made me fall in love with you?"

I gasped. "Yes." I balled my fists to stop my hands from trembling. "Remember when I told you about my neighbor, the one who suddenly turned nice that morning? I used magic on her as well, inadvertently, and now she's a changed person. I'm so afraid."

His gaze never left my face. "What are you afraid of?"

I gulped. "I'm afraid that people don't really like me. And if I trust them, I'll get hurt if the magic wears off."

Taran took my hands and covered them with his. "I know what you mean about being afraid. I am too. But I'm not sure I understand everything you're saying about magic."

"It's the umbrella." With my chin, I pointed at the handle that hung over my arm, not wanting to withdraw my hands from his. "It's an heirloom from my grandmother. She left it to me and my three cousins, and we're to keep it for three months each before passing it on. We all thought she was crazy. However, it's a magic umbrella. You won't believe me, but whenever I share it with someone, that person becomes infatuated with me."

His eyes widened. "This is incredible. Are you quite sure?"

"Yes." I nodded. "I tested it, and it really works. Scientifically speaking, though, it is just an ordinary umbrella. I tested that, too."

He looked at the innocent thing on my arm. "You think my feelings for you are only there because we shared some space underneath a magic umbrella?"

Something blocked my throat, and my eyes burned. "I think so. Isn't it terrible? It . . . it makes it so . . . so cheap."

He narrowed his gaze and gripped my hands even harder. "Hang on a minute." He stared down at the blinking city lights below the parapet, then looked back at me. The light from the street lamp next to us showed the line of his determined jaw. "No, that's not right. My feelings for you are not due to any magic, at least, not more magic than falling in love usually is."

I tried to draw a breath. "How do you know?"

"I just recalled that scene. I remembered seeing you at the checkout, noting your face, thinking that you reminded me of a Japanese Manga girl."

"A cartoon character?"

"Yes." His smile was tender. "With a heart-shaped face, huge eyes and loads of spunk. I wanted to get to know you, but I was too deep in my rut to react to that instinctive feeling. It was only when I was outside that I realized I had just missed a chance, maybe the chance of a lifetime. I had never felt this urge before. So I turned on my heels and tried to find you, but I must have run straight past you because when I turned around again, you were in front of me, just leaving." He gave me a crooked smile. "I did not plan to tackle you to the floor, though. That really was an accident, and I felt I couldn't admit that I had come back for you because you might think I had thrown you to the ground on purpose, to make you stop and talk to me."

"So the attraction was there before you opened the umbrella?" My voice sounded rough. My heart hammered as if I had run all the way up to the castle.

The corners of his mouth crinkled in a slow smile. "It was."

Relief spread through me and lifted me. I felt I could detach myself from the ground and soar over Edinburgh, umbrella in hand, much like Mary Poppins. I beamed at Taran, happiness spreading through my every pore.

He pulled me closer until my nose was almost pressed against his jacket. "How about you?" His voice was soft. "How does the umbrella work on you?"

"Not at all." I tilted back my head so I could see him. "Funnily enough, I'm not touched by its magic."

He looked at me, a frown in his eyes. "I think you're wrong there. How likely is it that you would have allowed me to accompany you home if you had not been influenced by the umbrella?"

I blinked as I remembered that strange feeling of being completely relaxed with him, right from the beginning. "You mean it's magic?"

He shrugged. "Magic. A miracle. Whatever you want to call it."

"Wow." I nodded. Then I freed my hand and pulled out my list. "Do you have a pen?"

"What for?"

I gave him a half-smile. "So I can cross out the last point on my list, the one you wrote down for me. It's done."

A slow smile spread across his face. Instead of giving me a pen, he pulled me closer and kissed me with so much tenderness that my feet left the ground, and only his arms kept me from floating away into the air; I swear it. I had fallen in love, with or without the umbrella's help. I didn't care. It was strong, and it was real, and it would last. I now knew it without a doubt, and my happiness spilled over. I relaxed, falling into his kiss. At some point, the umbrella slipped from my sleeve and fell with a clatter onto the pavement.

Taran let go of me and picked it up. "The handle fell off."

"Never mind. It happened before." I took the crooked wooden piece from his hands and stuck it back on, remembering to turn it to its correct position this time. I didn't want to talk about the umbrella. I wanted to kiss Taran. But just as I turned back to him, a sudden memory came to me of Mrs. McDowell walking toward me on the garden path right after I'd screwed on the umbrella's handle the wrong way. The handle had been pointing at my stomach, and my hand had tingled when she and Tony touched it, as if they were sending little love rays at me through the curved wood, as if it were a conduit. Could the handle's direction have had anything to do with the way the magic worked?

I shook my head. It didn't matter anymore. The only thing that mattered was the man in front of me and our feelings for each other. I smiled up at him.

Taran pulled me close. "Now, where were we when we were so rudely interrupted by your wayward umbrella?"

I smiled at him and pulled his head closer until his lips touched mine. "Right here."

Ainsley

Edinburgh

Three Months Later

The letter landed with a satisfying thud on the tiled floor in my hall. My Saturday morning had just begun, and I was busy making the first cup of tea for Taran and myself. Taran was still asleep, and I loved to wake him with a cup of tea in the mornings. His face always lit up when I inched closer and held the steaming mug underneath his nose, his mouth smiling and welcoming me even before he had opened his eyes.

Now, curiosity drew me to the front door. That thud had sounded too solid for an ordinary bill and too light for a catalog. Maybe it was a real, handwritten letter, like the ones my grandmother used to send me from Paris? I hadn't gotten one of those for ages. But who would write to me now?

When I picked up the letter and saw the French stamp, my heart stopped beating for moment. Could the letter be post-dated from my late grandmother? A message from beyond the grave? I flipped the envelope over and saw the sender's name on the back. *Anatole Plessis.*

Interesting. What would Toli write to me about? Did it have something to do with the umbrella?

It had been weeks since I'd passed the umbrella on to Josie, and I had often wondered how she'd fared with it. Before passing it on, I had continued to use it, careful not to let anyone else come into contact with it. The feelings it had started earlier with my coworkers and neighbor had remained to some extent but slowly abated. I was still good friends with my neighbor Mrs. McDowell, and the head of the buying department smiled at me whenever I turned around the corner. Even Bruce beamed at me in spite of our hastily interrupted dinner whenever he saw me from afar. I took good care never to get too close again. Most important of all, though, I was still in love with Taran, and he with me. I figured that the umbrella had done its job for me.

Of course I was dying to know how my cousins had dealt with the magic umbrella, but I'd forced myself not to get in touch with them, sticking to Grandma's rules. Far be it from me to interfere with the magic. I had only to keep my curiosity at bay until May. Then I'd see my cousins again, and we could discuss all that had happened to us.

A sudden gust of wind buffeted against the house, and a draft pushed through the crack under my front door. I drew my sweater closer around me. November had brought early winter storms with hail to us in Edinburgh, and with them freezing temperatures. Suddenly, I realized that my feet were icy. I snatched up the letter, got my two mugs of tea and rushed upstairs.

Unfortunately, Taran was awake now, so I couldn't nudge him and watch that delicious smile emerging over tea. He looked at me and immediately said, "What's so exciting?"

I had long ago stopped asking him how he could read me so well. I handed him both mugs, pulled the letter from the waistband of my pajamas and waved it in the air. "I got a letter from Anatole Plessis. Did I tell you about him? He's the old lawyer and family friend who grew up with my grandmother in the same village. We used to spend our summer holidays together in my grandmother's old house in Brittany."

"Sounds lovely."

I sighed with longing. "Oh, yes, it was. Toli, as we used to call him, was always around. He taught us how to fish and cook. He's a real gourmand."

"And what does he write to you?"

"I have no idea. I haven't read the letter yet." I slipped underneath the cover and snuggled my cold feet against his warm calves.

He winced. "Darling, please add furry slippers to your shopping list. This habit of yours of hopping out of bed in the early morning, only to return with iced feet, is not healthy."

"But I also return with hot tea," I pointed out.

He grinned. "True, and I have to say you're spoiling me." He pointed at the letter. "Are you going to open the letter this morning or do you want to put it on your list as a task to do in the afternoon?"

I gave him a gentle kick, slid my fingernail along the creamy envelope, and fished out several sheets of thick paper that were covered with beautiful handwriting in black ink. "Wow. It's really long." I leaned against his shoulder. "I'll read it to you:

My dear Ainsley,

This letter will come as a surprise to you, but I hope it will be a pleasant one. You see, I plan to get married in May next year.

I sat up straight. "Married?"

Taran grinned. "What's so unusual about that?"

I turned to him, shaking my head in astonishment. "He's the most confirmed bachelor I know. He's never been in a relationship, not even once, as far as I can recall. In fact, Carlo once asked grandmother how it came about that she had two husbands when everybody else only had one. He was five at the time, I believe. It has been a family joke ever since."

"What did your grandfather say about this arrangement?"

"Oh, don't get me wrong. Grandma didn't have an affair with Toli. At least, I never got the impression that there was jealousy or anything of that kind on my grandfather's side. No, Anatole's love was from afar." I shook my head again and looked at the letter in my hands. "And now he's getting married. This is unbelievable. I wonder if it has anything to do with the umbrella? Or maybe my grandma's death released him to love again." I turned back to the rustling pages and resumed reading.

When your grandmother died, nothing could have been further from my mind than romance, but on the very day of her funeral, when I went to her house to retrieve the umbrella for you all, I met Anne, and I have to say that ever since, my life has not been the same.

"I was right!" Excitement fizzed through me. "It does have something to do with the umbrella!"

"What else does he say?"

I continued reading aloud:

At any rate, last week I realized that at my age, it doesn't do to dawdle, so I asked Anne if she would marry me. I felt so honored and happy when she said yes, but when I learned how many plans she has for this wedding, I felt a bit as if I was on a roller coaster. Do you remember how I hate those things?

I smiled. "Gosh, don't I. One summer, he took all four of us to an amusement park. He went on one of the smaller roller coasters with us and turned quite green. I mean, really green. We'd never seen anything like it and couldn't stop talking about it for ages."

"Go on." Taran took a sip from his tea. "I'm hooked now."

I returned to the letter.

You see, my dear Ainsley, Anne was never married, and she has so many ideas about what she'd like for this wedding, and I love her so much that I really, really want her to have them all realized, but quite frankly, this whole wedding scares me more than I can say. Her family far outnumbers mine, and when she suddenly took it into her head that my reluctance to discussing wedding details has its roots in a reluctance to marry her, I knew that I needed help.

I smiled. "Poor Toli."

Taran made a wry face. "I feel for him. Quite a few guys have been in his position before."

Our gazes met. "Have you, with your late wife?" I could still be as direct and open with Taran as during our very first meeting, and this knowledge felt like a treasured warm fire deep inside me.

"My wedding was one hundred percent tradition-al, and I admit that I was glad when it was over." He cocked his head to the side. "How about you? What would be a perfect wedding for you?"

I could feel my face going hot. "I have a recurring fantasy. It's a bit odd, I admit, but for some reason, it's stuck in my mind."

He lifted his eyebrows. "I'm intrigued."

"I want to get married barefoot."

His jaw dropped. "Won't your feet get cold?"

I laughed. "Sorry, I started at the wrong end. I pic-ture my wedding on a beautiful beach during sunset, and me barefoot in the sand, but with full wedding dress." I looked at him, suddenly shy. "Is that too odd?"

His smile did something strange to my breathing. "Not odd at all. I quite like the idea and will keep it in mind."

Flustered, I turned back to Anatole's letter. My voice shook a little as I continued reading.

I told Anne that it was all the details and all the fuss that made me so nervous, but that it had nothing at all to do with her. I really want to be married to her. I just wish it was already done.

So Anne, who's a wizard at finding solutions when I see none, said that we should find a wedding planner, but nei-ther of us knows the first thing about where to start. And suddenly, I thought of you and your lists and how well you organize everything, and I've been wanting to invite you and your cousins to the wedding anyway, because you feel like my children, and I'm out of my depth here, so here it is in short, my humble question: Would you like to organize

Anne's and my wedding? We would of course reimburse you for your time.

I caught my breath. "Oh, how wonderful!" In my excitement, I bounced up and down on the bed.

Taran gave me a teasing smile and held his mug to the side. "Tea overboard. All men on deck."

"Never mind about the tea! First, we have to find a location. Where's my pen? I need a piece of paper." I threw back the covers and jumped out of bed. "In fact, I already have an idea—we could have the wedding at my grandma's house in Brittany. It's absolutely charming. You will love it."

Taran lifted his eyebrows. "Oh, am I invited?"

"Of course you are. The wedding invitations will say: 'You and your significant other are cordially invited.' Because I have a feeling that my cousins will not be single anymore by the time we celebrate Anatole's wedding." I gave Taran a mischievous smile. "That umbrella has not made the rounds without a reason."

Josie

Paris
December

"Aren't you going to open it?" my boss asked me. He's the head of sales and marketing at Esportiva, the sports shoe company where I've been a marketing coordinator for the past two years. He nudged my arm in encouragement. "You should offer your umbrella to Mr. Delorme. He looks like a snowman."

We were standing with a handful of our coworkers under the Eiffel Tower on a chilly December day, trying and failing to escape a snowstorm that had taken us by surprise. Today was the day before the big international shoe convention we were all scheduled to attend, and it was my job to give our visiting colleagues a tour of Paris's main monuments. But as luck would have it, the weather wasn't cooperating.

I gave a nervous cough and quickly slid the collapsed umbrella back into my bag. "An umbrella won't help in this wind. I suggest we find a cafe where we can take shelter."

"Josie," my boss hissed near my ear, "our guests want to finish the tour. And Mr. Delorme needs something to cover his head."

I hesitated. My thoughts were still fixated on the red and ratty umbrella I'd stashed away. I hadn't expected to find it in my handbag just now. The last I remembered, it was safely stowed under my bed.

"Forgive me," I said at last. "I would rather not lend anyone my umbrella." I cringed as the words left my mouth. In France, you must never challenge your superior.

My boss's watery eyes bugged out. "Why not?"

"I don't want to lose it."

This was a fib. The truth was I didn't want anyone to know about its—well, its power. That's why I'd hidden it under my bed after receiving it by post from my cousin Ainsley last month. I know this is hard to believe, but as I'd learned from careful observation, the umbrella had matchmaking abilities. When two people step under it at the same time, they fall hopelessly in love. I hadn't figured out yet how long the "love" lasts. My roommate who'd fallen victim to it, for instance, was showing signs of waning interest in her new beau, our early morning garbage collector, an ex-convict.

And now here I was, being asked to offer the same umbrella to my idol, Mr. Jean-Louis Delorme, the most versatile and talented shoe designer I'd ever had the pleasure to admire from afar. He stood a couple of yards away from me now amid a swirl of snow. Ski-tanned, athletic, smart, suave, thirty-one and generally a feast for the eyes, Mr. Delorme was a Swiss man who worked out of our Brussels office, where our design talent was based.

And where someday I hoped to work.

At the moment, he was talking to our star catalog model, Rob Dalyac, an American guy whose flight from the US had been delayed. Rob had just joined our little pre-convention tour, wheeling a suitcase behind him, his broad shoulders straining under his jacket. Rob had the kind of looks I liked—dark hair and vivid blue eyes, but I wasn't really attracted to him; he was a model, after all, and our models tended to be vain. Besides, I'd heard through the grape vine he was gay.

Mr. Delorme shook hands with the newcomer. "It's nice to finally put a face to the feet."

We all laughed, even my hissy-fitting boss. Being in the shoe business, we're desperate for any and all foot jokes. *It's only shoes* is our mantra. Otherwise, with the competition as stiff as it is, we'd take ourselves too seriously and crack under the pressure.

Rob the foot model laughed as well, showing strong white teeth and a broad American smile, the sort that most Parisians would find silly or insincere, but not I. Having spent holidays in the US as a kid, I knew he meant every inch of that smile.

His grin still in place, he set about greeting each person in our group, shaking their hands.

My boss, meanwhile, would not stop worrying the umbrella bone. "Everyone saw it in your hand," he whispered. "Remember the cultural sensitivity training? I must insist that you lend our guests your umbrella. And smile, Josie. Smile!" My boss grinned like a demented garden gnome. He had internalized much too much of the cross-cultural training seminar we'd been sent to—sponsored in part by the French government, I might add. The feds were trying to get us Parisians to be more user-friendly to tourists.

"Josie?" my boss said when I hadn't replied.

I kept my eyes lowered, biting my lip, saying nothing.

"We'll talk later, *Mademoiselle.*"

My heart fell. I knew what "talk later" meant. It meant my boss would find a way to shunt me off into a less international department, that is, if he couldn't demote me first. In France, we take our centralized hierarchies very seriously. If you step out of line even for a moment, you fall off the corporate ladder. I murmured my apologies, but it was too late. I was now an official inhabitant of the no-promotion-zone.

"And you are?" someone said beside me.

A loser.

I looked up to see Rob the foot model extending his hand. I grasped his warm palm as if clinging to a lifesaver.

"Joséphine Collomb, from international marketing and sales," I said. "We spoke on the phone a few times about travel arrangements."

"Yes, yes. That's right. Please call me Rob." He pumped my hand for far too long, an American peculiarity. "Sorry I'm late for your tour." He gestured toward his suitcase, which was held together by shiny industrial tape. Bits of brightly colored clothing stuck out at the side. "The airline demolished my luggage and then conveniently 'lost' it. And when I pleaded my case, they conveniently found it again." He grinned. Strong, healthy teeth. But they'd probably been professionally whitened. "The only thing holding this baby together is string and a prayer." He patted his suitcase as if it were an old friend.

I returned his smile. "I see you've mastered the French art of getting by, or *se débrouiller*."

"Exactly." He switched to French. "All you need to do is grovel and give customer service reps a sense of personal power, and they'll go to the moon and back for you."

"Your French is quite good!" My boss pushed between us, putting out his hand for a shake. He shot a look at me that said, *Where are your manners? You didn't introduce him to me as an inferior to a superior.* "I'm Betrand Pignon, head of international sales and marketing."

They exchanged a few pleasantries, while I wished myself away. I pictured myself as a tiny snowflake somewhere high above us amid the iron grid work of the Eiffel Tower, looking down on the obligations and humiliations of my life. But instead of flying away—perfect and safe—my snowflake collided into another flake, sticking to it, and these bunched up with thousands of others until they drifted down and flew into my face. God was throwing snowballs at me and laughing.

"May I, *Mademoiselle?*"

I jerked slightly to see Rob's arm near my face. As he unfurled a black umbrella, a scent of light aftershave rose from his jacket, mixed with something salty. A second later we were both under the dome of his jumbo umbrella, walking with the others through the snow on the Champs de Mars park. My boss had announced that, given the blizzard-like weather conditions, we would reschedule our tour of Paris and retire to a café a few blocks away.

Mr. Delorme sauntered alone in front of Rob and me, his black hair speckled with snowflakes, his wide shoulders covered with snow. My hand itched to brush the flakes away.

Why, oh, why hadn't I offered to share my umbrella with him when given the chance? I would have solved so many problems with that gesture; I'd have appeased my boss and created the perfect opportunity to talk to my idol about my apparel design training, my real reason for even taking a marketing job at Esportiva. And if Mr. Delorme were to fall in love with me, why, wouldn't that be utter and complete happiness? But what was I thinking? I shuddered at my imagined audacity. I had actually considered matchmaking myself with my idol.

Our little group arrived at a corner opposite the café and waited for the traffic light to change. Across from us, the café's yellow ceiling lights twinkled, and the steamed windows promised warmth.

"Oops," Rob said beside me.

I glanced to where he stood beside me. His suitcase was hanging open, the tape around it flagging in the wind. A trail of clothes dotted the snow behind us.

The traffic light had just changed to green. Rob waved us on. "Go get warm. I'll join you once I've got this thing in one piece."

"Let me help." Mr. Delorme moved to pick up the first article of clothing that had fallen out.

It was a dress.

A long, pink dress with wide shoulders and a scooped neckline, it fluttered to full length in Mr. Delorme's hands.

Oh, my. I stood stock still, unsure what to do. If Rob was in the closet as everyone said he was, calling attention to the dress would embarrass him.

Mr. Delorme's cheeks flushed nearly as pink as the dress. "Here you go." He handed the garment to Rob. "Excuse me."

Rob's face had turned crimson. "Ah! This is for a friend. I got her some freebies after a photo shoot." He pointed at a couple of other bright clothes in the snow. "They were in the same studio right before my shoot—tall and plump gals, up for grabs. Not the gals, of course. I mean the dresses. The dresses were up for grabs. Okay, now I'm babbling." Eyes wide, he glanced at the group of other colleagues who'd turned to see what the commotion was about. Rob waved them away. "Just a broken suitcase. We'll be there in a sec."

They'd seen the dress too but didn't look fazed. They turned and crossed the street.

"Miss Collomb," Mr. Delorme said to me, "maybe we should join the others. These are Mr. Dalyac's private belongings. Excuse me, again," he told Rob.

"Not a problem." Rob's blush had crept to his neck and forehead. "There's nothing in here you can't see."

But Mr. Delorme would not hear of it. He extended the crook of his arm to me. "Shall we?"

A thrill of hope ran through me. He wanted to touch me! I slid my arm around his. But as we made our way across the street, guilt made me cast a backward glance. Poor Rob was running around in the snow and stuffing clothes into his suitcase. Should I have offered to stay and help? He'd wanted the others to go ahead, but had said we could stay. And yet clearly, his blush showed his befuddlement.

It was so hard to read people, so hard to know the right thing to do. I sighed and continued to cross the street with Mr. Delorme.

The rest of the afternoon turned out less promising than I'd hoped. In the café, I was seated at the far end of the table, away from the movers and shakers. Instead of talking about the company's new directions and my ideas for going mass-fashion with our snow boots for women, *à la* Ugg boots, I was subjected to hours of gossip by a sales manager, Emmanuelle Courteau.

"Oh, he's definitely gay," she said about Rob the foot model. "I can't say who told me, but it was someone who ought to know."

"He doesn't seem gay; not that I'm always right about these things," I said.

"You never can tell," she said.

Personally, I didn't agree with that—there *are* subtle signs, as I'd learned the hard way with my ex, Michel—but it was no use arguing with Emmanuelle about it or going into detail. Anything private I might reveal to her would immediately enter the office gossip mill.

After our hot drinks and snacks, I took the metro home alone. My roommate was out on the town with her new boyfriend, and my best friend couldn't be reached by phone. Exhausted from the long day, I fell into bed early, forgetting about the umbrella in my bag, and dreamed of waking up in a snowbound cabin and having to dig myself out with my bare hands.

"What do you think? Are these not the most well-formed toes you have ever seen?"

An amateur foot model stood before me in high-heeled sandals, one of her legs extended as she pivoted her spray-tanned foot under the florescent lights of the Esportiva sales booth.

Today was the first day of *La Foire de la Chaussure,* which, unfortunately, was open to the public. Usually they weren't allowed in until the weekend, this being a trade show, but the Parisian government was doing everything it could to attract more tourists to our fair city, and our convention was now the "circus" part of their bread-and-circus strategy to keep locals happy and visitors entranced.

"Your feet look great," I said, "but really, I'm not the person who makes the modeling decisions. You'd need to have your agency send—"

"And look at this one," she went on. "This is its best angle. Three quarter view. Perfect for your sports sandals lines, *non*?"

I didn't have the heart to be angry at this woman. She was like me, just trying to get somewhere in life, but she didn't have any good connections. You have to start somewhere, right? I handed her my card. "Listen, in a few days, send me your portfolio by email. I'll forward it to the person who makes catalog decisions. But there's no guarantee they'll get back to you. They prefer to work with agencies. And honestly, I have very little clout in this company. In the meantime, do everything you can to get an agency to represent you."

She gazed at the card I'd given her, and when she looked at me her eyes shone with tears. "Thank you. Thank you! You are the sweetest person I've met here all day. I know I have good feet, but most people just don't have eyes to see it. You do!"

"Like I said, there's no guarantee. I wish I could be more encouraging."

"But you are; you *are* encouraging. A thousand thanks." She pocketed the card, gave me a few over-joyed air kisses with her good-byes, and swayed away on her high heels.

I sighed as I turned back to my binder of samples. The woman had seemed so oblivious to the rules, un-aware of the *comme il faut* of how you're supposed to break into the business. She was like a babe in the woods. And wolves eat babes.

"That was a kind gesture."

I looked around. Rob the foot model was standing a few yards behind me by a display of rock-climbing shoes, looking dashing in a well-cut suit. I blinked a few times, suddenly befuddled. My God. This guy looked like a movie star. I could practically feel the charisma rolling off of him in waves. "I made an ex-ception for her," I said. "I don't know why. She seemed pretty clueless."

"You should have seen me when I got my first break. As clueless as they come." Rob strolled to my side. Under his finely tailored jacket, he wore a dark gray shirt and black silk tie. Once again I was struck by the intense blue of his eyes, contrasted with the black of his hair and lashes. If he'd wanted, he could have done face modeling too. Maybe he already did. A shy smile curved his lips, as he shook his head. "I thought the guy who discovered me was a foot freak." He chuckled. "I'm not into that by the way. I assure you."

Why was he telling me all this? Maybe he was still embarrassed about the dress incident yesterday. I decided not to allude to any of it. To spare his feelings. "How has the fair been so far for you? Any new job offers?"

"A few. And you?"

I coughed. How did he know to ask me this? I hadn't told anyone I was looking to switch departments within Esportiva. "Pardon?"

"Just a wild guess. Who wouldn't want a new job with the way your boss treated you yesterday?"

"Ah, I see." More I would not say. The grape vine has a way of wending its way back to latch onto listening posts that shouldn't be in the know.

I checked my watch. The display read 6:31 p.m. Hurrah! It was time to close my booth. Already there was a great shuffling and scuffling going on all around, as the booth staff locked up their most precious sales equipment and gathered their coats. Hoards of tourists still roamed the aisles, searching for freebies of any kind—free pens, free cloth bags, free key chains—it didn't matter what.

"Closing time. I'd better get going." I unlocked the cabinet where I'd kept my handbag with the umbrella.

"Any special plans?"

I glanced up. Had Rob come to the booth especially to ask me this? I studied his face. His eyes seemed
especially focused on me, keen to hear my reply, or
was that worry I saw written there? He scuffed his
feet, as if nervous. Then I remembered he had an appointment with my boss. Of course Rob was nervous.
My boss had that effect on people.

"No special plans," I said casually as I opened my
bag and glanced inside. The red umbrella was safely
tucked behind the flap beside my e-tablet. "I was
thinking of catching a lecture by Mr. Delorme."

What an understatement. I hadn't merely been
thinking about it; I'd been obsessing all day about Mr.
Delorme's panel talk. I had a notion that afterward, I
would wait in line to ask him my questions, and then
find a way to be invited to wherever he was planning
to go for dinner or drinks. I had my portfolio pictures
cued up on my e-tablet, ready to show him at a moment's notice. I had spent many an hour debating
whether to send my samples via email to his Brussels
office, but I'd always heard that making a personal
contact first is the best way to get a promotion, so
that's what I was going to do.

"There he is," someone said beside me, "the man
with the best-looking feet in the western hemi-
sphere." It was my boss, who'd just arrived. He shook
hands with Rob.

"Not the best-looking feet in the world?" Rob
quipped. "I've already practiced my acceptance
speech if there's an awards ceremony. *Thank you,
thank you.*" He mimed teary-eyed joy. "I'd like to

thank my mother for her well-formed pinky toes and my father for his high arches. And of course, the company to which I owe it all, Esportiva. You guys are the best!"

We three laughed our desperate, help-I-work-in-the-shoe-industry laughs. Talk about pitiful. I wiped a tear from the corner of one eye. I really needed to get out of the office more often; I was too easily entertained by anything that made fun of shoes or the funny-looking appendages that filled them.

Rob and my boss went off for their meeting, and I was discreetly checking my makeup in a compact mirror a few seconds later when I happened to see a familiar figure striding at a diagonal away from the booth. It was Mr. Delorme, heading to the open coffee stand a row away! My ears started to buzz, and my heart rate soared. Here was my chance to talk to my idol alone. Would I have the courage this time? Half-blind with panic, I grabbed my e-tablet from the counter and race-walked to the coffee stand. I got in line a few people down from Mr. Delorme. So far, so good. I was only a couple of yards from him. Should I call out to him now? No, I should wait until we saw each other's faces. That would be more natural, as if I'd just happened to bump into him. He ordered coffee and then sat down at a nearby table, his back still to me. *Perfect.* I waited my turn in line and when I finally reached the counter, I looked down for my purse and—*oh là là.* My shoulder was disturbingly free of weight.

I didn't have my handbag with me.

A surge of adrenaline seared my nerves, propelling me back toward the sales booth. I spied something red there on the front counter. It was my umbrella—safe, thank God.

But my handbag was gone.

No! I grabbed the umbrella and looked around, heart hammering. A tall man in a black suit was striding away from the booth, weaving among the tourists and holding something brown under his elbow. It looked like a rugby ball. Or my handbag.

I launched after him. "Thief! Stop that man in the black suit."

Not the smartest thing to shout in a Parisian crowd. There were at least ten men nearby wearing black. I zipped past them, pursuing my target.

The man in question turned around. When his eyes met mine, they widened. He whipped forward and ran.

I ran too. "Him! That's the guy! He has my handbag."

Not that this did me any good. The thief darted to the right, dodged a display of platform heels, and whizzed outside through an emergency exit.

Of course, no alarm went off. Just my luck. I surged after him, my breath coming in spurts as I shouldered past the emergency exit door.

Outside I found myself in a parking lot. Snow flakes pelted my face, blinding me for a second. I looked down, and there it was on the ground—my handbag. The thief must have ditched it. Had he taken only my money? My credit cards? Or was he hoping not to be caught with anything on him? I lunged for my bag. But instead I skidded on ice. I went down in an awkward arc, my arms wheeling, and landed on a patch of snow, bumping my head on the ice. There was a blissful moment of peace as I lay there looking up at the white sky. Then came a deep, melodious voice.

"Joséphine?" Above me the angelic face of a man came into view, slightly blurry; the dark shape of his hair and angular planes of his cheeks stood out against a red halo behind his head. "Are you all right?" he asked. "Can you sit up?"

His voice floated into my ears like music from the heavenly spheres, the most beautiful sound in the world. It filled me, surrounded me, connected me to all that was and all that had ever been.

"Of course I can sit up," I said, and I did just that. I rubbed my forehead. It ached a bit, but not too badly.

"Let's take her inside," some woman said behind the angel's head. "It's cold out here."

"Not until we're sure she's okay," the man said.

I recognized his face now. It was him—Rob. The most beautiful, intelligent, kindhearted man in the world. *Who is also gay*, a tiny voice nagged from some reasonable part of my brain. But I ignored that for now. I beamed at him. "What are you doing out here?"

"I knew you were in trouble when I saw you running away from the booth after that guy."

Rob took off his coat and wrapped it around my shoulders, then he pulled me to my feet with a steady hand, a hand I wanted never to release.

"Did he hit or push you?" he asked.

"No." All at once I remembered my umbrella.

Oh, God. The umbrella.

Rob was holding it in one hand, sheltering the two of us under its tiny red roof.

I groaned; no wonder I felt as if I were drunk. I'd been match-made with Rob. "No-o-o-o."

"Glad to hear it," he said, referring to the thief. He guided me into the exhibit hall and took me to the nearest empty sales booth. "We should get your head checked out."

"No need. I'm fine. A little dizzy, that's all."

"I insist. I called the fairground paramedics. They'll be here any second." He sat me in the nearest chair and turned to the woman beside him, whom I recognized as my company's gossip, Emmanuelle. She was holding my handbag and my e-tablet. The screen shone with light.

Sudden panic made me sit up. Would Emmanuelle see my designs? I held out my hand. "Does my tablet still work?"

She gave it to me . "Looks like it."

"That's a relief." I switched it off and accepted my handbag from her as well. "Did he take my wallet?"

"I don't know. I haven't checked."

My fingers trembled as I rummaged through my bag. I went through every pocket, but in the end, I had to accept that the guy had grabbed my wallet and made a run for it, leaving the handbag behind to stop me from following.

I silently cursed my bad luck. Even worse than the loss of my money was the fact I'd missed my chance to have coffee with Mr. Delorme. Maybe I could arrive at his talk late and sit in the back. But before I could do that, I had to call the police and cancel my credit cards.

I was still worrying along these lines when the paramedics arrived. They set about examining my head, and I sat there on the booth chair, protesting. "I'm fine. Honestly. It's just a little bump."

"As a precaution, you should rest for a time with an icepack on that bruise," the paramedic said. "Are you staying in the convention hotel?"

Ugh. More delays. "No. I live in Paris."

"I'm staying at the hotel right next door to this hall." Rob said. "She can rest in my room while I'm at a cocktail event I have to go to." He turned to me. "Would that work for you?"

I bit my lower lip. Should I refuse? I didn't want to impose on him or risk being around him too much now that we'd shared the umbrella, but then again I really did need to lie down for a few minutes to figure out my next plan of attack for meeting Mr. Delorme. And icing a bruise is always a good idea. "Okay," I finally said. "Thanks, Rob."

I gathered my things and let myself be escorted by him and Emmanuelle to his hotel beside the convention center. When we arrived at Rob's room, Emmanuelle took her leave for some event she'd been invited to, and I sank onto one of the cushy double beds and stayed in that position as I phoned the police and the credit card companies.

Once I'd handled all the logistics, I heaved a sigh of relief and handed Rob his phone, averting my gaze, but this only made my fingers swipe his hand by mistake. I felt heat rise in my cheeks. I glanced up at him. I couldn't help it. I had to see his face. "Thank you," I said. "You've been very kind."

"It's the least I can do." He stood beside the bed, looking down at me, his pupils wide and dark, a dazed expression on his beautiful face. The poor man was a goner, smitten with someone who wasn't even the right gender. He fished something from his wallet, a fifty-Euro bill, and gave it to me. "Will this cover your cab ride home?"

"This is too much. I only need a few Euros for the metro."

"I insist on a taxi. But take your time."

I considered his words. He was right. I really should take a cab. "I'll pay you back tomorrow."

He shrugged. "I'm here all week." He headed toward the bathroom. "I hope you don't mind. I need to freshen up before an event tonight. I'll be in here for about fifteen minutes. Do you need it first?"

I smiled—too flirtatiously. Immediately I frowned to counteract it. "No, I'm fine out here."

He nodded and went into the bathroom. A minute later the rushing sound of shower water drifted through the thin door along with Rob's humming voice. He started to sing some love song I'd heard on the radio. I closed my eyes, put the bedcovers over my head, and tried not to think about the fact that at this very moment hot water was running in clear sheets over Rob's skin.

I sat up and rubbed my temples, as if that might help me to think clearly. I needed to assess the situation. Okay, yes; I had been under the influence of the umbrella at the same time as Rob, but my feelings for him weren't so strong now that he was in the next room. So, all I had to do was avoid being around him during the convention, and soon this weird attraction would pass, or at least wouldn't be an immediate problem.

Feeling in control again, I got out my e-tablet. It booted right up, thank goodness. I clicked on the convention website and navigated to the live streaming area, where I clicked on the icon for Mr. Delorme's talk. I saw a moving picture of Mr. Delorme pointing at an image on a projected screen, but then his image froze, and a message appeared on my tablet telling me to try again because the streaming had been interrupted. *Merde.* I clicked and clicked. Nothing. I was still clicking away when Rob came out of the bathroom a few minutes later dressed in black jeans and a white buttoned-down shirt.

My entire body perked up, but I ignored it. I forced myself not to see the masculine curve of his shoulders under his shirt seams. My gaze went instead to his eyes, which seemed to glow, drawing me in. I swallowed the lump in my throat and focused on the terracotta wallpaper beside his head. "Could I borrow your tablet?" I asked the wallpaper. "I want to see if I can get live streaming from the conference website."

"Sure." He retrieved his computer from the desk and gave it to me.

I repeated what I'd tried on my own computer. Nothing. Just the same error message.

Rob came to stand beside me, looking over my shoulder. The air along my arm near him felt a few degrees warmer. "If you log in to Twitter," he said, "you can follow the talks live there. The convention website lists all the hash tags."

I brightened. "That could work."

And it did. Hurrah! There were plenty of tweets about what I'd missed. Scrolling through them, I glanced at the time display on the computer screen. There were only about thirty minutes left before Mr. Delorme's talk ended.

Rob meanwhile had been looking at his phone. He gave a low whistle. "Uh-oh."

"Everything all right?"

"The snowstorm is getting worse. It says here that most of the streets in Paris are closed."

I bolted upright on the bed. "What?"

"There are traffic jams everywhere. It says not enough people have chains on their wheels. People are leaving their cars in the middle of the street for the night and taking the metro or walking home." He glanced up. "Do you live in this district?"

I shook my head. "On the other side of Paris, in the suburbs. It would take a couple of hours to walk there." I pictured the chaos of the metro, and groaned. Getting home tonight would be like riding in the Tokyo subway during rush hour, being pushed and squeezed into the train by grumpy people in a panic. I leaned back against the headboard, sighing. "I'm screwed."

"You can stay here. I have two beds, and I don't snore." He laughed. "Not that I have recent objective data about that."

"I couldn't impose on you."

"I'll be out most of the evening anyway at this stu-pid cocktail party. I'd invite you along, but the invita-tions are numbered. Your competitors are snobs like that."

I hesitated. What should I do? I had no credit cards, nor any cash except for the fifty Rob had lent me. My apartment was too far away, and I was snowed in. In Paris! I tried not to think about the fact that I'd be in the same room all night with a gay guy who resembled a Greek god and whom I found al-most irresistible. If I just pushed that thought aside and relied on my famous self-control, the very self-control that had made my exes call me uptight, I should be fine. "Sure, I'll stay. It's better than freezing to death," I said, trying to make light of the situation.

He grinned and shouldered into his jacket. "Good. I'll be back in a few hours, but who knows how long this thing will go on. Feel free to order room service and sign it to the room."

I thought of the chance of dining with Mr. De-lorme after his presentation. "I was thinking of going out for dinner, actually."

"Here's the extra room key for whatever you de-cide." He set a plastic card key on the desk beside him.

I nodded, still ensconced under the warm covers of my bed. It occurred to me that if we lived together, Rob and I would have this sort of conversation often, one of us leaving for a work thing, the other still at home busy with something before going out, too. I shuddered, banishing the thought. What was hap-pening to me? Maybe I really was the "fag hag" I'd once been teased about when I was at design school, a woman who gets crushes on gay men because she feels safe from getting involved in a physical love relationship that could lead to rejection.

Rob was still standing by the door, looking at me with rounded eyes as if he might be thinking the same thing. "Good night then," he said.

"Good night."

His hand was on the door handle, but he didn't move. An unreadable expression passed through his eyes. He blinked, as if confused, and continued gazing at me.

I gazed back, and dammit, we were fascinated by what we saw.

He broke off first. "Sleep tight."

"Will do."

He was out that door so fast you'd think he was a frightened buck in the woods, and I was the sneaky hunter.

Fifteen minutes later I had made my way to the convention center. I stood now outside the conference room where Mr. Delorme was giving his talk, my hair fluffed over the bump on my forehead, my fingers on the door handle. But I couldn't move. I was like Rob before he'd left the hotel, stalled by some indefinable hesitation. What had happened to the confidence I'd had in design school? I'll tell you what'd happened to it: rejection after rejection during a grueling job search for suitable work.

I closed my eyes, concentrating. I could do this. I could talk to Mr. Delorme without my voice shaking or sweat stains seeping into my blouse. I pushed open the door. Inside, about a hundred people were sitting on folding chairs, their backs to me. Mr. Delorme's back was also turned as he pointed at something on a large screen.

I eased onto a chair at the back and whipped out my tablet, clicking into the Twitter stream again.

Five minutes later, I'd read the rest of the tweets about the talk and heard Mr. Delorme's summary. A round of hearty applause filled the air, and the lights came up. My heart thumped hard against my ribs as I shuffled to the front of the room and took up position near the conference table. As I'd planned, I was the last person in line. When I reached the front, Mr. Delorme squinted at me for a moment.

"Wonderful to see you again." His gaze darted to the name tag I wore near my shoulder. "Mademoiselle Collomb."

Gulping, I stared into space for a moment, searching my brain for what I'd planned to say. "I wanted to ask you about— about—"

"Yes?" Mr. Delorme placed his e-tablet into a bag and slung it over his shoulder.

"—about any design software certification programs you may know of for employees. I know all the major programs—" I rattled off the names of the leading design software. "I'd like to learn Iconoplast as well."

We were alone now, entering the enclosed thoroughfare that connected the conference area to the convention center.

"I'm impressed you know those programs. Do you use them in sales and marketing?"

Hurrah! This was the opening I had been hoping for. But would he think me too forward? "Actually I trained as a shoe and handbag designer. I took a job in sales to learn more about the business. What I really want, though, is to work my way back into design." And so saying, I peeked at him out of the corners of my eyes. Would he take my tailing along with him now as an imposition?

"Ah. Do you have any experience?"

"Just an internship during my studies. But my portfolio got top marks in school."

Not that it had landed me any design assistant jobs. But I'd been working hard on my own to add better pieces to it.

"Ah," he said.

Show it to him, I silently ordered myself but I was too shy to get out my e-tablet. The two of us had reached the wide sliding glass doors that led outside. A flurry of snowflakes filled the air, making the sky almost as white as the ground. Dark shapes of people with hunched shoulders darted about, holding colorful umbrellas.

Mr. Delorme rummaged through his bag. "*Oh là là.* I lost my umbrella again." He sighed. "I need a day off. I've become too forgetful."

Perhaps that was why he'd forgotten my name. From overwork, and not because I was forgettable? I gazed into his brilliant green-brown eyes. Tiny specks of yellow glittered on the surface of his irises, putting me in mind of an autumn lawn strewn with freshly fallen leaves. *Offer him your umbrella, I thought, come on, do it. You know you want to. You knew from the moment you discovered its power, you wanted to use it on him.* I'd only ever seen Mr. Delorme from afar in hallways and briefly in a company break room when he visited the Paris office for meetings. But I'd researched everything about him that I could. I knew he enjoyed hiking and reading (at least according to his company profile on our website), and yes, I even created a fake Facebook account and befriended him there. I know, I know, I sound like a stalker. But I'm not. Just too scared to be rejected by people to my face.

"Say, didn't you have one of those little collapsible umbrellas yesterday?" he asked. "A red one? I remember I thought it a bold design statement." He chuckled.

"Yes," I heard myself say. *Bring it out. It's in your bag. Share it with him. That might counteract what happened with Rob.* But still, I stood there like an ice sculpture, doing nothing.

"Do you have it with you?"

"Y-y-es."

"Could we use it to get to my car?"

"You're planning to drive? I take it you haven't heard. Most of the Paris streets are closed. People have abandoned their cars in the snow for the night."

"I know. I wanted to fetch some equipment from my car to take up to my hotel room." He glanced at my bulging handbag, as though wishing for something to cover his nice suit during the long trek to his car.

There was no way I would use that umbrella on him just to get a job. To get a date, perhaps, but not a job. If he liked my shoe designs, then maybe, just maybe I'd push my luck with him. I drew in a deep breath for courage. "First may I show you my portfolio?" I took out my tablet and turned it on.

"Now?" he asked.

Oh, God. He thought I was pushy.

Maybe I *was* pushy. Maybe that's why no man wanted to stay with me. But what could I do? Most men were in higher positions in the work world. How are you going to get anywhere if you don't even try to impress them? "Please forgive the suddenness, but I may never have a chance to speak to you like this again. Here's the first one. Snow boots with outer fake fur that unzips and comes off. And look, you can take the second soles off, too. See? Inside there are skinny, fashion-boot leg coverings for après-ski socializing indoors."

He paused, eyes flicking over my designs. "I like it."

"Really?"

"Certainly."

Was he only being polite, so that I would shut up and go away? I peered at his face. His smile seemed genuine enough, stretching out in a warm arc, but his eyes held some reserve. Or did my self-doubt make me think so? I clicked on an image of high-heeled sneakers, a concept that in itself is as old as the hills, but my innovation had been to have the shoelaces tie up around the entire leg, ending at the top of the thighs in a bow. I'd also put a locked storage area inside the platform heels. And a way to activate an alarm by kicking down on a certain spot. "I'd love your thoughts on this one, too. It's all about staying safe while you're being chic. I call it 'Mean Streets'."

"They're quite good."

Quite good? What did that mean? It could be a compliment or an insult or a noncommittal brush-off. Unsure how to take his comment, I decided to switch off the tablet. "I'll show you the rest some other time."

"Why not over a drink right now?"

An inner rush of joy pulled me to attention. *Yes, yes, yes.* I'd received his invitation all on my own, based on my design talents, without having to use the matchmaking umbrella. *Or maybe he just wants sex. You know how some men are at conventions away from home.* I pushed the nagging worry aside. I would let nothing ruin my good luck. In fact, I was going to help it along. Mr. Delorme was after all probably single and straight. I'd learned that much from his Facebook posts. My chances were naturally better with him than with Rob. And didn't I deserve love and happiness as much as the next person? Lord knows I'd had a string of bad luck lately.

"I'd love to," I said.

"Wonderful." He moved forward, and as we stepped between the sliding glass doors together, I brought out my umbrella. Quickly, so I wouldn't change my mind, I pushed open the spokes and began to raise it. I know, I know; I was being an opportunist.

I was using the umbrella without telling my crush about it first. A big mistake; but don't we all make mistakes? I was desperate. I was lonely. I'd never belonged to anyone, not really, except to my grandma, and now she was gone. And hadn't Mr. Delorme asked me to attend a company reception with him? I was only helping our love along.

At least that's what I told myself as I lifted the umbrella to the sky and took shelter under it.

He stepped in beside me. "I'm taller. May I carry it for us?"

"But of course."

We stood there, face to face, both holding the handle of the umbrella. His hands felt cool on mine. His pupils widened. He blinked several times.

"Joséphine."

That was all he said. But it sounded like a symphony. My heart quickened; my fingers loosened their hold of the curved handle as I let him take the umbrella. Was this how love felt? Like being drunk and disoriented and giddy? I'd experienced nearly the same sensations when Rob gazed down at me earlier, and *that* couldn't be love. I gave myself a shake. How could I even think of Rob at a time like this?

"Mr. Delorme," I said, as if his name were some deep existential insight and fascinating fact. The air had gone quiet outside the shelter of our umbrella, muffled by a whirlwind of fluffy snow.

He smiled. "Call me Jean-Louis."

"Jean-Louis and Joséphine."

"Our names sound good together," he said in a reverential whisper.

"Like left and right shoes."

Okay, I'll admit we were dripping with sentimental sap. But the longer we stayed under that umbrella, the more normal our cheesy expressions of affection sounded to my ear. By the time we'd walked to and from his parked car and reached the front of the convention hotel, we were practically cooing like a pair of doves on a windowsill.

He paused in the hotel lobby. "I almost forgot. I'm supposed to attend a cocktail party soon. Would you be my guest there?" He pulled out two paper cards from his pocket. "Here's your invite."

I glanced at the card in my hand. There was a number in one corner and the Cliffhangers logo emblazoned across the other. My heart started to do a drum solo against my ribs and my palms broke out in a sweat. What if Rob would be at the same party?

"Cliffhangers?" They were our main competitors.

"That's right. The behemoth among sports shoe companies. And we're going in." We'd reached the bank of elevators. He punched the button and it lit up. "I feel like Indiana Jones braving a snake pit."

"I thought no one from our company was invited to their reception."

"Don't tell anyone," he said, tugging me along into the elevator. He clicked on the concierge-level button. "They're making an exception for me. And my guest."

All well and good, but I couldn't chance that Rob would be at the same party. What if the love magic made me cause a scene with both of them? I couldn't trust myself to keep my head. "But—"

"I know what you're thinking," he said. "What am I doing, going behind enemy lines?"

That wasn't what I'd been thinking but I said nothing, caught up as I was in my struggle to reach an analytical zone in my brain.

Jean-Louis leaned close to my ear. "Between you and me, they're headhunting me."

"They are?" My heart sank. Just my luck; whenever I bonded with a man I would learn he was leaving in some way or impossible to reach by his very nature. Or maybe men always left *because* I'd bonded with them. "If you work for Cliffhangers, you'd be based in the US, right?"

"Not necessarily. I'd be able to work from anywhere I want. That's what attracted me to the position."

I glanced at the elevator buttons, my stomach falling as the elevator rose. The seventh floor button lit up. We were almost to the top, and I hadn't figured out a polite way to decline the invitation to tonight's do. I couldn't take the chance that Rob or I might involuntarily flirt with each other in front of Jean-Louis.

"Cliffhangers is our fiercest competitor," I said. "Some of their people stopped buy our booth today. They'll recognize me and think I'm a corporate spy."

"Nonsense. Just say you're with me and let them stew. If they want me, they'll have to accept my choice of partner."

Partner. My pulse quickened. He made "partner" sound as if I would be either living with him or working on his design team. I glanced at the elevator buttons. We'd stopped at the eight floor, and several people in suits got in.

I leaned close to Jean-Louis's ear, whispering. "What do you mean by partner?"

A pink flush crept beneath the stubble on his jaw. "I suppose I'm getting ahead of myself," he whispered back. "I thought— Well, it seemed to me that you might be interested in—" He lowered his voice further. "—in becoming my design assistant. I'll teach you everything I know."

Whoa. I could only gulp, struck speechless. This sudden good luck had to be the result of the umbrella's magic. A jolt of guilt ripped through me at the thought, but still I couldn't refuse his offer. I'd never get a chance like this again.

The elevator had stopped on the eleventh floor, letting in more people.

"That's very generous of you." I happened to glance at the invitation in my hand. On the reverse side was the handwritten name Sophie.

Sophie? My heart sank. I'd been wrong about Jean-Louis being single. He probably had a girlfriend named Sophie who couldn't make it to the convention, and now here he was crazy-in-crush with me and wanting me to be his "partner" because I'd used the umbrella on him. What a fool I'd been. "This invitation is for someone else in any case." I held it out for him to take back, but he waved it away.

"Don't worry. I'll handle everything."

"But who's Sophie?"

"Sophie . . . Sophie . . ." He looked off to one side, as if trying to place the name. "She's my ex."

"I see." I wanted to press for more information, but that would be indiscreet.

"You have nothing to worry about on her account. She's ancient history. We broke up last week."

I felt my jaw fall open. He called a week ancient history? But now that I thought about it, seven days did seem like ages ago. The umbrella had changed everything, including my perception of time.

Like most hotels, this one had no thirteenth floor. The button for the fifteenth floor lit up. *Ding.* The concierge level. The elevator doors slid open. Jean-Louis went into the hallway first, but I held back, one hand pressed to the automatic door to keep it open. Last chance to get out of this cocktail party. "I can't go in there. I don't belong." The truth of this statement made my heart clench. I didn't belong anywhere. With anyone.

His eyes softened. "Please? For me? You'll be helping me to land the job. It's good to show I'm in a stable relationship."

Relationship? I gaped at him. This was all moving so fast. And yet, as soon as he'd said it, "relationship" sounded like the right word for what we had. I gazed into his pleading eyes. How could I refuse him when he looked like a lost puppy dog and I was his waiting home? How could I be so cruel? Whatever rational faculties I had left vanished and in their place came my reply. "If you put it that way . . ."

A minute later, having shown our invitations to a woman at the door, we entered a spacious suite decorated in beige, light brown and mauve. I glanced around warily, searching the crush of well-dressed bodies for a sign of Rob's white shirt and broad shoulders. No sign of him. Phew. Maybe he'd attended some other reception.

"I need to use the ladies' room," I fibbed, after Jean-Louis and I had hung up our coats. In reality I wanted to do a quick tour of each of the suite's rooms to make sure Rob wasn't in there, either.

"Hurry back, darling." Jean-Louis leaned toward me, puckering his lips for a kiss.

For a wild moment, I felt my lips jut out and my torso lean forward. I caught myself in time, backing away. "Will do."

What a close call. My nerves jangled as I made my way through the elbow-to-elbow crowd; I didn't know whether to be flattered or concerned that my first kiss with Jean-Louis would have been in public, in front of potential gossipers. People might say I'd slept my way into whatever new job opportunity he'd been talking about. That wasn't true! I needed to put the brakes on my attraction to him and take things slowly, the natural way, so that if and when the umbrella's charm wore off, we'd still have a solid basis on which to build a relationship, whether it was a working one or romantic.

I stopped outside the doorway to the next room and peeked around the hall corner to scan the faces within. No sign of Rob. I repeated this procedure in the next room. Still no Rob.

I let out the breath I'd been holding and returned to Jean-Louis. "It's occupied," I fibbed. "I'll go later."

"But the bathroom is right here." He indicated a room beside him with its door ajar.

I felt myself blanch. What do you say when you're caught in a lie? For a timeless moment, I clasped my handbag more tightly to my side, aware with every fiber that the umbrella was digging into my waist. Never again would I touch the blasted thing. It was tempting me down a path of fibs and trickery. But I'd come so far and gained so much; I couldn't turn back now. I was finally being asked to belong to something bigger and safer than myself, something I'd missed out on as a child. I'd never belonged to my parents. I'd loved them spontaneously, like a friendly dog, but hadn't seen the love reflected back. I'd been their fifth wheel—someone to ridicule because I was so "needy" and "weak." "She's so sensitive," my step-mother had joked snidely, blowing smoke in my face.

"So *there's* the bathroom," I said to Jean-Louis with a brightness I didn't feel. "Someone told me it was occupied. I'll be right back."

I dashed into the bathroom, locked the door, and leaned against it to catch my breath. Okay, so I'd told another fib to cover a first fib. That was the last one I'd tell tonight. I went to the mirror, touched up my lipstick, and studied my face. My cheeks glowed pink, and my eyes stared back with a liquid, slightly fixed expression. I looked drugged.

"There she is, my better half," Jean-Louis said when I joined him a minute later by the buffet table. He handed me a glass of wine, turning back to the three other people with him, all much older than I, all wearing tailored clothes made of fine cloth, unlike me in my Polyester-blend knock-offs with less than straight seams.

"This is Joséphine Collomb. Talented young designer," Jean-Louis went on. "And my muse. Can't work without her."

I murmured my *enchantées* all around and tried not to faint when Jean-Louis told everyone he wanted to telecommute for Cliffhangers *from his family's goat cheese farm* in Switzerland. "It's always been a dream of mine to get back to nature," he went on, regaling our knot of partygoers while I stood there with my eyes bugging out. "Did you know that goats were my original inspiration for the Billy Goat climber shoes? There's nothing like that hoof shape in front for stability and grip. Have you ever seen a mountain goat hop up a path? It's like dancing."

As interesting as this anecdote was, I could only nod and glug my wine. I couldn't get past his mention of telecommuting from a goat cheese farm. This evening was getting more surreal by the moment, and not just from the wine. What was I going to do on a goat farm? I'd been to a sheep farm once as a tourist and I would never forget the pungent smell of unwashed wool. I'd needed a week to get it out of my clothes.

When we were alone again, I asked my new beau, "Could you tell me more about this goat farm you were talking about? Are you really thinking of moving there?"

"You'll love it. In fact, let's Skype my parents right now to break the good news to them." He glanced at his watch. "They'll still be up."

I hesitated, my thoughts reeling. We'd only just committed to our relationship and now he wanted to introduce me to his parents? But as soon as this thought occurred to me, the strangeness of it wore off. Of course I should meet his parents. As soon as possible. It was romantic. "I'd love to," I said.

We found a quiet spot at the back of the suite's last room, where we sat down on a sofa and Jean-Louis brought out his e-tablet. He dialed up his parents' account, and a few seconds later, a beautiful, Rubenesque woman of about fifty appeared on the screen. She wore a flowered house dress over a blue plaid work shirt, her dark hair loose around her shoulders, streaked with gray. Behind her I heard something bleating. Was that a goat? In her living room?

Yes, it was. A goat walked past behind her, head bobbing, beard fidgeting as it chewed its cud. It paused to nibble on a sofa cushion, munching thoughtfully. More bleating followed, this time from off-screen, sounding remarkably human, like lost children whose voices were too deep. Ba-a-a-a-a-ah. Ba-a-a-a—a-a-ah.

"Little Jean-Louis," the woman in the foreground gushed. "What a delightful surprise."

"*Bonsoir, Maman*, what are the goats doing inside?"

Okay, so I wasn't the only one who thought a goat as a house pet was odd.

"It's this blizzard. The barn is too cold for them tonight. What a terrible storm. Poor babies were freezing out there." His mother patted the neck of a goat that had ambled over and stuck its snout into the screen area, chewing slowly and staring with yellow eyes at the computer. "How is it in Paris?" his mother asked. "They said on the news all the streets are closed?"

"That's right," Jean-Louis said. "But we're safe in the convention hotel."

As he said this, a bearded man with hair as long as the woman's poked his head into the screen area from the other side, chewing with the same slowness as the goat. "*Salut!* We were just sitting down to dinner. Can't stay long. Introduce us to your lady friend."

"*Maman, papa*, this is my fiancée, Joséphine."

I choked on my wine. *Fiancée? Fiancée?* Had the umbrella's magic planted a false memory in Jean-Louis's head? My stomach tightened, and as I sat there agonizing, my mistake became crystal clear to me: I should never have used that umbrella on Jean-Louis. I had abused its power and now I had to find a way to get out of this alliance without hurting his feelings or completely messing up my career.

Meanwhile there was much cyber-rejoicing, and Jean-Louis's mother suggested we hold the wedding at the goat farm.

When I heard this, I could barely breathe. "Oh, let's postpone the wedding," I said. "My— my— grandmother just died."

"My condolences, " his mother said. "Of course we can wait until you're ready." She turned to her head toward her son. "Jean-Louis, remember that time we tied a big ribbon around Mathilde for your birthday? Wouldn't that be cute for the wedding, too?"

"Mathilde is our oldest goat," Jean-Louis explained to me. "You'll love her. She'll eat the shirt off your back if you don't watch out."

They chatted a bit more about the weather and the various goats and their personalities, while I silently communed with my wine and freaked out. Finally it was time to sign off.

"Don't be a stranger," Jean-Louis's father told me. "There's room here for plenty of guests."

"And grandchildren," his mother quipped. "At least six."

They all laughed, Jean-Louis the heartiest, and for a panicked moment I pictured myself surrounded by six squalling toddlers in high chairs and as many goats eating the very clothes from my back.

"That's a long way off," I said, coughing nervously. "I have my career to think of, too."

We said our good-byes, and afterward I sat beside Jean-Louis in stunned silence. Was this to be my life? A goat farmer's wife with six children? Not if I could help it.

"Hey, Joséphine!" someone said, startling me out of my daze. "Great to see you here. Feeling better?"

I glanced up. Rob's broad-shouldered frame towered above me. My chest tightened near my heart region, and my jaw flapped in a manner not unlike the goat snouts I had just seen, but no words came out. *Oh, Josie,* I thought, *what a tangled web you weave. Will two men expose you for the poseur that you are?*

"I'm still a bit woozy, thanks." I stood up quickly, too quickly, and the room spun faster. "In fact, I should probably . . ." I didn't finish my sentence. I'd wanted to say *lie down,* but then Rob might mention I was spending the night in his room, and I wasn't sure how Jean-Louis would interpret that.

Rob's swift glance took in the sight of Jean-Louis's hand reaching out to touch the small of my back. Rob frowned, eyes narrowing.

When I saw this, my upper lip started to bead with sweat. If only I could flee this place, a love-struck Cinderella hoisted on her own petard. But I couldn't leave. What if Rob and Jean-Louis caused a scene in my absence? That might ruin their chances of future work with Cliffhangers. I racked my brain for a solution. But what?

An idea struck me like an umbrella to the head; I would remind them both about Rob's gayness.

"I love what you've done with your hair," I told Rob in my most girly voice. "Can I borrow whatever product you use, tomorrow morning?" I turned to Jean-Louis. "Rob's letting me stay on his roll-out bed here until the storm is over. He's such a doll."

I really, really shouldn't have said "roll-out bed" because in fact there were two double beds in Rob's room, and Rob knew that, so now he probably thought I was trying to downplay the sleeping arrangement for Jean-Louis's benefit.

Rob glanced back and forth between me and Jean-Louis, puffing out his chest muscles ever so slightly. His nostrils flared like a bull's. What had the love spell done to him? "Sure. You can use my toothbrush, too."

No, no, no. Why had he said toothbrush? Why assert a prior claim over me when nothing had happened between us, and he was gay, for goodness's sake? Or maybe bi. Whatever he was, he wasn't good for me and he was about to ruin everything for all three of us. I gave a forced laugh. "Such a joker, this guy. Next thing you'll say, I can use your eye cream. Thanks, sweetie, but I'll pass."

Rob's face fell, and with it, my heart. I could literally feel the muscles and vessels in my heart contract. *Poor Rob!* I had hurt his feelings. I was a terrible person who should make it up to him right away. "Will you excuse me a moment, Jean-Louis?" I asked. "I need to tell Rob about something. I'll be right back."

Jean-Louis had stood up too, and if I wasn't mistaken, was perched a bit on his toes so he'd be taller than Rob. "Of course, *chérie*. Shall I fetch you another wine?" He said all this without taking his narrowed eyes off of Rob. The two bristled like gorillas. I wouldn't have been surprised if they'd started thumping on their own chests.

Oh, man. I absolutely had to get these guys away from each other and calmed down.

"How well do you know that guy?" Rob asked as soon as we reached the suite's hallway.

"It's not what it looks like. He's the head of the design department and he offered me an assistantship. He has a little crush on me too, but I can handle it."

"He's way too touchy with you. Where I come from that's called sexual harassment."

"It's different here. We're Latins. We have a touchy culture. Flirting is a way of life for a lot of us. But it's not usually serious, and if it gets out of hand, we just give the man a good slap or make a joke in front of other people at his expense. That usually puts a stop to anything creepy. And believe me, Jean-Louis is no creep. He's a gentleman, and I'm a grown woman who knows what's going on, so you have nothing to worry about, okay?"

"You shouldn't have to work under that kind of pressure from a man."

Rob's chivalry made my knees weak. Without thinking, I set a hand on his upper arm to soothe him, perhaps to thank him, and after a moment my hand noticed that his muscles were hard and huge, warm and round. I could not take my hand away.

Who was harassing whom now?

I jerked my hand off his arm. What was happening to me? Thanks to the umbrella, I had turned into some sort of two-timing tramp, the kind of woman I had always silently judged. I needed to concentrate on the matter at hand: separating these men and avoiding a scene. I gulped a few times to find my voice. "How about we talk about this more in your room? I'll just say bye to my future boss, then I'll meet you there in about five minutes."

Bingo. Rob's face relaxed. "Works for me. I need to touch base with someone first. Then we can order room service."

Yes! I'd defused the situation. I'd kept my head and I'd placated these unruly men. And I hadn't sunk my teeth into Rob's deliciously-scented shoulder muscle, either. *Winning!*

I was still congratulating myself on my self-control a second later when a tall blond woman walked up to us. And when I say tall, I mean taller than Rob by almost a head. She also happened to be stunningly beautiful, with wide-set, pale blue eyes, a dainty nose, and naturally full lips.

And she was wearing the same pink, plunging neckline dress that had fallen out of Rob's suitcase yesterday.

I couldn't help but perk up; so, Rob had been telling the truth after all. That dress really had been intended for a tall woman friend.

"Hey, sorry to interrupt," she said to Rob in English, "but they want to take your picture with the top brass."

"That's my cue," he said. "Time to hike up the trouser leg and show off the old ankles. They only love me for my feet."

We three chuckled. Rob winked at me and then hotfooted it to the main room, leaving me in the hallway with his model friend. I stood there a moment, smiling to myself. Here I was in the middle of a career and romance crisis, and Rob had made me forget my troubles, if only for a second. I turned to study the model's friendly face.

"I love your dress," I told her. "Where'd you get it?" I knew the answer to this, of course, but I was trying to confirm a theory about Rob.

"Why, thank you," she said, a light twang in her voice. I imagined she was from a southern state in the US. "Rob got it for me at a photo shoot. It's so hard to find dresses in my size. Thank God for post-shoot swag."

"How do you guys know each other?"

She put a finger to her chin. "You know, I can't remember. Probably at a shoot. Did you meet him at a shoot too?"

"Me?" I laughed, secretly relieved that she seemed unsentimental about how she'd met Rob. "I'm not a model."

"Could have fooled me."

"You have to be kidding. I'm too short, and too—well, everything."

"I'm too tall, even for a model, but I found a niche."

We chatted a while about finding your niche in any field and how hard it is to break into apparel design and modeling, and then I asked her what I'd been curious about all along. "So does Rob have a boyfriend or anything?"

Her eyes goggled. "A boyfriend? Rob's not gay."

It was my turn to gape. "He's not? But I thought—Everyone said— I had no idea he was— Are you sure?"

She snorted. "Honey, he's so straight you could use him to draw the border around Utah. And he's newly single. Want me to set you guys up?"

"No, no, it's not that. I had some false information about him. That's all." I hesitated. "Are you two a pair?"

Her eyes twinkled as though she could see right through my questions to my interest in Rob. "He's only a friend. But if I weren't already in love with someone, I'd totally go for him."

"He does seem like a good guy."

"The best. I've been having some problems with my boyfriend lately, and Rob has been there for me as a shoulder to cry on. Absolutely no sexual undertones, thank God. He sees people as people, not as a woman or a man or a useful contact, and he doesn't expect anyone to be perfect. That's rare. I should know; I'm too demanding. But that's going to change."

Her candor had my shoulders relaxing. There's something refreshing about American openness. Some French people find this trait lacks subtlety, but I say French irony can get old fast.

"I hope my questions weren't too personal," I said.

"No worries. Any friend of Rob's is a friend of mine."

"Can I give you my card? I promised someone I'd be right back, and I've been gone too long."

"Sure." From her purse she fished out a business card, handing it to me. "I hope you'll stay in touch. I'm in Paris pretty often. It'd be fun to hang out."

"I'd like that."

I gave her my card as well, and after we'd exchanged cheek kisses, I navigated my way among the wall-to-wall bodies toward the back room. Halfway down the hall, I bumped into Jean-Louis, just coming out of a side room. "There you are! Here you go, one glass of wine for my lady."

"Thank you." I accepted the glass, avoiding his eyes. If I looked into them, I might lose myself again in "love."

"Everything all right?"

Guilt twisted at my insides. How could I bring up the subject of the umbrella's magic? I had to choose my words carefully. "It's all been so sudden, this courtship," I told his shirt front. "It's like a dream. I'm still reeling and I'm not quite sure how it all happened."

"I had the same feeling. When I was waiting for the drinks, I thought, wait a minute, did I even ask her to marry me? Don't misunderstand; I still want to, but I don't remember asking."

I felt his palm on my cheek. Despite my resistance, he lifted my chin, bending his head to look into my eyes.

I glanced away, but for a moment we had connected gazes. And *zing*. That feeling was back. The dizzy, wondrous, drunken feeling—much more volatile than the steady attraction I'd felt with Rob.

"I believe the lady would rather *not* be manhandled," came a menacing whisper behind us. I glanced back. Rob was standing about a yard from us in the suite's hallway, his jaw muscles tweaking, his eyes ablaze in fury.

My heart thumped hard in my chest. "Rob, please. There's a perfectly understandable explana—"

Jean-Louis jostled past me and got in Rob's face. "You! I've seen the way you look at her. I let that pass, but now it's time for you to leave, *Monsieur*. She has made her choice, and I am that choice."

"Oh, I'll leave all right," said Rob, "but you, *Monsieur*, are coming with me. Care to step outside?"

I groaned. I had to put a stop to this. "Let me explain why this is happening. You guys aren't yourselves right now, and it's all my fault. See, I've always wanted to fit in, to be a part of a couple and be respected in my field, and I have this umbrella. . . ." I launched into the story about my grandmother's heirloom, but neither of them was listening.

"Let's take it to the roof," Jean-Louis said. "To avoid scandal."

"Agreed." Rob followed him out of the suite.

I hurried after them, catching up near the stairwell. "Guys, listen to me! You're in some sort of testosterone-induced, altered state of consciousness. It's the umbrella talking."

They both looked at me as if I were speaking Swahili backwards. Shrugging, they faced off again, brows lowered in angry scowls.

Rob went into the stairwell first, bounding upstairs, with me and Jean-Louis in his wake.

A minute later we were on the roof. Brisk air slapped my cheeks as we entered a snowy tempest. Snowflakes swirled and danced, blinding me for a second. I brushed the flakes from my eyes. When I could finally see clearly, my gaze landed on my two men. They were circling each other in the center of the rooftop, looking like a couple of animated snowmen.

Oh, brother. What nonsense. I positioned myself between them, my knees trembling, my voice raw. "Now you guys listen to me! Stop this right now or I'll call hotel security." This was a bluff, of course. But it got them to stop and listen to me, their heads cocked to one side. I put my hands on my hips. "If the news of this incident gets out, your reputations as professionals will be ruined."

"Jean-Louis?" a woman's voice called suddenly from the stairwell door. "Rob? What's going on?"

I peered through the thick falling snow. A tall blond woman stood silhouetted in the doorway, her shapely body shivering in the cold. My jaw dropped further. The woman was the model I'd talked to earlier! What was she doing up here and how did she know Jean-Louis by name?

"Sophie?" Jean-Louis said to the blond.

Sophie? That was the name on the invitation Jean-Louis had given me. She was his ex-girlfriend! I staggered a bit in the snow and regained my balance.

"Jean-Louis," she said, "can you forgive me those things I said? I do want to be with you. I could live part-time on the goat farm. We can make it work."

My brain went into overdrive. I had to figure out how to get these two back together. How? How?

Then it came to me: I could use the umbrella on them. It might wean Jean-Louis away from me and—with any luck—me away from him. It was worth a shot. I grabbed the ratty rain gear from my bag.

Sophie had sidled up to Jean-Louis. She was brushing snow off his shoulders and cooing in his ear. "I've been doing some thinking. Who says we have to live with each other year round?"

Jean-Louis looked more like a guppy than a man. He stammered and gulped for air, glancing from Sophie to me and back to Sophie, confusion written in every cranny of his face.

Here was my chance. I darted over to them. "You guys need protection. Use this." I pushed open the umbrella above them, careful to stand well back.

A red glow bathed their heads under the red dome, and their faces went soft, their eyes bright. Their lips parted as they gazed at each other.

Yes!

I pressed the umbrella's handle into Jean-Louis's palm, and I stepped away. The last thing I heard was their murmured apologies and nicknames like *mon petit chou* (my little cabbage) and *mon gros chou* (my big cabbage). That's right; we French think cabbages are cute. With their heads bent together, their lips approached, touching. They shared a kiss that lingered for some time.

Rob was beside me now, wrapping his arms around my shoulders and pulling me close. His chest radiated heat and his breath was sweet near my cheek. "How can she forgive him so quickly?" he asked.

I found myself snuggling closer. "Remind me to tell you sometime."

"Yeah, first we need to warm you up." His hands, so strong and firm, explored my back. "Your dress is too thin."

I glanced around for a warmer place. "There's no snow in front of that vent. It could be a heating duct."

"I bet you're right."

Leaving Jean-Louis and Sophie to their kiss, we drifted to the raised metal opening and warmed ourselves in the steam coming from the open slats. Rob wrapped his arms around me even tighter and buried his face in my hair. "Nothing like the smell of a woman's hair on a cold night."

I noticed that my own nose was exploring his shoulder seam and the top of his chest, the hollow of his neck. Dang, he smelled good. Sweet and spicy at the same time. I could drink his scent. I could bite it too. I found myself kissing his neck a little too enthusiastically. I pulled back, laughing. "Sorry, I think I'm hungry."

"Have you had dinner?"

"No. You?"

"Nothing substantial."

I looked around the rooftop. We were alone now. Alone but for the half-open umbrella lying in the snow like a rose on an enormous white bedspread. "It's just you and me up here."

"And the snow and the sky." His breath was hot in my ear.

I raised my chin and tilted my head to one side, closing my eyes.

There's nothing like a warm kiss on a cold night. And snowflakes that melt on your cheeks. Joining with your tears.

Travis

Gilford

January

The last note of our song hung in the chilly garage air, a reverb drifting up to the rafters. All I could hear now was the whirr of the electric space heater beside my guitar case and the wind as it whistled against the side of Leila's house. It was the sound of a California winter, mild as usual, and surprisingly dry.

I waited in respectful silence for the other guys in my band to mentally digest what we'd just done— what we'd heard ourselves do with the aid of whatever muse it is that helps musicians. Then I said, "Talk about tight! We've never been so good. Did you feel it, too?"

"In every blistered wrinkle of my hands." Stinky tossed his drumsticks into the air and snatched them back like a baton twirler. Sweat rolled off of his lean, muscled arms and glistened across his spiked tattoo. Like the rest of us in our band, he'd been working out with weights at the Gilford YMCA for the past six months, holding true to his promise to get buffed for our new sexpot look. He'd been an inspiration to Jud, Bo and me for how much a person can change his appearance when he sets his mind to it. It was as if we'd been training for the music Olympics. Our jogs and workouts had sharpened not only my muscle defini-

IT'S RAINING MEN

tion but also my musical instincts. And Leila's love had given those instincts new wings. Wings with soft feathers and tough, flexible spines.

I glanced at the wall clock above the old fridge. "We're still on schedule. Leila should be home in about ten minutes." I pointed toward the garage's back door that connected directly to Leila's house. "She'll be in the kitchen. That's where I'll pop the question. Jud, you ready?"

He nodded as the rest of us wiped down with towels. We put on clean shirts, and Jud got out his violin case. I'd persuaded him to provide romantic background music for the big event. That's right; I was going to ask Leila to bind herself to me for life. Was I crazy? Maybe. Was I in love? Yes. And I felt sure it was lasting love. I based my conviction not only on the strong feelings I still had for Leila but also on observations I'd made of my band members.

Case in point: After two weeks, Stinky's infatuation with his middle-aged laundress had worn off, along with his enthusiasm for kitschy music. On the other hand, Bo and Jud's feelings for their girlfriends had remained strong—less loopy and more stable, yet they had gladly turned away from the boy band concept and that style of music, and Jud's ex-cop girlfriend—now our manager—had returned the spandex outfits for a full refund. As far as I could tell, the matchmaking umbrella gave reluctant people like me the push we needed to take the plunge into the heady waters of infatuation. But it was only a push. After about two weeks, we had to learn to swim through real love on our own. If a love match was meant to be, it would survive the trial period. If the match wasn't meant to be, it wouldn't.

My fingers trembled as I buttoned up my cotton shirt. Man, was I nervous! What if I caught Leila off guard? What if she wasn't ready to talk marriage yet and I was moving too fast? My band and I would be leaving on tour soon, thanks to our agent. I wanted to make sure Leila knew beforehand that I was a one-woman man, and no amount of willing groupie attention could tempt me to stray.

Jud took out his violin and tuned it with a few tentative chords. Before he'd learned to shred a guitar, he'd won a bunch of violin awards as a kid, and he was still amazingly delicate and versatile on that instrument. I'd written many a song for our band featuring his strings. And now he was going to feature as the background music to my proposal. That is, if I had the guts to go through with it.

I checked my pocket for the engagement ring. The familiar round shape met my fingers with reassuring solidity. But what if I had a hole in my pocket? What if I were to lose the ring before I made the proposal? I took a deep, calming breath. *Get a grip, Travis.* My brain was looking for any excuse to panic.

Bo and Stinky had stashed their instruments and were leaving now by the garage's automatic door. "Don't worry," Bo said to me as the door slid down. I could see only their knees and feet. "She wants you too."

"I hope you're right," I said. Sure, Leila had shown me almost every night how much she wanted me. But desire wasn't the same as love, obviously. What if the matchmaking magic had only worked on me, and Leila had some reservations she hadn't told me about?

Jud came to stand close to me. "Okay, so when do you want me to start playing?" he asked in his usual sleepy drawl.

"When I say to Leila, 'There's something I need to tell you'."

"What?"

"Your cue is 'There's something I need to tell you'," I said more loudly for the benefit of his bad hearing. His tinnitus had been acting up lately, one of the health hazards of playing in a band.

"What do you need to tell me?" he asked.

I snorted. "No, no, that's what I'm going to say to Leila. That's your cue to start playing."

"That's what I'm asking. When is my cue to start playing?"

Oh, brother. I sighed. Jud had gone cold turkey with his pot habit and had been clean for months, but his thoughts still got scrambled at times. I gave it another shot. "Okay, here's the plan. When Leila comes home, she and I will chat in the kitchen a bit. You'll stay around the corner just off from the kitchen. After a few minutes, I'll say, 'There's something I need to tell you,' and *that* sentence will be your cue. Got it?"

"Ahhhh. I get it."

We hurried inside through the garage's back door, entering directly into the back of the kitchen. Jud took up position around the hall corner, while I lit the tapers and set them on the linen table cloth. I checked that the champagne was chilled in its bucket of ice, and then I put Leila's engagement ring on my pinky finger. My idea was to make a lot of obvious gestures showing off the ring until Leila asked me about it, and at that point, I'd have a fun way to bring up the question I'd been hoping to ask her for the past month. Fate hadn't handed me the right opportunity on its own. It was time to seize Fate by the scruff and make it happen.

"Honey, I'm home."

It was Leila's voice in the hall, making a joke about our domesticity. She always said that when she came home, as if she were the traditional husband and I the waiting wife. Well, this house-man also had a back-breaking job out in the garlic fields every morning, fire-weeding for an organic farmer and helping to plant next year's crop, one bulb at a time.

"I'm in here." My heart felt like a bunch of garlic now, about to burst its skin, beating so hard I couldn't hear myself think. Fingers trembling, I adjusted the silverware on the table, so the forks and knives would be more evenly spaced.

Leila came into the kitchen, and when she saw me by the candlelit table, a smile lit up her face, dimpling one check. Her long, thick hair had been swept to one side by the blustery winter wind. I wanted to touch it, to touch her and keep her safe and warm, but I stayed put, so she'd see the ring on my pinky.

"Welcome home," I said with a flourish of my hand.

Her large green eyes were aglow in the warm light; they weren't looking at my face but at the candles on the table. "How romantic." She sighed. "I have it so good."

"No, I'm the one who has it good." I came around the table and gave her a sweet and lingering kiss.

After we'd come out of our kiss trance, she set a stack of mail on the side counter. "These came for you today. One of them looks important. Like a formal invitation."

I waved the mail aside. "That can wait. Champagne?"

She nodded. "Oh! I almost forgot. There's something I need to tell you!"

At that moment a single violin chord started up around the corner. It was Jud right on cue. Or rather, *wrong* on cue.

"Not now, Jud," I called.

The music stopped, and Jud's straggly-haired head appeared around the corner. "Oops, sorry. I got mixed up." His head drew back behind the corner as quickly as it had appeared.

Leila's mouth was hanging open. "What was that?"

"Just Jud being Jud. You know how he gets. I'll explain in a sec." I handed her a glass of champagne, extending my pinky with the ring on it, wiggling it for attention. "Here you go."

"Why, thank you."

Dang. She hadn't seen the ring. I set my pinky finger on my chin and pretended to be deep in thought. "Hmm. I wonder what we're having for dinner tonight. Could it be the one of two dishes I know how to cook? Or could it be catered?"

"Oh, oh, could I tell you my news first?" She was almost jumping out of her high heels. "It's going to blow your mind. It blew mine."

"Okay, but first there's something I need to tell *you*, something I've been meaning to tell you forever." I paused, waiting for Jud's violin. Nothing doing. *"There's something I need to tell you,"* I said a bit more loudly, cocking my ear. Still nothing. "Jud!"

There it came, finally, Jud's violin, a sweet and floating melody I'd composed just for this occasion.

Leila turned her ear in the direction of the music. "That's beautiful."

"I wrote it for you. For tonight."

"You did?" Her eyes shone in the candlelight, liquid with emotion.

Here it came. Time to pop the question. Heart hammering, I sank to one knee and drew the ring off of my pinky finger. I reached for her left hand. "Will you join your life with mine? Will you be my wife?"

Her chest was rising and falling quickly, and her eyes filled with tears, shimmering. A drop spilled over and slid down one cheek. This had to be a good sign. My eyes went warm in response, and the image of my beloved's face swam before me.

She nodded. "Of course." She knelt beside me on the kitchen floor, and her soft body shook against mine. She was crying into my shoulder, and then kissing my face with her wet cheeks and mouth. She must have wanted me more than I knew. She must have been holding herself back too.

The song I'd written for us came slowly to an end. After a time, Jud sauntered around the kitchen corner, his eyes dreamy, maybe even a bit red around the rims. Had he been crying?

"Congratulations." He sniffled.

"Couldn't have done it without your amazing interpretation of that song," I said. "Thank you, Jud."

He nodded, and as Leila and I got to our feet, he let himself out by the front door, mumbling something about wanting to go buy a ring now for his Alice.

After Leila and I finished off the champagne in our glasses, I asked, "What was it you wanted to tell me?"

"Oh, that. *That.*" She shook her head to herself in amazement. "Remember my sister Maxine?"

I squinted, trying to figure out what she meant. Leila had four sisters. "Which one is she again?"

"The one who started that app company. The online matchmaking algorithm? Well, she reached a million beta users yesterday, and to celebrate she sold the company. And—get this—she gave me some of the stock. If I sell it, I can afford to stop renting and can buy a house. For us."

"Wow. That's great." I gave her a hug.

"I'll never forget this day. When it rains it pours, eh?"

"And when it shines, it goes supernova." I went to the hearth to check on the warming dishes there. "Are you hungry?"

"Famished."

We sat down to eat, and as we did so, my eye was caught by the sight of the thick envelope that Leila had brought to me earlier. I recognized the cursive handwriting. It was from Ainsley. I picked up the letter. "This is from my cousin in Scotland. Maybe she's tying the knot too."

"I hope so. I love weddings."

"I'll open it after dinner."

"Aw, why not now?"

"Do you mind?"

She grinned. "I'll mind if you don't. Patience is not my strong suit."

I shrugged and scraped open the envelope. The card inside was thick and cream-colored, covered with gray, printed calligraphy. I set the card up against the salt and pepper shakers so we could both read it:

Major General Jacques Pluchot
and
Madame Julie Plessis
request the honor of your presence
at the marriage of their children
Mademoiselle Anne Marie Pluchot
and
Monsieur Anatole Eduard Plessis
as they happily unite their hearts,
their lives and their families through marriage

"Now I've seen everything," I said. "Anatole is getting married!"

"Anatole?"

"He's my godfather, an old friend of the family." I shook my head and gave a low whistle. "Anatole the dyed-in-the-wool bachelor is getting married. There's hope for all of us now."

"Look; the wedding's in France. I've always wanted to go there."

All at once I remembered I'd spent my savings from my new job on Leila's engagement ring. "We can't afford the flight," I said automatically.

"Of course we can. Did you not hear my news earlier? I'll cover the flight."

Guilt zapped me in the gut. Guilt and male pride. "I couldn't ask that of you."

"We're getting married, silly," she said matter-of-factly. "Fifty percent of anything I bring to the marriage is yours."

I stared at her in wonder. I had spent so long living below the poverty line, working at minimum wage and singing for my dinner, it had never occurred to me that life could be any other way. "That's not how it works," I said. For some strange reason, I had an idea that men were the ones who brought the money to a marriage, and women got a part of it, not the other way around. I guess this was sexist thinking on my part, but mostly it was just me not thinking about money very often at all, because it had never been a big part of my life.

"Yes, that *is* how it works." She smiled. "Don't worry. It'll all even out later. Your band is going to be big."

"There's no guarantee of that."

"You're right. There's no guarantee of anything. We could drop dead tomorrow in a car accident. But that's no reason not to try. Or to believe."

How right she was. She'd caught me out again in my old defeatist thinking. I reached over the small table and cupped her cheek in my hand. "Have I told you lately you're my muse? My godsend. My everything and all I need?"

"Only every day." She took my hand into both of hers and kissed my palm, sending a warm shiver to my spine.

"Well, get used to it, sweet cakes." I came around the side of the table and lifted her in my arms. "I'm only getting warmed up."

Carlo

Florence
February

The parcel arrived on Saturday morning, February seventh, and it couldn't have had worse timing. I had only just returned from another exhausting business trip to China some hours previously. When the bell started to ring, I was in the middle of an unpleasant dream that had me chasing an elusive programming error in one of my textile machines, and for the life of me, I couldn't figure out where the problem was, while five anxious Chinese customers hovered behind my back and whispered amongst themselves.

I groaned and turned around in my bed. With my plane being delayed, I had barely slept three hours. Disoriented, I prized one eye open and tried to remember where I was. It didn't feel like Beijing. The air wasn't right.

R-R-RING!

I knew that high ringing with the metallic note that always grated on my nerves. I knew it well. Home. That was it. I was home in Florence, and this was my bed.

R-R-RING! I hated that bell. It had something that set my teeth on edge and filled me with unaccustomed aggressiveness. Every time it rang, I decided to get some melodious bell as a replacement, but then, I wasn't home all that often and few people rang my bell anyway, so I had never come around to fixing it. I pressed my lips together and stumbled downstairs to the door. My house is somewhat unique, even for Florence, which has its fair share of odd architecture. Basically, it fills a gap between two larger houses and consists of just two rooms piled on top of each other, with a kitchen squeezed in on the first floor and a bathroom on the second.

Stabilizing my reeling body against the hall wall, I pulled the heavy wooden door open and glared at whoever was outside.

The postman. Or rather, postwoman, if I interpreted the long, dark hair correctly. She held out a longish parcel. The packaging was torn in the middle, and something bright red with white dots peeked out. *Oh, no.* I knew what it was, though I had almost managed to forget it in the months since grandma's funeral.

"I apologize for the torn packaging," the postwoman said.

I couldn't avert my gaze from the dreadful pattern. "It's a pity you didn't lose it."

"I'm sorry?"

"Never mind." I held out my hand.

She gave me the parcel and held a technical device underneath my nose. "Please sign here."

I grabbed the plastic pen she held out to me, thinking of nothing but a quick return to my bed, but suddenly, a subtle perfume, sweet and alluring and totally wrong for my concept of a postwoman or courier woman or whatever she was, wafted over to me, and I became aware of my bedraggled state. I probably smelled like a panther.

I took a step back and for the first time, lifted my gaze to her. My blurry vision improved with something of a jolt. She had the longest eyelashes I had ever seen. They had a curious shape, longer in the middle, almost like a triangle. She was still looking at the parcel, and the lashes threw a soft shadow on her cheeks. I became aware of the stubble on my chin and the fact that I was only wearing a pair of boxer shorts.

"Would you like to check the content first?" she asked.

"What?"

Those amazing lashed lifted, and her gaze met mine. "I probably shouldn't say so, but the parcel looks somewhat battered. You don't have to sign if you're not sure that it's acceptable."

A sudden idea flashed through my head. If the umbrella should be broken, and by no mistake of my own, I couldn't be held responsible. I could tell Anatole that it had not been in my power to salvage it. After all, nobody could expect me to walk around with a broken umbrella for the better part of three months. Best of all, I had an independent witness who could confirm that it had already arrived in a state beyond repair. "Good idea." I took another step back. "Will you come in? Give me two minutes, will you? I'm sorry; do you have that much time?"

She nodded and followed me just inside my entry-hall-slash-downstairs-room, leaving the door open behind her. "You'd better get a pair of scissors. Someone used a whole roll of string to fix the ends, but that didn't prevent the packaging from opening in the middle."

I ran upstairs to the bathroom, splashed my face with water, used some mouthwash, and threw on a T-shirt and jeans. Feeling almost human, I returned downstairs with a pair of nail scissors. "Let's see."

It took longer than expected, but finally I managed to extract the umbrella. It was even more unattractive than I remembered. When I shook it to unfurl the material, a note fell onto the floor.

I picked it up and read the terse text. "Stick to the rules. It's worth it. Josie" I had always had a soft spot for my little cousin Josie in Paris. She was quite a few things, but a stickler for rules had not been so far one of her typical characteristics. *Strange.* What was it with this umbrella? I had not talked to Ainsley or Travis yet, but that wasn't for want of trying. They'd both proved to be extremely tight-lipped about this whole umbrella-rigmarole, sticking to Grandma's rule of not revealing anything, as if their lives depended on it. An uneasy shiver slid down my spine.

I looked up and realized only when I saw Eyelashes' astonished look that I had read Josie's note out loud.

"It's a— a bet," I improvised. "A family bet."

"I see." She gave me a look as if she was wondering about the sanity of my family.

As well she might. "Let me just open it to make sure that none of the spokes are broken." *I hope they are smashed to pieces.* I gave the thing a shake and pushed it open. It worked like a charm. Crooked, yes. Shabby and worn, yes. Broken, no. *Damn.*

Eyelashes came closer and stood next to me, looking up at the umbrella above us. "Good. It's all right." She gave me a huge smile that revealed small teeth. A streak of sunlight from the window fell through the red material of the umbrella and colored her cheeks a soft rose.

I narrowed my eyes. "Why are you so happy about it?"

Her face started to glow. "I— why, I'm just glad that I don't have to file a claim."

She made it sound like a Herculean task. Once again, she whipped out her electronic device. "Would you like to sign now?"

"Sure." I signed my name with a sigh.

"Why do you look so disappointed?"

God, but she had sharp eyes. "It's nothing." I shrugged. "I'd only hoped that I wouldn't have to go through with— with the bet."

"What is the bet about?"

I looked into her eyes. "I have to keep that dreadful umbrella with me for three full months."

Her mouth twitched. "Not exactly a nice accessory."

She had that right. Particularly for me, that umbrella was an insult and a professional problem. I come from a family that has worked in textiles for half a century now. That is, my father is from that family. My French mother married into it, and we were fighting hard to keep the company going in spite of the Chinese competition. So far, we were doing okay. By specializing in making samples and small productions for fashion shows at lightning speed, we'd hit upon a formula the Chinese couldn't match.

I'd always enjoyed taking stuff apart, so my father suggested a degree in engineering which sounded good to me. A year ago, I'd finished my studies and was now working for a company that supplied special parts for textile machines to China. Dad said the job was a good foundation for the future and that I had to stand on my own feet before starting at his company. Anyway, in our industry, dressing well is more than a matter of *"fare una bella figura,"* as we Italians say, of looking good. It's part of being taken seriously at your job. And now I was saddled with the ugliest parasol on earth and had to schlep it around as if I was some impossible tourist. I mean, red with white dots. That's just too hideous for words.

"Well, good luck with it." She grinned, and in the next moment, she was gone.

I put the umbrella on my table and contemplated it with something akin to hatred. I would not allow myself to be ridiculed. On the other hand, I'm a little bit superstitious. Not much, and nothing to write home about, but I'd rather not do anything that calls bad luck onto me. I know, I know, it's unreasonable, but I just can't fight it.

Theoretically, I knew that nobody could control what I did with the ugliest accessory on earth. I could hide it in my storeroom and forget about it until the three months were over. However, I had a strange feeling that Grandma was watching me from above or wherever she was. Her instructions had been straight-forward, and they had not sounded like a joke. So going against Grandma's rules wasn't an option. *Crap.*

I poked a finger at the flimsy material. If only it had a decent color. If only . . . I drew in my breath with a hiss. Nobody had said that I wasn't allowed to mess about with the umbrella. I could dye the thing a respectable color. Like black. A nice, intense black that would cover the red and the spots and everything. My heart already felt lighter.

I dressed in unusual haste and hurried outside, to the closest supermarket. Thank God that Eyelashes had woken me before all the shops closed. Half an hour later, I was back in my house with three different types of dye. Might as well do this thing as thoroughly as possible. I put the plug into the sink and had just started to read the instructions in grim determination when I came across the note "submerge the material for several hours." Several hours? Grandma's rules said I was supposed to stick to the umbrella at all times. Did that mean I would have to be stuck inside my bathroom for hours on end? Or maybe the rules were to be taken a bit more liberally. Maybe the umbrella wasn't to be treated like a newborn baby. Maybe more like a bigger child—you could leave them alone in their room but not alone in a house.

Damn. Why hadn't someone enclosed more specific instructions with this stupid umbrella? I would never sell a machine with such scanty input. Never. I lifted my family heirloom and resisted the temptation to throw it out of the window. Instead, I placed it into the sink and realized immediately that it would never fit sufficiently to be totally submerged—a part of it would always stick out. I should have thought about that before. Dismayed, I looked at the tub. Would I have to dye this stupid thing in the tub? I pictured a tub filled with pitch-black water, and a shiver crawled down my back. Disgusting.

Shaking my head, I decided not to worry too much and just to go ahead, so I threw the umbrella into the tub, scattered the black powder over it and filled it with water until the umbrella was totally submerged. At least, that was the goal, before I realized that my heirloom from hell could swim. It rose to the surface and fanned out like a bird covered with oil. Yuck. How could I weigh it down? Stones. I needed stones. But I didn't have any in the house. I was starting to sweat. This project was already turning into a full-time occupation, and I'd only had it for one hour. What on earth had grandma been thinking when she'd made such a stupid request? She'd been one smart lady, but maybe a sudden, eccentric streak had gripped her when she'd written the will?

I dipped my finger into the water and dunked the umbrella. Maybe it just had to soak and then it would stay down by itself. I waited two minutes and withdrew my hand. The umbrella floated up like a balloon—and my finger was black as if I had played with coal. Perfect. Cursing under my breath, I scrubbed my index finger with soap until the bubbles covered half my arm, but my finger stayed black.

I groaned. Maybe it was a curse, this heirloom. Maybe I had done something to grandma that she had never forgiven me. Had I written to her enough? No. Had I called her? No. *Damn.* I had liked her, but I had never bothered to tell her so, had never bothered to keep up the relationship. Too late now. I went down-stairs to the front door. Hiding my right hand in my pocket, I looked up and down the street. Just to the left of my entrance, a cobblestone had become loose. I'd noticed it weeks ago, when I'd tripped over it. Since then, I'd tripped at least fifteen times, but had never gotten around to fixing it. I knew it made no sense to ask the city to do something about it. They were busy fixing the medieval *palazzi* that were falling apart—no time for modern-day repairs. Experimentally, I kicked the stone. Yup. It was still loose. I was bending forward to pick it up when a voice behind me chirped, "Why, Carlo, I had no idea you were back in town!"

Cleopatra. You heard that right. Her name really was Cleopatra. Her American mother had had some kind of fixation with the Roman Empire, and thus Cleopatra had gotten her name. Poor girl. I jumped half a meter into the air and dropped the stone, straight onto my foot. "Ouch."

Her blue eyes widened. "What happened to your finger? Oh, my God, did you smash it against that stone? How on earth did that happen? Do you want me to call a doctor?"

I gripped her arm. Of course she had to come along the very second when I couldn't bear to have her around. "Calm down, Cleo. My finger is all right."

"Really? But it looks dreadful. As if . . ."

I hid my hand from her view. "It's nothing. Just a little experiment gone wrong."

"Oh." She looked at me with her huge eyes. "What experiment?"

"Something to do with my textile machines," I lied. "The ones I program, you know."

Her eyes glazed over. "Oh."

She was remarkably fond of saying "oh." This habit of hers had started to get on my nerves even before I'd left for China. But how to tell her so?

"Will I see you tonight?" she asked. "At Gina's party?"

I jumped. Tonight. The umbrella wouldn't be done by tonight. Or would it? "I'm sorry; I'm bushed. I've only had a few hours of sleep and really have to catch up." Now I sounded like an old man.

Her eyebrows climbed. "I see." The corners of her mouth turned down.

I really had to make clear that I wasn't interested in a relationship, but I had no idea how to do this without hurting her feelings. I bit my lip. If I was being perfectly honest with myself, I'd admit her feelings didn't matter as much to me as my Dad's feelings did. For some reason, he had decided that Cleo would be the perfect wife for me. I admired my Dad and really tried hard to make him happy, but binding myself to Cleo went against my every instinct. I stared at her, wondering where that lucid thought had come from. So far, I had never admitted my true feelings about Cleo to anyone, least of all to myself. "Actually, I have to go in again. I'll call you! Ciao!" Before she could reply, I retreated inside the house and closed the heavy wooden door with all possible speed. *Phew.* I leaned against it and waited until I heard her high heels retreating. Then, to be on the safe side, I waited another few seconds before I opened the door and peered out. *Nobody. Good.* I slipped through the doorway, shivering in a sudden gust of cold wind, and picked up the stone. It had a nice weight, perfect for submerging my umbrella.

"Carlo Carrelani!" A voice boomed out from somewhere above me.

Startled, I slipped and almost fell onto my nose. "Oh, it's you, Edoardo!" I turned my head like an owl until I could see my substantial neighbor standing on his balcony to my left. Edoardo was a tenor, and he liked to sing in his bathroom, usually at nighttime, in the mistaken belief that his walls were more or less soundproof. Unfortunately, the acoustics in his bathroom were everything but soundproof; in fact, they were excellent, with the effect that I was more familiar with several opera arias than I wanted to be. But apart from that, Edoardo was a treasure, someone to go to when the fridge was empty and nobody else was awake in the middle of the night.

"Did I just see you sending that beautiful woman away? You must be joking!" His voice easily filled the tiny street and reverberated from the ancient houses.

I hid my black finger with the stone behind my back and threw my head back to see him properly. It was unusual to see him on the balcony when the sharp February wind was whipping down the street. He usually took great care not to risk damaging his voice in cold weather. However, I was glad to note that he had protected his throat with a bright red scarf. "I only returned from China some hours ago, Edoardo. A man has to sleep at some point."

He leaned over the balustrade until his ample girth was pressed against it in a way that somehow made him broader than he was high. With his red scarf flying in the wind, he now looked like a Christmas tree ornament with a string. "But you can't sleep alone, Carlo. That's not the right way to live at your age."

"Trust me, Edoardo. I can, and I will." The idea of Cleo in my apartment made me nervous, and not in a good way. "Good night!" I grinned at him and slipped inside, pressing the stone against my side in the faint hope that Edoardo wouldn't spot it from above, but when I pulled the door closed behind me, I heard his well-trained voice say as clearly as if he was reciting something at the Teatro Verdi, for all its thousands of visitors to hear, "And what do you want with that stone? Who needs a stone in bed, eh? Tell me that."

I pretended not to hear him.

Back in my bathroom, I dropped the stone with care onto the umbrella and heard it go down with a satisfying gurgle. There. Job done. I returned to my room with a spring in my step. Part one of the operation was successfully completed. Now I could go back to bed.

Five hours later, a call from my father woke me. "So you're home again," he said in a gravelly voice. Most people thought it sounded like a pilot's voice. To me at the moment, it sounded like a deep, dark alarm clock.

I suppressed a yawn. "Yes, I got in last night."

"Ever think of calling?"

"Dad, I've been asleep most of the time."

"Your mother is always worried when you're in China."

"Tell her everything's fine." I was becoming aware of an immense hole in my stomach. It was probably only hunger. But it always started when I talked to my dad.

"I met Cleopatra this afternoon."

"Really?" I prayed that she hadn't mentioned our brief meeting this morning.

"She's a nice girl. And well-connected, too. Her family has a lot of influence in Florence. I think she likes you."

My heart sank like a stone. "She does?"

"Yes. You could do worse than her, you know."

My stomach twinged again. "Dad. I'm not looking for a wife."

"You should. When I was your age, I already had two sons."

"Good for you." It slipped out before I could think it through. I needn't have worried. He ignored my bad manners.

"I have to admit it sounds nice," he said.

I frowned. "What does?"

"The alliteration. Cleo and Carlo."

"Gosh, Dad. Can we please drop the subject?"

"Are you interested in another woman? Is that it?"

For some reason, the image of Eyelashes flashed through my mind. "Possibly."

Of course, that kind of response didn't go down well with my Dad. Ambiguity is not for him. "What does that mean, 'possibly'? Tell me about her!"

Deliberately, I said, "She's a postwoman."

With satisfaction, I heard him gasp. He's not exactly a snob, but he likes to see the bigger picture. When he gets to know someone, he always tries to find out how to fit them into his network. I hated it that I had come to think like him; I was trying to shake it off, but it was difficult. Dad would find it hard to get anything useful from a postwoman. That much was sure, and for some reason, that made her profession very satisfying.

"What's her family name?" His voice had become a tad sharper.

"I don't know." I didn't mention that I didn't know her first name, either.

He made a sound like a bull that's seen a red flag. "Cleopatra said she would be at Gina's tonight and that she hopes to see you."

"I know."

"Will you be there?"

"I'll think about it." Time to change the subject. "Listen, Dad, I have to go. I'll be in touch on Monday, all right? Ciao!" I hung up before he could protest too much. My stomach grumbled as I went into the bathroom. The conversation had unsettled me. Dad had been blunter than his usual blunt self. What on earth had Cleo told him about my relationship with her? It's not as if there had ever been much of a relationship anyway. I had known her for years, as part of the gang I used to hang out with, and one night last month, I stayed over at her place. It had been a mistake, I knew that even while I was there, but for some reason, I didn't leave while I still could. Probably some subconscious need to please my father. I had always tried to please him, had tried to make up for the loss of my older brother who died in a car accident when I was a kid. We rarely talked about my brother; it hurt too much, even after all these years. But I had tried all that time to be twice the son my Dad dreamed of having.

My gaze fell on the black mess inside my tub. The plug had not stopped the water from leaking, and now, the tub sported a black rim, and the umbrella looked like a super-sized raven. Disgusting. I slowly opened the umbrella and left it upended inside the tub to dry. Black drops rolled off the fabric and fell with a hollow sound into the tub. I checked the fabric and was pleased to see that while it wasn't as pitch black as I had envisioned, at least the hideous red had been transformed to a uniform dark green tinge, and the white spots had disappeared. I could take this umbrella with me without risking my reputation, as long as I took care not to open it in public. *There, Grandma. Hope you're satisfied.*

I dressed with my usual care and was happy to take out my old favorites again: A white shirt by NaraCamicie in thick cotton quality that felt good on the skin and looked exactly how I liked it: quality combined with understatement. A little bit of blue at the inner part of the collar and half hidden behind the buttons gave this shirt an extra something. On top of that, a blue cashmere sweater to keep out the February chill. Combined with my dark-blue trousers and loafers, I knew I was well dressed and would enjoy walking through the streets of my hometown neighborhood. In my bones, I could still feel the weariness that comes from a long trip across several time zones, but my spirit was bouncing, and even the dark scarecrow at my side, now finally dry and fit to be taken outside, couldn't destroy that good mood.

I was just stepping into the street when I heard Edoardo's voice above me to the left, as if someone had installed him as a sort of human door bell, to appear whenever I opened the front door to my house. "Where are you off to, Carlo?"

I turned my head to him and held the umbrella closely to my side, so it wouldn't show too much. "Just going for a walk and to do some shopping."

Edoardo bent forward until his red scarf hung straight from his neck. "Do you have something to do tonight?"

"Not really." I had not yet reconciled myself to going to Gina's.

"Why don't you come to the Teatro Verdi? We're playing the opera *La Traviata* by Verdi. I still have some tickets. Bring that friend of yours, the one you sent away this morning."

"Cleopatra?"

He chuckled. "Is that her name? Poor thing. Thank God she doesn't have the nose to match. Yes, bring her."

Again, the image of Eyelashes rose in front of my mind. Darn it all. What was it with that girl? Had she bewitched me, just because she had triangular eyelashes? With something of a jolt, I realized that I wanted to see her again.

"Carlo? Did you drift off? I have to go back inside; it's too cold for my voice. So, are you coming?"

"Yes, I'd love to." I could always go to Gina's later.

"Fantastic. Hang on. I'll give you the tickets."

I waited until Edoardo appeared at his own front door two steps to my left and held out the tickets. "Enjoy the evening," he said. "If you wish, you can come to the Trattoria dei Artisti afterwards. We'll have dinner there. It's right behind the theater."

"That sounds very nice." He had never invited me out before. "Is there a special reason? Is it your birthday or something?"

He chuckled. "No, no, nothing of the kind. In fact—" he looked up and down the street and shifted his weight from one side to the other as if nervous, "I'm expecting a friend from out of town. She said she might either come to my house today or to the Trattoria after the performance. Actually, I'm a bit scared she might not show up at all, and in case she doesn't, I'd like to see another friendly face instead."

That explained his unusual loitering on the balcony on a cold winter day. I had to smile. "I'll be there."

"And you'll bring that girl, won't you?"

I frowned. "Why?"

Again, a fleeting expression of embarrassment crossed his face. "She—" He broke off and cleared his throat. "She looked kind of sad when you told her to go away this morning."

"But you didn't see her face. She was walking away from you." Unless she had turned around after I had closed the door. I didn't get it. Why did he care?

"I saw her shoulders and the way she walked. Discouraged. And I felt for her because I'm in a similar—" Again, he broke off. "She's a nice girl, isn't she?"

I swallowed. A nice girl. Yes, that much was true. A nice girl who didn't do a thing for me. A girl who didn't make my heart beat any faster; a girl who got on my nerves the second she opened her mouth and said, "Oh." I hated that "oh." It had a curious inflection, as if she was a half-wit, didn't get what I had said. I bet Eyelashes would never say "oh" in that terrible way.

Great. Now I was fantasizing about the postwoman, and all I could remember about her was the subtle fragrance of her perfume and her amazing eyelashes. Enough to build a fantasy woman with, but not much more. *Get a grip, Carlo, will you?* "All right," I said. "I'll bring her."

After all, what harm would it do? Maybe I was judging Cleo too harshly. It couldn't hurt to try again with her, and it would please my father who would never in a million years reconcile himself to a postwoman as his daughter-in-law. I stopped myself short at that thought. Marriage had never been a focus for me. What on earth was happening to me? Had the postwoman bewitched me into thoughts of matrimony in just a few short minutes?

I put the tickets into my wallet. "I'm off to the shops."

Edoardo nodded. "Why are you carrying an umbrella? It's not raining."

I cringed. "It might start any moment."

Edoardo gave the windswept, blue skies a surprised look but didn't protest.

Thank God. I hurried away with a casual wave before he could ask more questions. "See you tonight!"

To avoid the icy wind, I ducked my head and charged through the ancient streets without glancing at the buildings that make the tourists faint in ecstasy. For some reason, I felt driven to see Eyelashes again. But how? I didn't even know her name. How could I contrive another meeting? One when I was dressed and fresh, not wrinkled and tired, looking like wilted spinach. I shuddered at the memory.

All at once, an idea presented itself to me, and I stopped dead. That was it. I would send myself another parcel, so that she could deliver it.

I'd turned on my heels to go back and prepare the parcel immediately when I realized that during the week, I wouldn't be home to welcome her. Instead of following through on my impulse right now, I would have to time it carefully so that she'd deliver the parcel next Saturday. And this time, I would be ready, with croissants and freshly brewed coffee, and I would invite her to stay for a cup. All by themselves, my lips curved into a smile.

And what would I put into the parcel? The stone that had held down the umbrella? No, better not. I didn't want it to be too heavy. I would put a sweater inside, so the parcel wouldn't be too cumbersome. I wanted to organize the shipment immediately, but I knew that I had to post it on Thursday evening if I wanted the box to arrive on Saturday. Or maybe I had to send it off on Friday morning? It was hard to predict how long a parcel took in general.

Impatient with myself, I shook my head. I felt like kicking something, but that might scratch my good shoes, and I wasn't going to risk that. I would post the parcel on Thursday morning and send my least favorite sweater. The rest was up to fate. Feeling satisfied with the decision taken, I managed to buy the food I would need for the week. The umbrella proved to be a nuisance as I shopped. I stuck it underneath my arm whenever I needed both hands, and twice, I managed to inadvertently sweep some stuff from the shelves. Blast this thing. How was I going to survive three months with such a handicap?

I returned home, dumped my bags in the kitchen, glared at the umbrella, and was steeling myself for the call to invite Cleo when the door bell rang. *Eyelashes.* My heart started to beat faster. Maybe she had another parcel for me? I opened the door, a welcoming smile on my face, and felt it freeze. "Cleo. What a coincidence. I was just going to call you."

Her blue eyes lit up. "Oh, really?"

Did Eyelashes have blue eyes, too? I had been too distracted by the fringe around them to notice. With an effort, I concentrated on the conversation. "Yes. I was given two tickets for an opera at the Teatro Verdi tonight. Would you like to come?"

"Why, I'd love to!" She beamed at me.

I felt like a louse. "Cool. I'll pick you up at seven-thirty, all right? We might go to a Trattoria to meet the singers afterward. My neighbor gave me the tickets. He's a tenor, and he'll be performing tonight."

"That sounds lovely." She made a move as if to come in, but I blocked the door.

"So, what brings you to my doorstep?"

She blushed. "Oh, I was just passing by. And I thought . . . I thought maybe you'd slept enough and felt like going out or having a cup of coffee with me."

I stared at her. Had I ever been attracted to her? Was my father right that we two were made for each other? Something grabbed me by the throat and choked me. "I'm sorry, Cleo, but if you wouldn't mind, I'd rather not do anything this afternoon. I'm still exhausted. Would it be all right if I picked you up at seven-thirty tonight?"

Now her whole face was bright red. "Of course." She turned on her heels. "See you tonight. Ciao."

"Ciao." I felt terrible about sending her away like this, but I just couldn't face the idea of spending the whole day with her. I needed time for myself. Time to readjust. Time to decide what I really wanted, independently of my father's wishes for me.

When Cleo opened the door to me that night, I could tell she'd made an effort to impress me, styling her long hair into an elaborate hairdo and wearing a sleek black dress. She would look good at my side. "You look great." I slid the curved handle of the unspeakable umbrella further into the crook of my arm, hoping she wouldn't notice it. I needn't have worried. She looked at me like a drowning woman, as if I was her only hope and salvation. This should have made me feel like a hero, but it only made me uneasy. "Shall we go?"

"Yes." She placed her hand on my free arm, and together, we started to walk to the theater. It was only two streets away, and with parking the issue it was in Florence, it made more sense to go on foot.

Unfortunately, it started to drizzle as soon as we'd gotten to the end of the street.

Cleo chuckled. "How clever of you to bring an umbrella."

I cringed. Oh, no. Now I had to open the ugliest accessory I had ever called my own. "I think it's too windy. The umbrella is not very strong, and it might fold."

She gave me a surprised look. "But there's hardly any wind at all." She stretched out her hand, and the rain fell like a soft curtain in a gentle pattern on her skin.

"There'll be gusts." I knew I had my back to the wall. "I was using the umbrella earlier, and a sudden gust almost blew it out of my hand."

"Oh." Cleo gave me a look that told me I was unchivalrous to the point of being rude.

I gave in. "All right, let's give it a try." I opened the umbrella, grateful that night had fallen and that the yellow street light didn't do much to dispel the dark.

Cleo snuggled up to me, and we walked on. The raindrops on the fabric above us made it sound as if we were walking in a bubble. I looked down at Cleo. She smelled nice, of some perfume. Could it be the same as the one Eyelashes had used?

She lifted her gaze to me. Her lips opened in a trembling smile.

The world started to turn around me, slow at first, then faster and faster. I saw an image of Eyelashes as she had looked down at the parcel, saw the shadows of her lashes on her cheeks. The image came closer and receded, and the world moved in whirling circles around me. The fragrance of the perfume became stronger and filled my senses until it almost overpowered me. I stumbled and had to grab Cleo's shoulder to steady myself.

"Carlo? Is everything all right?"

I couldn't look at her; it made me dizzy. "Yes, yes." I fixed my gaze to the pavement and marched on. The shaky feeling lingered. What had happened to me? Was I having a nervous breakdown? Low blood pressure?

"Are you ill?"

"Not at all. Just a passing—" I broke off. A passing what? I couldn't tell what it was that had come over me, but it was too strong for me.

The umbrella tilted to the side. I realized the rain had stopped. Relieved, I dropped Cleo's arm, closed the umbrella, and hung it back on my arm.

The dizzy feeling disappeared as if someone had snapped a finger.

I blinked and stared at Cleo.

She looked back, her blue eyes huge. "Better now?"

"Yes." I shook my head in disbelief. Did the umbrella have something to do with this?

"Why are you shaking your head?"

"It's nothing." I took her arm again. "Let's get a move on. We're running late."

The Teatro Verdi was magnificent. We arrived five minutes late, so the musicians were already busy tuning their instruments. I looked around. The rows of red seats were surrounded by a half-circle of elegant tiers with golden curlicue decorations, bathed in a muted light from the lamps fixed in regular intervals on the tiers. The excited hum of the audience mingled with the sound of the instruments.

I was still a bit shaken by the strange experience underneath the umbrella, but I managed to guide Cleo to our seats on the first tier. We had an excellent view of the stage. I wasn't much of an opera buff, but I had come to like the songs I heard Edoardo practice. Maybe my passing interest was just a lack of familiarity with the genre.

As the opera unfolded, I was surprised that Edoardo played one of the starring roles. He sang the part of Alfredo, Violetta's lover. My modest neighbor had never mentioned he was a star.

But this was nothing compared with the excitement that gripped me when Violetta's servant Annina came onstage. I bent forward until I threatened to fall over the balustrade of the first tier. I could not believe my eyes. Could it be—was this my postwoman? It was hard to discern her eyelashes at such a distance. Some people below me were using lorgnettes. Damn. Why didn't I have one? And what was the postwoman doing onstage when only this morning, she'd been delivering parcels? Or did she have a double life? I was so excited, I found it hard to wait until the curtain finally fell for the last time. I immediately stood to go.

"You forgot your umbrella." Cleo got up and held it out to me.

I sighed. "Thank you."

"I loved the performance. Wasn't it heart-wrenching?" Cleo held onto my arm as we descended the stairs.

Thank God she hadn't noticed my reaction to the actress playing Annina. I wasn't going to admit that I'd hardly noticed the events onstage. "Well, if you can believe the premise that a woman with a serious lung condition can still sing loud enough to blast half the audience away, then it was indeed a nice play."

She squeezed my arm and laughed.

I wondered if I was betraying her. Was it morally right to go out with a woman and to think of another one every single minute? It sure felt wrong. I decided to call off the charade as soon as possible, but I'd already told her about the Trattoria, so I couldn't accompany her home and hurry back to the restaurant without her, to find out if Annina was Eyelashes. No, I had to take Cleo along tonight, unless I could convince her it would be too boring to go.

"Oh, it's raining again." Cleo looked at me. "Would you open the umbrella? I think it's quite safe; the wind has settled."

I eyed the lumpy accessory in my hand with misgivings. First of all, too many people were around to see me underneath it, and second, I wasn't convinced that all was well with the thing. It seemed to have some kind of influence over me, and I wasn't sure I liked that.

Cleo smiled, took it out of my hand, and opened it. "See? It's not so difficult, is it?"

I didn't reply but followed the tug on her arm, entering the street.

"Where is the Trattoria you mentioned?" she asked. "I can't wait to see all the singers. It'll feel like mingling with celebrities." She made a little skip like an excited child.

Guilt made me sigh. There went any hope that I could stop her from coming.

"It's not far." I glanced at her, and in that very second, the strange feeling came over me again. The old stones beneath my feet seemed to tilt, and I found it hard to keep my balance. In a panic, I looked around, but none of the other theatergoers seemed to have noticed the earthquake.

Was it just me?

I clutched Cleo's arm and kept my gaze on the street to steady myself, but the world turned around and around. I had to do something. Now.

"Carlo? What is it?" Cleo's voice was filled with alarm.

I let go of her arm and slipped away from the umbrella. The moment the rain hit my head, the earth steadied again. I took a deep breath.

"Carlo? You're getting all wet." She came closer and tried to hold the umbrella over me.

I dodged away as if she was trying to hit me over the head with the wicked bundle. "No, please don't." I realized my voice had taken on a panicky note. "I'm fine. I just need— some air. I'm fine, really." And I was. The second the fabric wasn't spanning over me, my world was back to normal. Something was wrong with the umbrella, and if this was the magic my grandmother had wanted me to experience, then she had definitely been looking for revenge. I really should have spent more time with her. Was she watching me from somewhere, chuckling about my panic? "I . . . need to feel the rain on my face." I improvised with a growing feeling of desperation. "After . . . after all the time in China and on airplanes, with that recycled air, I love to be outside." I lifted my face to the rain. A drop of cold water trickled beneath my collar. I suppressed a shiver. I had to see Eyelashes again alone. But how?

"Oh, I understand completely. Whenever I come back from the US, I feel the same." Cleo stopped waving the dangerous accessory and leaned it against her shoulder. They looked like perfect mates, as if she'd come straight from a musical rehearsal of 'I'm singing in the rain'. Why did the umbrella affect me and not her? Did it only work on family members?

I dug my hands into the pockets of my coat and strolled along, taking care not to slip underneath the umbrella by mistake.

When we arrived at the Trattoria, the place was packed with people. A strong odor of wet wool mingled with the scent of spicy tomato sauce and aromatic herbs. The scent of herbs I could understand but where did the wool come from? Then I saw it. Just inside the narrow entrance, the wardrobe was piled high with wet coats, scarves, and umbrellas. A smile curled around my mouth. Maybe this was my chance to rid myself of the umbrella. Maybe fate would have mercy on me and someone would steal it. I found a hook for both our coats and managed to leave the umbrella in an ideal position for theft, leaning casually against the door frame. Anybody who didn't have an umbrella would grab it instinctively if they came to the door and saw the drizzle outside. I'd had to force myself to touch it, but luckily, touch alone didn't make me shake. Apparently, the black magic only worked if I was right underneath. I shook my head in bewilderment. When Eyelashes had brought me the parcel this morning—was it only this morning?—I would never have believed it possible that I'd come to fear this rickety structure of steel and cloth.

Speaking of Eyelashes ... with a growing feeling of excitement, I searched the room. As far as I could tell, she wasn't there. However, Edoardo was waving at us from across the room. He sat at a large table with several empty places. We joined him; I presented Cleo, and we ordered a my favorite Chianti wine.

"Let's hold off ordering the food." Eduardo said. "I'm early today because I'm hoping to meet a friend, but the others will soon join us." He folded his checkered napkin with nervous fingers and talked more than usual.

"Does the whole cast meet here after the performance?" I tried to look as if the answer didn't matter.

Eduardo shook his head. "Not all of them, no."

My heart sank, and every attempt I'd made to be subtle went over board. "How about Annina? Violetta's servant?"

Cleo gave me a strange look.

Eduardo shrugged. "She might come; I'm not sure. It depends."

"Depends on what?" I couldn't stop myself; I had to know.

"She has a grandfather who's sick, and sometimes, she has to go home." Edoardo looked surprised. "You know her?"

"I'm not sure. She reminds me of . . . of a friend, but I was sitting too far away, so I couldn't be sure."

"Is she important to you?" Cleo's voice had a bit of steel underneath the velvet tone.

"I don't know." My throat was parched.

Cleo opened her mouth to say something, but before she could utter a word, Edoardo jumped to his feet.

His chair wobbled and would have crashed to the ground if I hadn't snatched it at the last moment.

"Excuse me." In spite of his bulk, he moved through the restaurant with the ease of a falcon, intent on his goal. His red scarf fluttered behind him.

I smiled. The lady must really be important to him. I wished him luck. Then I glanced at the door, and my smile froze. Someone had opened my umbrella and had fixed it in the narrow entrance above the coats, so that everyone who walked in had to pass beneath it. Why on earth had they done that? In a misguided attempt to dry it? Several other umbrellas were fixed in a similar manner, but mine was smack in the middle. It looked like a weird decoration scheme gone mad.

Edoardo had stopped right beneath my umbrella.

I winced. What would happen now?

He helped a tall lady out of her coat—Gucci, no less. Her hair was cut stylishly short, and she looked as if she knew exactly what she wanted and how to get it.

I could tell from the way Edoardo moved that he was nervous. He hung up the coat with jerky movements, yet with as much care as if the garment were fragile, then he turned to face the lady.

She looked at him and smiled.

It took my breath away. The smile was an invitation if ever I'd seen one, and I don't mean an invitation to be kissed. It was an invitation to her life, her soul, everything.

Edoardo only hesitated one second. Then he took her into his arms until she all but disappeared, and he kissed her as if he never wanted to stop.

In fact, he didn't. The door to the restaurant opened, people were brought up short, standing half inside, half outside in the rain, but nothing could stop the couple, totally engrossed in each other. A hush fell over the restaurant as more and more people realized what was going on.

Our waiter looked up and frowned, then moved forward as if to break them up. I stopped him by catching his sleeve. He looked down at me, his eyebrows lifted in a mute question.

I shook my head. "This is important."

He nodded, then smiled at the waiting people on the other side of the couple, lifting both hands, palms up.

They laughed.

I settled back in my chair, filled with a mixture of wonder and bewilderment. Edoardo had not been sure of his reception; that much had been obvious. I was ready to bet my best suit that he was as surprised by this kiss as I was. Had it something to do with the umbrella? If only I could understand how it worked. Why did it cause romance for some people and only made me dizzy? The image of Eyelashes floated up in my mind; the way she had looked at the parcel, with the soft shadow of her lashes on her cheeks. I wished I could remember more, but that was all my brain had retained. It had only been an instant, but that instant had been enough to capture my heart. And if I remembered correctly, we had both been underneath the umbrella at that all-decisive moment. Of course. My sudden obsession with her had been caused by the umbrella. What a weird situation.

"*Mamma mia*." Cleo blinked.

I gave a start. I had totally forgotten her.

"What passion." She sighed.

It sounded as if she would voluntarily have switched places. "Quite." I refilled her glass, more to have something to do than anything else.

Edoardo must finally have realized that he was blocking the entrance because he came up for air and led the lady of his heart to our table. "I'd like you to meet Laura." He looked at her as if she was a cross between royalty and a shooting star—something enormously beautiful, something to be revered.

I felt a twinge of envy, and when I looked up, I realized that half the restaurant must have felt the same way, judging from the looks he got.

We started a conversation, but it was obvious that something earth-shattering had taken place and that their minds were still in the clouds.

I felt out of place and wondered how I could escape without being rude. Then again, no. I had to wait for Eyelashes. I had to know if the Annina actress was her, had to see her up close.

Apparently, Cleo felt a similar need to get away from the loving couple. She'd found a woman's way out. "I've forgotten my lipstick in my coat pocket." She jumped up. "I'll be back in a second."

From the corner of my eye, I saw her going to the door. She stopped beneath the umbrella and started to look for her coat in the pile of clothing at the wardrobe.

The door opened, and an extremely tall and muscled man came into the Trattoria. He almost dislodged the umbrella but ducked his head just in time. I'm not quite as tall as the average Italian and have to admit that I frequently wish I was a bit taller, so I couldn't help noticing that this man looked as if he was a basketball star. I'd have bet he had his suits especially made, and probably half his furniture, too.

He looked at Cleo, and though he could see her only from the back, he stopped as if some magic wand had rooted him to the ground.

My jaw dropped.

Cleo had found her lipstick; at least she was clutching something slim and gold in her hand. She turned around, smack-dab into his broad chest, and tilted back her head to say something with an apologetic smile.

It was too loud in the restaurant to understand her words, but it looked like a normal apology. Then she took a step back, maybe to get a better look at him without getting a kink in her neck, and then, something extraordinary happened. She just looked and stared, and so did he, and then she colored and opened her mouth to say something, while he took her hand and kissed it, without averting his gaze from her face.

That was it. The final proof. This umbrella was not normal. Deep inside my stomach, I felt a mixture of fear and excitement stirring. Funnily enough, I didn't feel jealous. If anything, I was relieved. If Cleo fell in love with this hunk, my Dad couldn't keep on suggesting that I should marry her.

Edoardo and Laura had not noticed anything amiss; they were fully occupied with each other. Cleo came back to our table, the handsome giant trailing behind her as if bound by an invisible rope. She was flushed, and her hand trembled as she pushed a strand of hair behind her ear. "Carlo," she said. "I . . . I've just met . . ."

"Tino." The giant stretched out his paw and pressed mine until it felt like mush.

"Nice to meet you, Tino." I indicated a chair. "Have a seat."

Tino lowered himself into the chair and immediately made it look like a child's toy. He fixed me with a direct gaze. "Let's get something straight right away. Are you in love with Cleo?"

I swallowed. He sure didn't waste much time. I gave Cleo an apologetic look. "I'm not."

"Good." He took Cleo's hand. "Then we won't have any problems."

Cleo looked at me with trepidation. "Are you sure that's all right, Carlo? I can't explain what happened."

"It's fine. Don't worry." I found myself grinning at her.

"You see, I've never had this sort of experience before, and—"

"And you'll never have it again." Tino kissed her cheek.

She gave him a trembling smile. "No, I guess not."

Tino grinned at me. "Do you want another glass of wine?"

I shook my head and got up. "No, thank you." Sitting between two couples that were love-struck by some kind of umbrella-magic hadn't been my plan for the evening. All at once, I felt tired. Eyelashes hadn't come. Maybe the singer who'd played Annina hadn't even been her; maybe my fevered imagination had projected her image onto the singer. "Have a good evening."

I waved at them and knew that as soon as I turned my back, they would have forgotten me.

Now all I had to do was get out of the restaurant. I eyed my umbrella from afar with misgiving and decided to take it back home. I had gotten clear orders from my family to keep it, after all. Besides, maybe it would help me to find Eyelashes. If I'd understood its magic correctly, the umbrella was responsible for my yearning.

I grabbed my coat and was just stretching to grab the handle of my umbrella, hoping I was not going to feel dizzy, when someone opened the door from outside and rushed in. We collided underneath the umbrella, and I had to grab her arm to stop us from falling. I looked at her face, saw the amazing eyelashes flutter, and my heart made a sort of somersault. Taking a deep breath, I forced myself to let go of her arm. "What's your name?"

She blinked. "Anna."

Had she said Annina? Laughter from a nearby table had drowned out her soft voice. "I don't mean the role you sing. I mean your real name."

She smiled. "It's still Anna. And you're Carlo."

Something warm shot through me. She'd remembered me. "Yes. And why do you deliver parcels in the mornings when you are an opera singer at night?" I felt I had to get the most important information right away. Who knew when she would slip through my fingers again.

She looked around. "I can't explain it here. Do you mind if we leave?"

"Not at all." Without thinking about it, I plucked the umbrella from the ceiling, convinced now that it would help to protect my fragile relationship with Anna.

Anna held open the door, and we left, with the umbrella arching above us.

Once outside, I took a deep breath of the cool air. It smelled of rain. Everything was steady, no dizzy spell threatened, and the night was beautiful.

She slipped her hand through my arm, and we walked a few steps in silence.

Inexplicable happiness filled me. I smiled at her, marveled at the shape of her cheek, saw her firm mouth with full awareness for the first time, inhaled her scent.

Then she began her story. "This morning, I helped out my grandfather. He's the postman in the Santa Croce district, but he's ill at the moment, and he still has to work another year before he can retire. Of course, it's illegal if I take his place, and I don't do it very often, so I don't like to talk about it, particularly if my colleagues are around." She gave me a crooked smile. "I really don't know why I suggested that you file a claim this morning. If you had agreed, I would have been found out. I've never done that before."

"Thank God you did." *Otherwise, we would never have been together underneath the umbrella.* A deep feeling of satisfaction coursed through me. I knew I had found my place in universe. And suddenly, I knew I could tell her my whole story, without reservation, and she would understand. So we walked through the city of Florence, through the silent, dripping streets that had seen so much history already. We didn't mind where we were going.

I told her everything, starting with Grandma's funeral, explaining how I had tried to be with Cleo only to please my father, and ending with Cleo's sudden new boyfriend. Anna looked up at that. "And that didn't hurt your feelings?"

"Not at all." I didn't hesitate.

A little shiver went through her. "But what would have happened if Cleo had been the first person to share the umbrella with you?"

I frowned in thought. "I have a feeling that the umbrella only works with the right pair of people.

When I walked underneath it with Cleo, everything was tilting; my whole world seemed upside down. It felt wrong, totally wrong. Cleo didn't seem to notice anything. Maybe it didn't affect her because she was already infatuated with me, the wrong guy. She seemed as love-crazy as ever."

We stopped in front of the Palazzo Pitti. The spotlights bathed the ancient building with a warm glow. I pulled Anna closer and buried my mouth in her hair.

I could feel her body yielding, molding herself against me. My arms tightened.

We held each other, and I closed my eyes.

At peace.

"Carlo." Anna said after a time. "If I'm not mistaken, the umbrella is losing its color."

I opened one eye and saw a fat drop of black water trembling at the edge of the fabric before gravity overcame its resistance, and it fell with a little splashy sound onto my shoulder. "Never mind, cara. I don't care." Then I kissed her, and the world around us seemed to disappear without a trace.

Carlo

Swiss Alps
Three Months Later

"*Cara mia,* may I tell you something?" I took hold of Anna's hand where it lay on the table between us and gently squeezed her smooth, warm fingers. We were in the dining car of a Euro-City train, heading north and crossing through the Alps. Our train had just emerged from a tunnel to a stunning view of Lake Zurich. Spiky, snow-covered mountains, even in May, soared up from the water's edge, reflecting the blue above and below, as if we'd plunged into two, infinite skies. Sunlight poured into our window, showing Anna's eyes to advantage—limpid pale green pools, clear and deep.

Her pupils expanded a fraction, and her irises quivered. "You can tell me anything. Except whether these jeans make me look fat." She tittered, a rich and musical laugh.

If a few months ago I'd been smitten with her eyes, now I was taken with her harmonious voice. Not that I was merely infatuated. No, this was love, and Anna was the love of my life. I hoped beyond hope that she felt the same way. My first few weeks with her had been like being constantly drunk; I'd never before felt my blood pumping through my body with such élan. But luckily, after these three months with Anna, the roller coaster of my emotions had become like a steady, well-run train, like this very train we were riding in today, wending a slow course through rough and beautiful country, always on a level track, always climbing or gently descending.

"I—" I broke off. I'd wanted to say *ti amo. I love you. I've loved you from the moment I set eyes on you.* But the words wouldn't leave my throat. Not for want of feeling, but for want of courage.

"Yes?"

"I like your new dress. You look beautiful." *Blast.* I'd messed up my chance to tell her my deepest feelings.

Anna smiled. "Thank you, *caro mio,*" She'd repeated my pet name for her, but changed it to the masculine. It was a game we played. Whichever pet name she used for me, I would repeat and vary, and she did the same. "May I tell *you* something?"

I leaned forward. "Anything."

She hesitated, as if collecting her thoughts, and for a panicked second I wondered if there was some trouble in our paradise. Not that Anna was in any way cool to me, but I had noticed that *I* could not take my hands off of her. Especially in public. Had I stifled her? I wanted to protect her, claim her, show all the other men she was mine. She had to know I did this out of passion and love, not because I was needy. But perhaps she'd misunderstood.

"I—" she began.

Just then my blasted telephone rang. I glanced at the screen. It was my cousin Josie. I ignored it. "Keep going," I told Anna. "I'll return the call later."

"No, please. You said you'd take Josie's calls this morning. It could be important."

Usually I turn my phone off when I'm with Anna, but today I'd made an appointment with my cousins to be available all morning, so the three of us could nail down the last details of our godfather's wedding arrangements. There were certain decisions we needed to make together.

"Are you sure?" I asked Anna.

"Of course." She picked up her camera and aimed it at the window. "I want to take some pictures of the Alps while I can."

"Okay. Thanks, *cara*." A couple of people in the dining car shot dirty looks at me about my ringing phone. I grabbed it and clicked it on. "Hey, Josie. Just a sec. I need to go to a part of the train that allows calls."

"Sure."

I got to my feet, kissed Anna's cheek (yes, I was definitely the pursuer in this relationship; I had near-hourly proof!) and hotfooted it out of the restaurant wagon into the small area between this car and the next. "So how are you doing?" I asked Josie in French, the language we grew up talking together every summer. There was something about speaking it that made me feel like a teenager again. "Did you get that job you interviewed for?"

"I did! You are now talking to the assistant junior designer at BubbleUp shoes."

I pressed one index finger in my free ear, straining to hear her over the train's racket. "Congratulations.

I'm glad to see that jobs are opening up in your industry."

"Actually, it's really hard to find work if you're fresh out of school, but I got a good recommendation from the head designer at my old job. So that helped." She paused. This gave me time to get out of the way of a man heading for the dining car. "Which reminds me," she went on, "do you have Grandma's umbrella with you? I'm going down the checklist Ainsley made for me, and that's the number one priority on my list."

The umbrella. That infuriating thing. "No worries. It's with my new girlfriend now in the next train car, at the bottom of her enormous handbag. I told her to guard it with her life." I gave a nervous cough. "Just kidding. In fact, I'd better get back to her now. We're just finishing up lunch." I glanced through the window of the sliding door to the restaurant car. Anna still had her camera out, happily clicking away.

There was another long pause from Josie. "Before you go, I wanted to ask you. Did you notice anything strange about the umbrella?"

"Apart from its dreadful ugliness? Oh, yes. I sure did." I paused. "Wait, are we allowed to talk about it now? I remember Grandma's will was quite strict. I'd hate to jeopardize our inheritance after we've waited so long."

"Ainsley and I were worried about the same thing. But it's been more than a year since Grandma's funeral, so we've already compared notes."

"How is Ainsley, by the way? Having a nervous breakdown with those wedding arrangements? I don't envy her that job."

"She can tell you herself. She's staying with me. I'll put her on speakerphone."

A second later, I heard Ainsley's precise Scottish accent in French. "*Salut*, Carlo. No time to chat. I have to make another call in a second. Do you have the umbrella?"

"Yes. It's wending its way through the Alps with me as we speak."

"And the fabric for the reception tables?"

"Check. I sent them from my dad's factory. They should arrive in Erquy by tomorrow. I'll be there to sign for them."

"Thanks, Carlo. That's a load off my mind."

"About the umbrella," I said, curiosity getting the better of me. "Josie said you guys have been comparing notes?"

"That's right." She paused. "We were wondering if anything unusual happened to you with it."

"You'd better believe it. I fell in love." I held my breath, hoping they wouldn't think I was nuts.

As if they'd timed it, my cousins squealed and laughed simultaneously.

"Same here," Josie said. "It's a love charm. We're convinced of it. Ainsley fell in love too, with a wonderful Scottish man. And I've just moved in with my American boyfriend. He moved to Paris for me!"

"That's fantastic."

"And this girlfriend you mentioned," Josie continued. "Is she the one you were sort of dating before? Did your love deepen?"

"You mean Cleo? I never really dated her. She was someone my dad kept trying to get me to marry. No, I've met the love of my life. Her name is Anna, and I couldn't be happier. You'll get to meet her at the wedding."

"So glad she could come after all," Ainsley said. "I remember you said she might have a performance?"

"That's right. But it all worked out."

"*Alors,*" Josie said, drawing out the word. "Ainsley and I have been trying to figure out exactly how the umbrella works. Some of the people we know who shared it with other people are still in love, but some aren't. My roommate, for instance. After two weeks, she lost interest in this ex-convict, garbage collector she'd been seeing."

"Same with a guy I dated once," said Ainsley. "He's back to normal. Slightly more friendly with me, but that's all. It's the same situation for my friend's father, my coworker, and my neighbor, all of them major grumps. They're a bit friendlier to me than before, but no longer acting as if I walk on water."

I laughed. "What? Did you run around trying the umbrella out on everyone?"

"It was by accident," she protested. "Actually, I think it had something to do with the handle. I had stuck it back on, facing the wrong way, and maybe that reversed the magic somehow. I thought it was way too scary, so you can believe me when I say that I wouldn't try to manipulate the power. Once I realized the umbrella had magic powers, I only tested it on one coworker. Luckily, nothing bad happened and the charm mostly wore off."

"Same here, except my motives going into it weren't so innocent," Josie said in a quiet voice. "But never again. I feel so stupid. I was desperate for someone at my company to give me a leg up, so I risked using the umbrella on the head of the design department. Thank God the infatuation wore off. Though I wonder if I'd have gotten that recommendation from him otherwise...."

"You would have," Ainsley said. "The umbrella got you to face your fears. To take risks. It can do only good. Remember?"

This piqued my interest. "Hold on a second. How do you know it can do only good? What if some tyrant or dictator got hold of it? He could do major damage." As I said all this, I cast a look into the dining car. Thank God nobody could overhear this conversation. Anna was still taking pictures through the window, smiling to herself.

"I had the same worry until a few days ago," Ainsley said. "But then Josie told me about the message she found rolled up inside the stem of the umbrella."

My ears perked up. "A message? I didn't see any message."

"It's in there," Josie said. "I stuck it back in before I sent it to you. It was handwritten on paper that had then been laminated. Someone had rolled it up and slid it into the long steel part of the umbrella."

"In the stem? How did you think to look in there?"

"I didn't, actually," Josie went on. "The handle fell off by itself. I was putting it back on when I saw something sticking out of the end of the stem. It was a note from Grandma."

"Are you sure?"

"It's in her handwriting."

"What did it say?"

"It said, 'This umbrella may have become lost, but now it's found. Take it with you on your journey. It can do only good. When you need it no more, forget all about it. Pass it on'."

A warm shiver passed down my back. "I wonder why Grandma kept it to herself all these years? Or did she?"

"I'm not sure," Josie said. "For all I know our parents may have met under its influence. Anatole did tell me, just in passing, that when Grandma was dying and talking about our inheritance, she'd said something like 'Hubert would not have wanted it,' but then she refused to explain what she meant. Maybe Grandpa wanted to keep the umbrella out of circulation, but Grandma knew better."

"She definitely knew better," Ainsley said. "Grandma was a woman of her generation, so she would have respected Grandpa's wishes. But she was not to be trifled with."

I laughed. "You can say that again."

"She was a force of nature," Josie said.

"There's something to that part in the note about needing to forget the umbrella," I mused. "I can't tell you how many times I've forgotten it somewhere during the past couple of months. It was as if the umbrella *wanted* to move on, *wanted* to be forgotten."

"The same thing happened to us," Ainsley said. "I think it's a sign that it's time to release the umbrella."

"The question is how? Where?" I asked.

"Yeah. We're stumped too," Josie said. "We tried to ask Travis about it but couldn't reach him. I think he's on tour."

Ainsley said, "We could leave it in a park. In a restaurant. But that seems so lonely. And what if no one sees it?"

"I have no doubt someone will find it. It knows how to call attention to itself." I chuckled at the thought.

We were silent for a moment, and then an idea came to me. "We could hide it under the bouquet that Anatole's bride will carry. I went to a wedding once where the bouquet had long strands that hung down nearly to the bride's knees."

"That's brilliant," Ainsley said. "And when the bouquet is tossed, whoever catches it will already start mentally associating the umbrella with love. We probably shouldn't tell that person about the umbrella, though. I think Grandma's edict was a good one."

"I agree. The magic doesn't work if someone tells you about it first."

Both my cousins said simultaneously, "Are you sure?"

"Yes. I told Anna about it, and she gave it to her best friend, explaining what to do. Nothing happened. Nothing at all."

"Wow," said Josie. "So that's why we weren't allowed to talk about it until we each had our three months."

"Yes. Grandma was one amazing woman," I said with a sigh. "I wonder how she learned about the umbrella's powers."

"Personal experience, probably," Ainsley said.

"And she always was a bit psychic," Josie added. "I had the feeling she could tap into other realms."

I scoffed. "I wouldn't go that far, but then again, I can't deny what happened to me."

"It's a mystery," said Ainsley.

"It is," Josie agreed. "At any rate, we can talk more at the wedding. You need to get back to your girlfriend now, Carlo. We've kept you too long."

So we said our good-byes and confirmed that we'd meet the next day in Anatole's home town of Erquy, where the wedding would take place in three days.

After ringing off I went into the dining car and hurried to Anna's side. "I'm sorry about that. My cousins and I had a lot to settle for the wedding. I'm all yours now. The phone's off."

Anna's sweet smile swept away my guilt. "All mine. I like the sound of that."

Our gazes met, and a tingling feeling went all the way down to my feet. "Me, too." I bent forward to kiss her; and then, by a superhuman effort, I concentrated on more mundane matters.

"We'd better get our things. We're almost in Zurich." I set a few bills on the table to cover the cost of lunch. Then I remembered something Anna had said before I'd gone off to take my call. I sat down across from her and took her hand. "But first, what is it you wanted to tell me?"

"Oh, that." Another smile, this one mischievous. "I wanted to tell you that I feel the same way."

My heartbeat raced, and a warm lump formed in my throat. "The same way as what?"

She stood up, wrapping a cardigan around her shoulders, and came to stand beside me, bending for a kiss. "I love you, too."

Anatole

May
Erquy, Brittany

I stood near the altar alongside the other men in the wedding party, my mouth dry, my heart in my throat. This was to be "the wedding of weddings," or so Ainsley had promised, but for me it was an intimate family reunion. Gathered here in the old church in Erquy was everyone I'd ever known and loved.

The first notes from the organ intoned, and all the faces in the church turned toward the back of the nave, eyes searching for the bride.

Anne stepped into view beside her father, silhouetted against the light shining in from outside. With one slender arm interlaced in his, she sailed across the flagstones, her skirt billowing like a galleon at sea.

My breath caught in my chest. Never had I seen such a beautiful bride. Because she was mine. My own dear Anne.

Her father halted in the middle of the aisle to greet someone, giving me time to glance at the guests all around. My family members were here, at least those who were still alive. And of course my family-in-spirit had come from abroad as well, the children and grandchildren of my dearly departed friends Charlotte and Hubert.

Beside me, my mother stirred. I'd escorted her according to custom into the church and was supposed to guide her to her seat in the front pew soon, but as the bride and her father were still only a few steps into the nave, we'd had to wait.

"What's taking them so long?" my mother whispered, squinting down the aisle. At ninety, her eyesight wasn't what it used to be. "Has the old fool been doing his salutes again?"

"Indeed he has."

I chuckled. My future father-in-law, a thin, stooped man of ninety-four, had from the moment we'd picked him up this morning been under the impression that he was participating in a military parade. He'd taken one look at my former officer's jacket and those of my best men, and had tried to take command of the party, addressing us as soldiers.

Outfitted in his naval uniform from the previous century, he had stopped now in the church aisle to salute the crowd.

Poor Anne smiled gamely and tugged on her father's bony arm. She had assured me her mother had been sharp as a tack right up until she passed away. Her reassurance was unnecessary. I would always love Anne, even if fifteen years from now she mistook me for a hat rack.

I smiled back at her, glad of the delay with her father. This gave me more time to admire her figure, her grace, her eyes behind her veil, twinkling at me from afar. How good it was to slow down the tornado that was this day and be still with her at the center of our storm.

In her free hand, she carried a bouquet of mixed flowers that I couldn't name if my life depended on it. Some of them hung low in long strands around her hand, partially covering the handle of an umbrella.

It wasn't any old umbrella. I knew this one. Knew it well. It was the folded-up umbrella that my friend Charlotte had bequeathed to her grandchildren. For reasons known only to that eccentric family, her grandchildren had insisted that the bouquet be attached to the compacted umbrella, to be thrown into the crowd during the wedding reception.

I'd only laughed at their superstitious requirements. Mine was not to question why. Mine was to survive this wedding on the terms of anyone who cared to organize it.

At last, Anne and her father reached the altar. We guided our parents to their places in the front pew and then ascended the short flight of steps to the low prayer chairs that had been set out for us to kneel upon.

Easier said than done when you're both a little bit older than the average bride and groom and have bad knees. But we did it, lowering ourselves one leg at a time.

The priest raised his arms in greeting and proceeded to read aloud a passage about the Lord protecting us from whatever evils might rain down on us in our remaining days on this earth. I barely followed the rest of the ceremony, nervous as I was. My ears had filled with a roar, and my hands shook as Anne and I set the rings on each other's fingers. Our kiss, so familiar and warm, brought me back to my senses. And once again we were swept along on the tide of events planned for us by Ainsley and her famous checklist. Not that she carried it about anymore. She had that thing memorized.

Outside the church, rice was thrown over us and laurel leaves were strewn on the stone steps, even though clearly Anne and I were no longer a fertile couple.

A sudden roar of engines filled the air, and a second later, six Harley Davidson motorcycles rounded a bend in the road, stopping in front of the church. Anne's biker club of middle-aged ladies had arrived to escort us to the reception. Specially for this day, Anne had persuaded me to learn how to drive a motorcycle. Me, of all people. Anatole the scaredy-cat.

With an effort, I slid my leg over the padded seat of the machine that had been made free for me and waited as Anne removed the outer skirt of her gown to reveal long flowing culottes. She straddled her own bike, and we were off.

"If I'm to marry at all," she'd told me when I asked for her hand, "it will be in style. With full motorcycle cortège. Then I want to dance all night. And after that, I'd like a taxi ride to the local airport and a honeymoon in a tropical locale. My family will pay for it, of course. Please don't feel you must."

I would have agreed to anything to have her in my life. And so here I was, with a ton of vibrating steel between my thighs and a beautiful woman of sixty-six at my side. We toured the streets of my hometown under a bright May sky, all horns honking as we waved at the few old classmates who remembered me from grammar school days.

If only Charlotte had lived to see this day. She must have known I'd been hopelessly in love with her. But those days were long gone, and I was free to love again.

The wedding party arrived in front of a large fisherman's cottage, Charlotte's and Hubert's old place, which had been around since the seventeenth century. The house had been cleaned and freshened up for the bridal party, the light blue shutters standing out well against the gray stones. The garden looked immaculate with an elegant alley of box trees in terracotta planters all the way up to the road, surrounded by smaller planters with white flowers.

As soon as Anne and I dismounted from our rides, one of her lady friends came up to us, her helmet tucked under one arm. "May I steal Anne for a group shot? It's not every day we've all had our roots dyed at the same time."

Anne turned to me, an apologetic smile tilting her lips. "Sorry, darling. This should only take a few minutes."

I kissed her. "I need to check in with my people too. I'll meet you for the first toast in . . ." I checked my watch. ". . . about twenty minutes."

"See you then, lover boy." Another sweet kiss, and she was dragged away by her friend.

"Photo opportunity on the bikes!" the friend cried.

As the rest of the ladies rallied round them, I made my way to the wide lawn beside the house. Above me, a couple of white clouds scudded swiftly inland, leaving the sky tinged with sea mist. I breathed in the salty air and sighed in contentment. It was good to be home.

Ten tall cocktail tables dotted the lawn, each wrapped in fabric provided by Carlo's family for the *vin d'honneur* reception. I made my way to the table where my four young friends and their guests were just gathering, champagne glasses in hand. I had promised them that today I would show them the letter their grandmother asked me to hold in reserve, but before I even reached the table, Josie came flying toward me and kissed me. "*Félicitations, mon cher Toli!*"

My heart swelled with happiness. It was so good to see someone being genuinely happy for me. Others had voiced their doubts about me being too old to change my ways this late in life, and I had trembled inside at the thought that they might be right. But only whenever Anne wasn't close. When she was by my side, the doubts evaporated.

"Come on." Josie took my hand and pulled me to the table. "I want you to meet my boyfriend, Rob." Her whole face lit up when she said the words "my boyfriend."

I smiled to myself, entranced by her enthusiasm, but my smile slid a bit to the side when she presented to me the most handsome man I'd ever seen. A man this gorgeous would be a welcome prey for any woman on the prowl. Was he going to be strong enough to withstand temptation and stick with my little Josie over time?

But then I saw the smile he gave to Josie before he turned to me and shook my hand, and I felt reassured. He was just as much in love with Josie as I was with Anne.

"Josie has told me a lot about you, Anatole. Congratulations on your marriage. I wish you much happiness." He spoke good French, even though he had a strong American accent.

"Thank you, Rob," I replied.

Josie slid her arm around his waist, stood on tiptoe and gave him a kiss on the cheek.

Ainsley, meanwhile, had taken me by the arm. "Toli, I'd like you to meet Taran. He only arrived this morning." She slid her free arm around a tall man who had very long, red hair. He was dressed in a kilt with all the trimmings, looking uncannily like the main actor in that movie *The Highlander.*

I blinked. I'd never have thought that Ainsley would choose a partner so very . . . unconventional. This guy looked as if he'd never made a list in his life. But maybe that was exactly why she had fallen for him. Don't they say that opposites attract? "I'm pleased to meet you."

We shook hands.

"You did a wonderful job with the organization of the wedding, Ainsley," I said. "Thank you so much."

She glowed. "I loved it. It was really fun. I'd do it again in a shot."

I recoiled. "God forbid. This is the one and only time I want to get married."

They all laughed.

"Are you in the music industry, too?" Travis asked the Highlander.

I had forgotten the Scot's name already, so "Highlander" would have to do until I could discreetly ask someone for his real name again.

The Highlander smiled and winked at Ainsley before he replied. "No, I'm sorry. I'm a painter."

Ainsley shook her head as if she was despairing of something, but she chuckled.

I didn't quite get the joke, but before I could ask, Travis turned back to me.

"I guess it's my turn now." Travis shook his bangs from his eyes. "Please meet Leila. She made it possible for my band to be here tonight to play for the wedding party." He pointed out a motley group of three young men standing at a distance, sipping champagne and looking quite out of place in their straggled haircuts and wrinkled suits. Travis grinned. "That's my band over there. Wait till you hear our new sound. You can actually dance to it now."

I took Leila's hand. "Why thank you, *Mademoiselle*. That is a very generous gift indeed."

"It's from us both." She was a brown-haired beauty whose wide smile made up for her stumbling words in French. She was standing beside a pale woman about her same age who had spent the entire time reading and clicking on her telephone.

Leila turned to the pale woman. "Maxine, won't you greet the groom?"

The girl continued typing on her phone, oblivious to us.

"Don't mind Max," Travis said to me in a whisper. "She's Leila's sister. I think she may be a bit autistic or something, but she means well. She's creating some app that does online matchmaking based on algorithms. She doesn't see the people behind the facts."

"It's no problem." I smiled.

Beside me, Carlo took a step forward. I could tell at a glance that he was wearing the best cut suit of all of us. He put his arm around the shoulders of a woman with beautiful eyes. "Let me introduce Anna to you." His pride was obvious.

"Ah. Now that's a name I can easily remember!" I smiled. "You sang at the ceremony. It was wonderful, most impressive."

"Thank you very much." Anna rolled the r in a very charming, Italian way.

I continued, swept away by the memory of her performance that had brought goose bumps to my arms. "I'd never have thought that such a small person could have such a big voice. In fact, you sounded like a professional singer."

Carlo gave Anna a little smile. "That's because she *is* a professional singer," he said, "though she freelances as a postwoman from time to time. In fact, she was the one who delivered Grandma's umbrella to my house."

A hush fell over them, as if another person had suddenly joined the table. The air became brittle with sudden tension.

Surprised, I looked around. "What's the matter?"

Carlo leaned forward. "What did you know about the umbrella before you gave it to us, Toli?"

I spread my hands out in front of me. "Nothing, I swear. I told you everything I knew. Charlotte was extremely secretive about that whole thing. I didn't get it at all. Why? What happened?"

They all stood without moving. The four partners of the cousins had not said much these last minutes, but I could tell from their faces that they knew something that I already half-guessed in the back of my mind but hadn't yet allowed myself to consider.

"No, wait," I said. "Let me guess. You think the umbrella is some sort of good luck charm, don't you?"

They all smiled, relief rippling through our little group like a wave receding from a rocky shore.

"Exactly," Travis said. "And because of it, we've all been lucky in love."

"Real love," Josie added. "Except when it's not meant to be. It's like a litmus test."

I couldn't help it; I snorted in amusement. These youngsters were even more superstitious than their grandmother had been. "So that's why you wanted to attach it to Anne's bouquet? To spread the love? Anne and I thought it was an odd idea for a bouquet handle, but we decided to humor Ainsley. We thought it was some sort of Scottish ritual."

"You don't believe us?" Carlo said.

"Does it matter whether or not I do?"

They exchanged glances, and two of them shrugged.

Ainsley stepped forward, smiling. "All that matters is that you're happy."

"Yes, I'm happy." I said it humbly, knowing that a day like this was a gift. Then I cleared my throat. "I think this is the right moment to learn about your inheritance. I have Charlotte's letter here."

Instantly, the mood changed. They shivered with curiosity, excitement in their eyes, even the guests who could understand French.

Carlo spoke first. "Let's hear it then."

"Here we go." I took Charlotte's yellowed envelope from my pocket, gently tore open the flap, and pulled out a slip of folded paper. Clearing my throat, I began to read out Charlotte's elegant handwriting.

My dearest ones,

By the time you read this, I'll be gone, and you'll have spent a year of discovery. You've carried around my old umbrella for a year now, surely wondering what I'd meant by asking you to do so, which I'll come to in a bit. First, it's time to claim your inheritance. As you may have guessed, it's my family's fisherman's cottage in Erquy. I know it's not much to look at, but the property is valuable and the site charming. It's for all four of you to with do with as you please. You may sell it, restore it, rent it out, keep it, enjoy it, or do nothing at all with it. I leave this for you to decide. Whatever you decide, I hope it will not involve any ill will. Life is too short to argue for too long.

You will find the deed to the house under the kitchen sink floorboards on the property itself. I ask only that you complete one more task before fetching the deed. Not to worry. This one is a simple task. I would wish that in the privacy of your own mind, in your own time, you would ask yourself what this year has taught you. What is it your life wants you to learn? That is a question I've asked myself often during the past few months. What is my life trying to tell me?

If you haven't already, I hope you begin asking yourself this same question. No one else can or should answer it for you—though, goodness knows they try!

With love,

Your grandmother

A hush had fallen over the table. Their champagne glasses sat on the linen, untouched, bubbles fizzing to the top.

"I know one thing my life is teaching me," Travis said. "I need more champagne."

Everyone tittered in relief.

I addressed the four cousins. "Do you already know what you'd like to do with the house?"

Almost in unison, they said they'd like to renovate it for their entire family. "We could reinstate the reunions we used to have every August. Remember those?" Carlo asked.

The others nodded eagerly, and while they and their partners began planning the new look of the house, I put Charlotte's letter back into its envelope. My work here was done.

"Who would like to keep the letter?" I asked them.

"I'll scan it and send copies to you guys," Ainsley offered, and when they all nodded in agreement, I handed the letter over.

"And now I must go do my groom's duties." I bowed my head and turned just in time to see my bride wafting toward me.

"Anatole. There you are." Anne was wearing her wedding skirt again, reattached to the bodice. She snuggled into the crook of my underarm, where she fit perfectly, the last piece in the puzzle that had been my life.

As I slid my hand around hers, my fingers brushed the bouquet's handle, and I felt a warm tingle. Could Anne feel it too? Or was this just the elation of being newlyweds?

About a hundred guests, many of them distant acquaintances from my hometown, had gathered around the main drinks table where the caterers were pouring champagne into rows of glasses.

We joined them and had our glasses filled too. It was time for the toast. I had prepared nothing to say, so I did as I always do on such occasions. I panicked and blathered.

The remaining hours of the reception passed in a blur. I only came back to my senses when we moved to the dinner venue, and it was time for the bouquet toss.

"Bouquet, bouquet," chanted Anne's friends. We were standing outdoors beside a beautifully converted stone grange that Ainsley had found for us to rent, the sunset's rays angling in through a neighboring apple orchard, filling the courtyard with a golden glow.

"Do you suppose they want the bouquet?" Anne quipped, and she sashayed onto the lawn. She took up position in the middle of the grass, facing away from the group of about ten single people, including a handful of men, who had gathered some ten yards behind her. Closing her eyes, Anne threw the bouquet behind her. It spun like a baton, rising high, rotating.

There was mad scramble on the lawn. Arms and legs became tangled. Laughter filled the air as everyone jumped up, reaching for the prize.

But then . . . silence. We all looked around to see who the lucky catcher was.

"Who has it?" Anne asked.

"It disappeared," said a young woman on the lawn.

A delicious shiver ran through me as I scanned the grass. Could the umbrella really have vanished?

"That can't be." Anne said. "It must have gotten caught in one of the apple trees."

At once, a bustle of activity began. About five men formed a group to discuss the best way to locate the missing bouquet.

"We need a long pole. Do we have any poles on the premises?" Carlo asked, his engineer's mind going to work at once.

"I'll check the storeroom." Travis dashed off, long hair waving.

The women meanwhile had begun throwing objects at the neighboring trees. The branches rustled on impact, but nothing fell from the leaves.

After some twenty minutes of this, we all decided another glass of champagne would be more fun. And so the search for the bouquet was abandoned.

"I'm inclined to believe it vanished after all," Josie whispered to me as she walked with me and Anne to the banquet area. "It's more romantic that way."

"And I'm inclined to believe you're right," I said.

We joined our party, and I took my place beside Anne at the center of the table, facing our guests. For the next few hours we feasted and danced, and then we danced some more to the beats of Travis's band.

Ainsley had promised me the wedding to end all French weddings, and she delivered.

Late that night when the stars came out and the moon hung full and low, we took the party back to Charlotte's cottage. At six a.m. my bride and I tried to sneak away for our taxi ride, but we were delayed by everyone who was still standing for the *charivari*, or as I like to think of it, another excuse to eat and drink. They banged pots and pans and demanded that we feed them breakfast.

Sleepy-eyed Ainsley came to our rescue and herded them all to a table on the lawn, where a breakfast buffet had been laid out beside a pot of traditional onion soup.

Anne and I were at last free to start out on our honeymoon.

About ten members of our wedding party gathered around us, as Carlo and Travis loaded our suitcases into the car and we got into the back seat.

Our taxi pulled away as the first rays of sun peeped over the horizon. The car climbed the hill beside the house, and I looked back. Sunshine reflected off the ocean and the windows of the cottage. Charlotte's grandchildren and their new partners were standing around the garden gate, waving. I took a deep breath, relieved that they were as happy as I was. Charlotte's crazy will had served its purpose.

As we reached the top of the hill, a small reddish-green shape appeared in the crowd, a circle of muddied color. Could someone have found the umbrella? The sky was free of clouds, but perhaps whoever had located the bouquet was now separating it from its artificial stem.

Our taxi crested the hill, and I cast a last glance at the cottage. The circle of red twirled to face east, like a spring flower turning to the sun. Was it the umbrella or only someone putting on a red sweater in the morning breeze? I preferred to think it was a sweater, and the umbrella had disappeared to join Charlotte wherever she had gone.

I reached for Anne's hand, which was warm and firm. We were both alive, and we both knew it, and this moment of pure joy would stay with us forever.

THE END

DEAR READER,

Thank you for reading our novel!

Word of mouth is crucial for an author's success. If you enjoyed *It's Raining Men*, please consider leaving a review online, even if only a short line or two. It would make all the difference and would be deeply appreciated. For example, you could leave a review on Amazon.com, which will then post it on their sites worldwide.

If you'd like to know when our next books are out, please sign up for our newsletters via the below link. Your email will never be shared by us, and you may unsubscribe at any time.

We hope to hear from you. . . .

Sincerely,
Beate Boeker & Gwen Ellery

Our Newsletters
http://eepurl.com/TXxuX

Links to two free stories from Beate & Gwen

Dead Men Don't Eat Quiche
A short, humorous mystery
http://www.gwenellery.com/go/freebies

Beauty and Beast E
A short romantic comedy
http://www.happybooks.de/29-0-Sample+Story.html

ABOUT THE AUTHORS

Beate and Gwen have three things in common: they both live in Germany, are both bilingual, and both have curls. That much they knew when they started to work on this novel together, but not much more. In the months that followed, they realized that working together is amazing fun, and they hope that you'll feel the same while reading *It's Raining Men*.

Gwen grew up in California and trained as an English teacher for expatriates. She married one of her conversation students and moved with him to Germany in 1998. Since then, she's been a full-time novelist and screenwriter, with two comedy film credits in Germany and several awards for her fiction, including sponsorship by the Arts Council England. She writes romantic comedy novels and sitcom-style novellas.

Beate has been a traditionally published author since 2008 with a passion for books that brim over with mischief and humor. Several of her novels were shortlisted for the Golden Quill Contest, the National Readers' Choice Award, the Best Indie Books, and the RONE Award. She writes contemporary romances and cozy mysteries.

You can reach Gwen and Beate via their websites:

http://www.happybooks.de
http://www.gwenellery.com

www.ingramcontent.com/pod-product-compliance
Lightning Source LLC
Chambersburg PA
CBHW020050180626
46812CB00006B/2260